"Why do you take my part, John?"

"You are my wife. I will always take your part." He leveled Helena with his gaze. "I may not always agree with you, but I will stand beside you. No matter what you do."

Helena blinked. John believed her. He truly believed her.

He pulled her to stand. In a gentle motion, he wrapped his arms around her, even though he had promised never to do that, even though she had sworn she would never let him. He left a proper distance between them, as if they were about to waltz, but this was nothing like a dance. This was an embrace. A true, real clasp of his arms around her back.

Helena closed her eyes. John smelled of starch and wood smoke and soap—so wonderful, she'd bottle the scent if she could and sprinkle it on everything she owned.

"'Tis all right, Helena," he whispered. "You are safe…"

Susanne Dietze began writing love stories in high school, casting her friends in the starring roles. Today, she's blessed to be the author of over half a dozen historical romances. Married to a pastor, and mom of two, Susanne loves fancy-schmancy tea parties, cozy socks and curling up on the couch with a costume drama and a plate of nachos. You can find her online at www.susannedietze.com.

Books by Susanne Dietze

Love Inspired Historical

The Reluctant Guardian
A Mother for His Family

SUSANNE DIETZE

A Mother for His Family

HARLEQUIN® LOVE INSPIRED® HISTORICAL

Recycling programs
for this product may
not exist in your area.

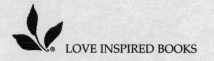

LOVE INSPIRED BOOKS

ISBN-13: 978-1-335-36953-6

A Mother for His Family

www.Harlequin.com

Printed in U.S.A.

Therefore if any man be in Christ,
he is a new creature: old things are passed away;
behold, all things are become new.
                    —*2 Corinthians* 5:17

To Debra E. Marvin,
with gratitude for your friendship, prayers
and encouraging help. If I could thank you by
taking you to the UK for scones and tea, I would.
Instead, we'll have to settle for Starbucks and
a BBC costume drama, which isn't so bad. Right?

With deep appreciation to my family;
my editor, Emily Rodmell;
and my agent, Tamela Hancock Murray.
Thank you one and all, from the bottom of my heart.

Chapter One

Perthshire, Scotland, July 1819

With no warning, the rain-soaked ground underfoot gave way, and Lady Helena Stanhope slid backward into the mucky trench. Landing at the bottom of it, she lifted the mud-soaked shred of fabric where her snowy hem used to be and burst into laughter. What else could she do? At least she matched now, inside and out.

Ruined gowns befitted a ruined reputation.

"Are you injured?" Gemma Knox, Helena's cousin by marriage, knelt at the edge of the ha-ha, some six feet up the slope from Helena. A naturalistic feature in the landscaping, the ha-ha prevented cattle and sheep from grazing too close to the house without impairing the view like a fence would—an obvious barrier to animals, but Helena had stumbled into it easily enough.

Even sheep were smarter than she.

"I'm well," she called, her face upturned to the rain. She didn't rise yet, though. Her right ankle throbbed. So did her pride, little of it though she had left.

Two boys with ginger-blond hair scurried down into the ha-ha with her. Young Petey Lyfeld's freckles faded into his flushing cheeks. "My fault, Lady Helena. I didn't mean to push you."

"You shoved her?" Eddie, two years younger than Petey's eight, gaped.

"No," Helena said with a smile. "I stood too close to the edge to see the world's largest earthworm and I fell, that's all."

Petey's arm had bumped hers, but Helena didn't blame the boy for knocking her off balance. Her unfortunate circumstances were her own fault—not just slipping into the ha-ha, but being banished to Scotland in the first place.

Even being out in the rain was her doing, because she'd been the one to suggest taking a walk to escape the tension in the house. The skies opened once they'd hiked a half mile or more, and now water dripped from the brim of her cork bonnet and the hem of her once-milky-white cloak. A glance at her ensemble assured her she was now brown-speckled as a goat. "Let's climb out before we turn to mud."

"Why is it called a ha-ha?" Eddie gripped Helena's hand and tugged her upright. "It should be called a no-no."

A shackle of pain fettered Helena's ankle the moment her foot bore her weight. "Thank you for your assistance, gentlemen, but I do not seem to be ready for the ascent yet."

"You *are* hurt." Gemma's lips pressed into a thin line.

"My ankle twisted. A tiny bit. In a minute or two, it will be better and I shall march up the slope like one of Wellington's men." But she didn't mind postponing her return to the house, where Papa no doubt paced and grumbled under his breath, as he had done since their arrival from London yesterday.

He had much to be frustrated about. His health was declining, and his disobedient daughter caused him no small amount of grief.

Her stomach tightened. "Go home and get out of the

rain. I'll be well enough here." In the trench. In Scotland. Alone and a little afraid.

Gemma's frown revealed Helena's trembling hadn't gone unnoticed. "Don't be a widgeon. Boys, fetch Uncle Tavin."

Muddying their nankeen pantaloons and miniature boots, the boys scrambled up the ha-ha in less time than it took Helena to envy their pain-free ankles. "Gemma, no."

"They're well on their way. I would pull you out myself, but I'm not so steady on my feet these days." Her hand rested over her protruding belly. "My husband won't mind."

Helena rolled her eyes. Of course Cousin Tavin wouldn't mind. He'd relish teasing her about it. Ever since she was a girl, he'd been merciless in his brotherly teasing—

But she wasn't a child anymore. Frederick Coles had changed that, too.

Then again, like an infant, she needed assistance if she was to escape the ha-ha. Just like she needed help to get out of her "devastating dilemma," as Mama called it. Helena's shoulders slumped as she settled to wait.

She glanced up. "You shouldn't be out in the rain in your condition, Gemma."

"I'm in the family way. I'm not rheumatic." Gemma wrapped her scarlet shawl about her.

A steady thudding rumbled through the earth. Hoofbeats. Wincing in pain, Helena hopped forward like a one-legged bird. How had the boys reached Tavin so fast? How had he saddled a horse and—oh.

The rider couldn't be Tavin.

The hoofbeats slowed as Gemma rose. Before she found her footing, a man in a tall beaver hat and deep blue coat was at Gemma's side, supporting her by the elbow.

Helena's pulse battered her rib cage. No, the man was definitely not Tavin.

The man stepped out of Helena's sight. "You gave me a

fright, Mrs. Knox, down on the ground. Are you unwell?" He said *down* like *doon*, and his *yous* were clipped and soft.

Helena's throat pinched shut. The man was a gentleman in appearance, manner and speech. And he'd been riding to the Knox house. That could mean only one thing.

Gemma's face reappeared at the edge of the ha-ha. "I'm in robust health. But I fear we've had a small accident."

"Ah. Which of the boys made mischief this *dreich* day?" He peered down, allowing Helena her first good look at him. He was a full head taller than Gemma, broad but slender. Dark blond brows scrunched in concern over light-colored eyes that widened when he saw her. He rushed down into the ha-ha, splattering mud all over his boots and buckskin breeches. "Are you injured?"

"No." Her cheeks heated. Surely she blushed so fiercely her wet clothes would steam.

"Yes," Gemma contradicted.

His well-formed lips twitched. "Either way, let's get you out of here, shall we?"

The last man to touch her was Frederick. But this man was not Frederick. She had no choice but to allow his help. "Thank you."

There was nothing lurid in his gaze as he assessed her one-footed stance and extended his arm. "Lean on me."

She placed her hand in the crook of his elbow and dropped her right foot. Pain shot up her bones. "Oh!"

"Forgive me." His arm fell.

"No. It is me."

He rubbed his square jaw with his leather-gloved hand. "I intend to carry you." It sounded like a warning.

"Say yes, please." Gemma brushed rain from the epaulettes of her spencer.

Helena sighed and nodded. The gentleman's arms went underneath her, swooping her from the ground. He'd carried her out of the ha-ha before she realized her face pressed against his spice-and-starch-scented lapels. A rather nice smell.

She jerked her head back. How improper to notice such a thing.

The gentleman peeked at her. "How did you fall down there?" There it was again. *Doon.* Would Helena speak like that soon, too?

"Clumsiness, I fear."

"No doubt the boys were with you." With steady steps, he marched to a black, white-socked gelding grazing a few yards distant. She might have been a sack of corn seed for all the intimacy of the act. "I'll put you on the horse, if you *dinnae* mind."

What she minded was encountering him in this sorry state, but ah well. She'd left her pride back in London. "Thank you for your assistance."

With no noticeable difficulty, he adjusted her in his arms and hoisted her into the saddle. She landed square on the horse's back, although it was an uncomfortable fit, sitting sideways on the standard saddle. It was far more suitable, however, than being carried in his arms all the way back to the house.

Although he had been everything proper. Even now, he looked away when she adjusted her sullied gown and cloak over her legs. It proved no easy task, for the drenched muslin of her gown clung to her damp undergarments, which stuck to her limbs, revealing the curves of her legs. And her cloak did not reach her ankles.

Mama would swoon at the sight.

Her rescuer removed his blue coat and held it up to her. It was on her tongue to refuse, but his expression brooked no argument. His eyes were soft, though. And such a nice shade of green, like the underside of a new leaf.

She unclasped her cloak and draped it over her legs like a blanket. Then she pulled his wool coat over her shoulders, at once enveloped in welcome warmth and his spicy smell.

"Thank you." Did he realize she meant it for more than his coat?

He nodded, then turned to Gemma. "Are you able to walk back, Mrs. Knox?"

"Oh, yes." She tucked her hand into his elbow. "What an exciting day."

Did Helena imagine it, or did the gentleman glance at her and smile? The evidence vanished as if washed by the raindrops pelting from the leaden sky. With a click of his tongue, he urged the horse to a walk.

"In my haste, I did not wait for a proper introduction." He tilted his head to Gemma. "Perhaps you would be so kind, ma'am?"

Gemma's hand flew to her face. "I beg your pardon. In all the activity, I forgot."

She then spoke his name, but Helena had guessed it the moment he appeared. How many landed neighbors of a certain age did Tavin and Gemma possess? His name was familiar to her. She had spent the past two weeks clinging to it like the rail of a rotting bridge over a turbulent river. Clutching it because, while she didn't quite trust its safety, it was the one hope she had to get to the other side.

He was John Gordon, the Lord Ardoch. The stranger she had come here to marry.

In less than an hour John Gordon, Lord Ardoch, had returned home, changed into dry clothes and ridden back to his neighbor Knox's house, and been shown with all haste into the blue-papered drawing room. Not one of his London cohorts in Parliament would dare call him inefficient, and if ever a matter demanded expediency, this was it. The task ahead was critical.

Unfortunately, it was also distasteful. Not the marriage, exactly, but the other part. Coming to terms with Lady Helena Stanhope's father.

"And the deed can be accomplished by when?" The powerful Duke of Kelworth stopped pacing a trail into the thick Aubusson rug and leveled John with a glare. Other men quaked under such a stare during parliamentary discussions at Westminster. But not John, which perhaps accounted for Kelworth's bristling manner toward him.

His future father-in-law. He stifled a grin. His peers in Parliament would drop a collective jaw when they found out John had married Kelworth's daughter. Romeo and Juliet made a less surprising match.

"I must post the Banns first, Your Grace." John sipped his coffee. Bitter, as he liked it.

"That will take too long." Kelworth shoved thinning blond hair from his broad brow in an impatient gesture. "This is Scotland. Marriages are performed by blacksmiths and butchers. Can't the deed be done today?"

The deed, as if his daughter's marriage to him was naught but a transaction. Most dukes expected a better match for their eldest daughter than John, true. No doubt Kelworth would have preferred a Tory, too.

"It could, but your daughter deserves better, and I've my own *bairns* to consider. A wedding in the kirk is best for everyone. I'll make special arrangements for all the Banns to be read at once during divine services this Sunday, and we can be married Monday." He set his coffee on the filigreed table. "By this time next week, it will be over."

For better or for worse.

A pinprick of guilt needled John. He was betraying his late wife's wishes by marrying again—she'd never said those precise words, but he'd understood her meaning. Catriona would understand him marrying *this way*, though, wouldn't she? Because it was not for love?

A brief knock on the door drew their gazes. The butler opened the door, admitting a rush of cool from the hall and a wide-eyed Lady Helena. "Forgive my intrusion."

John hopped to his feet. Kelworth stood, too. "No intrusion, daughter. The matter is settled. Ardoch is on his way out."

"I should like an audience with him before he leaves." Her words were for her father, but her clear gaze fixed on John.

"Well, then." Kelworth started to sit down.

"A private one." Her thumbs fidgeted.

"I should be honored, Lady Helena." John was eight-and-twenty, no green lad, but the idea of being alone with Lady Helena sent his heart thunking in his chest.

Kelworth's brows met in a fierce line and his face purpled, like he had choice words to sputter. Instead he succumbed to a fit of coughing.

John stepped forward. "Your Grace?"

Helena rushed toward him, wincing with each step. "Papa—"

"I'm well. Don't fuss." A few more coughs, and Kelworth's coloring returned to its normal hue. He stepped away from Helena's outstretched hand, avoiding both of their gazes. "Five minutes."

The moment the door shut behind Kelworth with a soft click, Helena hobbled toward John. He hastened to her side, arm extended. "Mayhap you shouldn't be walking yet." His wife would have stayed in bed for a week or more after taking a fall. But Helena was not Catriona, was she?

He shoved the dangerous thought aside and assisted Helena into the fireside chair vacated by her father.

"I'm already much better. 'twas just a twist." She'd changed clothing since her tumble into the ha-ha, and her high-neck gown of white covered her, throat to wrist. She looked the model of modesty.

Something they both knew to be an overstatement.

He pitied her and her mistaken choice to trust the wrong gentleman, and it was clear from her demeanor that she regretted it. But here she was, paying the price, without tears or wailing, and he couldn't help but admire her resolve. He took the seat beside her.

"How may I put you at ease?"

"You already have, more than you know. Agreeing to a, er, *convenient* marriage to me, sight unseen?"

In a fit of madness four weeks ago, he'd confided to Tavin how much he wished he had a wife—for the children's sake but no more—but he'd expected nothing to come of his admission other than relief at sharing his burden with a friend.

Tavin, however, knew of a female who sought a husband—who was rather desperate for one, as it turned out. When John learned the lady was amenable to a marriage in name only, he couldn't help but believe it an answer to prayer.

"You agreed to the same. We both have our reasons."

"As to that." She swallowed. Pinked like a cherry. Looked everywhere but at him. "Papa wished to rush the wedding in the event I was in a d-delicate state."

Oh. "I assure you, it doesn't matter to me if you are with child or not."

"I'm not. In a delicate state, that is. If you're to be my husband, you should know."

So she had no need of an immediate marriage, after all. Did that mean she wished to break their arrangement altogether?

Of course she did. Who would wish to bind herself to a stranger and raise his children?

Disappointment soured his stomach. He needed a wife. No one could replace Catriona for the children, but they needed someone. Needed her now, because he had failed so miserably.

But that wasn't Lady Helena's problem; it was his. He forced a smile. "I see. Fear not, Lady Helena. I shall speak to your father and tell him we decided to break our arrangement."

"No, you misunderstand. I'm willing to marry you. But you deserved the truth first. If you do not wish to marry me now that you've met me, however, I understand." She looked into the hearth, presenting him with her profile. Her blue eyes flashed silver in the firelight until the fringe of her dark lashes lowered, allowing him the freedom to truly look on her. She was dainty, from her fingers to her pert nose. Tendrils of blond hair escaped the pins at her crown to curl about her temples.

She was lovely, his bride-to-be. But frightened, too. Her fingers clutched the armrests of her chair.

She need never be frightened of him. "Our convenient arrangement might be unusual, but it suits me well," he said. "We may marry Monday, if it pleases you."

"It does."

This was nothing like his first proposal. His heart had skittered like a snared rabbit's that winter day nine years ago when his father arranged for him to speak to Catriona. They were both nineteen, the same age as Helena was now. A bit young, but his parents desired him to marry at the earliest opportunity. He must produce heirs, as many as possible, because children, as his family knew all too well, were fragile. And heirs were an absolute necessity.

He didn't resist his father's direction to marry Catriona.

She was a fair lass with a kind demeanor. He'd called on her at the appointed hour and asked for her hand. She had smiled, he had smiled. He gave her a chaste kiss afterward.

Now, betrothed once again, there were no smiles. No kisses, chaste or otherwise, would ever exist between him and Lady Helena. This was a business transaction, no more.

But they were in agreement. Relief soothed his stomach like a healing tonic, yet a niggling of fear would not be displaced. Would he come to regret this? Would she?

Her eyes were large, as if she expected something. Perhaps he should kiss her hand, if not her lips.

He stood and bowed instead. The scent of clean linen and rosewater emanated from her, fresh and feminine and more appealing to him than it should be. "Thank you, Lady Helena."

"Are we to forever thank one another for our sacrifices?" Her smile was weary. "We shall help one another. But there is one more thing we should discuss."

A token of his pledge, perhaps? Surely this duke's daughter would expect something expensive. A small price to pay, he supposed, for what he asked of her. He fingered his signet ring. "Anything."

"I wish to meet your children before we make an announcement."

Of course. That should have been obvious. What sort of father was he, to commit to marrying a stranger before he saw how she behaved with his children?

A desperate one, that was the sort of father he was. And he saw no other way to nurture his four charges than to provide them with a well-bred maternal figure to see to their needs. Tavin's recommendation of his cousin Lady Helena's character—disregarding the one grave error that brought her here—gleamed like a polished gemstone. She was a lady of breeding and bearing: educated, refined and gentle with her younger sisters.

"Tomorrow? It would be my pleasure to introduce you." His niece and three children were quick-witted and mannerly.

No doubt she'd love them on sight.

Chapter Two

They are just children.

Helena perched on the settee in her betrothed's drawing room awaiting his offspring, willing her hands to be still. She'd wear through her gloves if her thumbs kept up with this fidgeting.

They are just children. And Lord Ardoch is just a man whom you shall seldom see.

And this was to be her home, the oddly named Comraich. She was more than capable of running it, despite her youth, although the task was a trifle daunting. It was only natural, facing such prospects, for her stomach to stir as if a whirlwind eddied inside her.

But she had not expected to be daunted by *him*. Lord Ardoch was no longer a distant hope for redemption, but a real man with gold hair curling over his brow, his elbow propped on the arm of his chair, his index finger resting against his lip. Intelligence sparked in his eyes, and his broad shoulders bore an air of confidence. Her husband-to-be was self-assured, noble and handsome.

Handsome? Oh, dear. Her thumbs resumed fidgeting on her lap.

"Your home is a far more comfortable pile of stones than

I expected, considering its age," Papa was saying. "How do you feel about living in such an ancient manse, Helena?"

Her gaze flew to Lord Ardoch's. His brows lifted, awaiting her response. Heat flushed her cheeks.

"Comraich is lovely." And it was, with its blue free-stone walls and mullioned windows. "This is a pleasant chamber, too."

The drawing room benefited from southwestern exposure. Light spilled through the windows to brighten the cheerful green and cream decorating the walls and furnishings. A gilt pianoforte occupied the corner by the window, and Helena itched to touch the keys. Once Lord Ardoch left for London and she was alone, she'd play every day.

One side of Lord Ardoch's lips curved upward. "I'm gratified you think so. My late wife decorated it to her tastes, but you may do as you wish with it."

Alter his wife's rooms? Her hand lifted an inch from her lap. "I would not wish to overstep."

Lord Ardoch's gaze fixed on her hand. "It's not an overstep. You're to be the lady here. Change whatever you like."

What she liked was to change nothing. To be a grateful little mouse. She lowered her hand.

"Change is your way, isn't it?" Papa skewered Lord Ardoch with a glare. "I suppose you'll have some new bacon-brained notion for the House of Lords come January?"

Helena's thumbs fidgeted anew, but Lord Ardoch grinned, appearing almost gleeful. Her husband-to-be could stand up to Papa. Few could.

"Not *new* at all, Your Grace. I'm determined to introduce a plan to improve education."

Papa waved his hand near his nose, as if the notion reeked. "Do not think I'll support your notions because you are my son-in-law."

Lord Ardoch's smile turned impish, taking years off his

countenance. Was this what his sons looked like? If so, they no doubt got away with heaps of mischief.

"I would not have dared dreamt it so, Your Grace. But neither will I neglect my determination to see the children of Britain educated."

"All children?" Helena blurted. Did he mean the poor? Or just poor boys?

Papa stiffened beside her. "He'd insist the government school every urchin."

At a soft shuffle at the door, her fiancé's gaze riveted behind Helena. "Speaking of children, mine are here at last."

A flutter twisted in Helena's stomach as she and Papa stood. Would they like her? She would be their mother. Not in the real way, but she would try to make a worthy substitute. She'd always wanted to be a mother, after all.

Four children—two boys and two girls—assembled like infantrymen into a line, although the smallest girl needed the assistance of the young maid with mouse-brown hair and a beak nose.

Lord Ardoch made introductions, and the children performed precise bows and curtsies. "'Tis an honor, Your Grace," they each said to Papa. Mama would approve of their deferential bearing at being condescended to by a duke.

But Helena didn't wish them to feel condescended to *by her*. She turned to the eldest, a girl, and not Lord Ardoch's child. Margaret Allaway was his deceased wife's orphaned niece. A pretty girl, Margaret had the lean, angular look of an adolescent experiencing a rapid shoot of growth. The top of her reddish-brown head reached Helena's nose.

"How do you do, Margaret? I understand you are thirteen? My youngest sister, Andy—Andromeda—is your age."

"How do you do, Lady Helena?" Margaret did not return Helena's smile.

Next came the boys, twins, seven years old and—how would she ever tell them apart? They were identical, from their bright eyes to their pointy ears to the light brown hair curling over their collars. The first, Alexander, mashed his lips together as if to stifle a laugh. His brother, Callum, stared at her shoulder as if his life depended upon holding his gaze there.

Mayhap she should address them both at once. "I hear you are busy lads."

"Yes, Lady Helena." One side of Alexander's lips twisted up more than the other. It gave him a mischievous look. Callum grinned in exact imitation of his brother. Was there nothing contrary in their appearances?

A shaft of anxiety twisted in her abdomen.

She turned to the littlest girl, a round-cheeked blonde with clouded eyes.

"Louisa." Lord Ardoch's voice broke in before Helena could greet the child. There was a touch of something careful in his tone. "Lady Helena, Louisa is—"

"Five years old, I expect," Helena interjected. What had he been about to say? That Louisa was blind, in case she'd forgotten? When Lord Ardoch had written to propose, he'd told her his youngest could see nothing but light. Did he fear his daughter's blindness would bother her? Or did it embarrass him?

The back of his fingers stroked Louisa's rosy cheek. "Her birthday was last week."

No, he wasn't embarrassed. Just protective.

"Papa gave me a cradle for Tabitha, and the boys aren't allowed to touch it," Louisa announced.

Perhaps that was for the best, considering how Alexander and Callum stifled snickers. "Is Tabitha your doll?"

"She is indeed," Lord Ardoch said.

"From Mama 'afore she went to heaven." Louisa's statement was matter-of-fact.

At the front of the line, Margaret stiffened. Oh, dear. Perhaps Margaret missed her aunt, or feared being shuffled off because she was an orphaned relation. Well, Helena would give Margaret plenty of support during the adjustment. And surely, in no time at all, they would be a happy family.

Papa cleared his throat. "Very good, Lord Ardoch."

With a paternal nod, her betrothed sent silent approval to his brood. They executed one last bow or curtsy and filed from the room with the birdlike maid. He watched their backs as they went, smiling, like a loving father.

Helena smiled, too. Had he known her request to meet the children was a test? To see if he was a man of his word?

It wasn't the children she'd needed to observe. Rather, it was whether or not Lord Ardoch loved them. Because if he loved his children, his motivation for marrying her was true.

He wanted her for his children's sake. He did not want her for himself. And that was what she wanted above all. To not be wanted by a man, not after what Frederick did to her. If she was never going to be hurt again, she must spend her life alone.

Alone. John was so accustomed to silent corridors and solitary meals and empty arms, it felt almost strange to be at Comraich, with its noise and activity. How sad that it felt strange, too, to hold Louisa in his arms.

Her breath was warm and milky on his cheek as he carried her down the main staircase to the ground floor Monday morning. "You've grown, little one."

"I am five now. Of course I have grown."

"And in eight years, you shall be as grown up as Margaret."

Her brow furrowed. "Will I turn as sour?"

"Your cousin is not sour." Moody, perhaps, but that was the age. At the bottom of the stairs, he gestured to the bird-boned nursemaid, Agnes, to take Louisa. "We leave for the wedding at a quarter to eleven. Ensure the children are ready, please." There was still plenty of time for the boys to work out their fidgets, as they seemed to be doing. Over-head, their stomps reverberated across the oak plank floors.

"Yes, m'lord." Agnes's head bobbed.

He bid Louisa farewell and made his way outside. Dis-mal clouds thickened overhead, stirred by the chill wind nipping John's cheeks and nose. His wedding day would be damp, to be sure.

But not without all the usual trappings of tradition. He traipsed over the grass until he spied MacArthur, the wizened-faced gardener with a white forelock escaping a tweedy cap. The man had served here since his father's time, and had seen John bring one bride home. Now the gardener would see John bring another here, this afternoon.

MacArthur spied him and bowed. "M'lord."

"Good morning, MacArthur. Forgive my disturbing you, but where is the patch you mentioned?"

"On the nort' side of the great oak, m'lord. I'll fetch some for ye, if ye like."

"No, thank you. I shall see to the matter myself." Every bride deserved a posy, and it seemed fitting that a husband should gather the wedding blooms for her himself.

Comraich had traditions, although he'd neglected them for some time. When Catriona was alive, he'd been too pre-occupied in London to be home a great deal, and she didn't seem to mind overmuch. "You have your occupations, and I have mine," she'd say every time they parted, the wave of her hand more like a shoo than a farewell. Surely she meant to ease his guilt over his long absences in London.

At least, until Louisa's birth.

John winced as pain stabbed inside his cheek—he'd chomped it again. He shook his head and looked ahead for a glimpse of white close to the ground, but he couldn't shake the image of Catriona from his mind.

He should have spent more time at Comraich with her, but he had a duty to the Crown, and even though he'd not been eligible to sit in Parliament until the session started this coming January, he spent more time in London, it seemed, than he did at home.

So how could he know where the wedding blooms grew anymore?

He tromped through the wet grass, allowing the familiar smells of damp earth and cattle to fill his lungs. For all his absences, he loved this place. And by the end of the day, he'd have a wife who would care for it while he executed his duty.

His eye caught on something small and white. The wedding blooms. Although the stems were slim enough to snap with his fingers, he withdrew a slim knife from his pocket.

The cuts were precise and neat. Just like his life would be from now on.

Helena had never indulged in daydreams of her wedding day, but if she had, she would have hoped for sunshine, not the cloudy skies overhead. She would have also expected to marry a man she'd seen more than twice.

She was grateful all the same. Lord Ardoch was rescuing her. Marrying him would solve every problem she'd created.

She smoothed her hands over her snowy wedding gown, adjusting the gauze overskirt trimmed in green ribbon before she examined herself in the looking glass. She looked ready, to be sure, in the dress and with a short veil trailing behind her white bonnet, but her skin was pale, her eyes flat, her lips set in a line. She didn't look grateful.

She looked like ice.

A knock on the door startled her, rattling her teeth. Was she brittle as frost, too?

Barnes, her new dark-haired lady's maid, hopped to open the door. Gemma swept past her, her grin as sunny as her daffodil gown. "How lovely you are, Helena. Here, the finishing touch."

The bridal posy was unlike anything Helena had ever seen. Bundled and tied with a simple white ribbon, a sprig of white blooms lay atop a cutting of ivy, spreading a delicate but delectable spicy-sweet fragrance. "How thoughtful. Thank you."

"Do not thank me. 'Tis heather from Lord Ardoch."

A faint swooning sound came from the usually stoic Barnes.

Her maid was right: this gesture of Lord Ardoch's was thoughtful. The heather was a pleasant token, and far preferable to a more lavish gift. Papa had presented Mama with the Kelworth diamonds on their wedding day, but a convenient wife like Helena didn't deserve anything like that.

She sniffed the blooms. "I thought heather was purple."

"Most of the time. But white heather is special and not easy to find."

"Is it a bridal tradition?" She fingered the slick leaves of ivy trailing the heather. Rimmed in creamy white, the green foliage echoed the trim of her gown.

"I don't know, but I'm sure the ivy is not. I recall it is his family plant." Gemma patted Helena's arm. "'Tis a Scottish tradition, a way of him welcoming you to his family."

A gesture, which, if theirs was a true marriage, would make her heart swell. As it stood, this symbol was kind, but one more facade to mask the hollow shell that would be their marriage.

"I shall carry it with my prayer book." Helena tied the cuttings to the slim volume using the ribbon he had provided. Or, rather, his staff had provided. He wouldn't have bothered with such a chore himself.

Only a devoted man in the throes of love would pick blooms for his bride.

In her youth, she hadn't dreamed of her wedding day, true, but not so long ago, she thought she would marry Frederick. Sometimes when she thought of it, her grief compressed her chest like too-tight stays, and no matter how her fingers plucked and pulled at the laces, she couldn't loosen them.

Everyone thought she was here today because of her love for Frederick, because she'd made a grave mistake giving herself to him before they wed. Tavin, Gemma and her almost-husband seemed to pity her over it. Would they feel otherwise if they knew the truth, that Frederick forced himself on her? The facts hadn't mattered overmuch to Papa, although he was angrier with Frederick than he was with Helena. He just didn't know how to show it.

He also blamed her for her disobedience in falling in love with Frederick. Well, this was the day she would obey Papa, demonstrating her sorrow to God and her family by marrying a stranger. She squeezed the flowery prayer book and looked up into Gemma's expectant face.

"We mustn't keep everyone waiting. Shall we?"

Chapter Three

Helena pattered up the rain-puddled path to the village church on her father's arm, favoring her stiff ankle. The kirk's weathered stones blended into the landscape's gray-green palette of rolling hills, rain-heavy clouds, mossy gravestones and muddy grass. It was probably damp and drafty inside, but the moment Helena crossed the threshold, she didn't mind the cold swirling her ankles. The kirk *felt* like something, all right—warm and comfortable in a way that had nothing to do with the temperature.

It felt hopeful, something Helena hadn't experienced in a long while.

Was this from God? Did it mean this church was full of His love? Could some of it extend to her?

Someone must have noticed them arrive, because the murmured conversations of the guests quieted. A nervous thrill twined with the quickening she'd experienced in her body, but she was ready, especially now that she'd felt such comfort. She took a deep breath, filling her nostrils with the smells of every church she'd ever entered: stale air, musty pages, candle smoke and beeswax.

She squeezed Papa's arm as they paused at the threshold

to the aisle. She hoped he'd look down at her. Smile and squeeze her fingers. Tell her she made a beautiful bride.

Instead he looked ahead. "Come along, then."

The aisle was as lacking in length as the pews were in guests. A tiny female in dull clothing—the children's nursemaid—lurked in at the rear. Toward the front, a few others dressed in finer attire stared at her with unashamed curiosity. The familiar faces of Gemma and Tavin smiled at her from the left side of the aisle while their wards, Petey and Eddie, wriggled and tugged at their miniature neck cloths.

Lord Ardoch's children stood in the front pew on the right. The boys wore matching brown coats and impish expressions. Margaret, wearing sprigged muslin, a straw bonnet and a scowl, lifted little Louisa in her arms.

And beside the bespectacled, round-faced young clergyman at the end of the aisle, donned in a formal black coat, Lord Ardoch waited, hands at his sides, face impassive.

The sensation of peace she'd experienced at the threshold drained away.

Helena compressed her lips. *I do not know if I can address You like this, God, but You must know how sorry I am. Marrying will make everything right, won't it? Will You forgive me, once I do this? Will You even love me?*

When they reached the end of the aisle, Papa released her arm. She clutched her prayer book so hard her knuckles ached.

Glancing down at her flowery book, Lord Ardoch's eyes warmed to a deeper green and a soft smile lifted his lips. He must be pleased she'd attached his gift of blooms.

He was handsome, the sort of gentleman she might have noticed before she met Frederick Coles. But as Lord Ardoch was a lord of Parliament, the lowest rank in the Peerage of Scotland, her parents would have dismissed him as a potential husband.

In the end, however, rank hadn't mattered to her that much. Certainly not with Frederick.

Stop thinking of him. She forced her lips to lift into a slight smile. *Now freeze.*

She trembled. Perhaps in freezing her smile, she'd iced the rest of her, too.

The clergyman spoke of covenant, looking over his spectacles at them as if to impress on them the gravity of such a thing. But she wouldn't be here if she didn't understand. Her pledge was no small thing. It was forever.

A few more words, punctuated by one of the children's snuffles and someone's long sigh. Then Lord Ardoch faced her and took her right hand. *Steady,* she ordered her twitchy fingers.

"I, John Angus, do take thee, Helena Caroline, to be my married wife, and do, in the presence of God, and before this congregation, promise and covenant to be a loving and faithful husband unto thee, until God shall separate us by death."

As he spoke the vows, did he think of his Catriona, the wife he chose? He was marrying Helena out of convenience, after all.

Then his gaze met hers, its message sure. He would provide for her and shelter her. He would be a good husband in that way. Perhaps not *loving,* but good.

It was more than she deserved. A jerky swallow pained her throat as she took his right hand. Not too firmly. Nor too affectionate, or too scared, or however else he might interpret her clasp. She fixed her gaze on the precise knot of his neck cloth.

"I, Helena Caroline, do take thee, John Angus, to be my

married husband, and do, in the presence of God, and before this congregation—"

She glanced at Papa. His mouth was downturned, like a child's drawing of a rounded mountain.

"Before this congregation, promise and covenant?" The clergyman bore an indulgent smile. She must not have been his first overset bride.

"—before this congregation promise and covenant to be a loving and faithful wife unto thee, until God shall separate us by death."

There. She'd done it. Maybe God would absolve her now.

Her fingers squeezed Lord Ardoch's.

His brows rose.

Oh, dear. She meant nothing more in her gesture than relief. Assurance of their partnership. But perhaps he hadn't understood. Prickles of heat barbed her neck and cheeks. Her hands pulled back, but he held on, his grip far firmer than hers had been.

She couldn't lift her gaze from the buttons of his silver waistcoat while the clergyman spoke about the *fruits of marriage*. There would be none of that. The warmth of her blush washed away, from the crown of her head down, leaving her cold again.

After more prayers, Lord Ardoch slid a cold, polished ring with a deep red stone on the fourth finger of her left hand.

And then the one other thing. Their first—and last—kiss.

With one hand, he cupped her shoulder, and with the other, he lifted her chin. It was a light touch, enough to hold her steady. But more than enough to send her insides quaking.

He bent his head. His well-formed lips brushed the corner of her mouth, fleeting and gentle. Then he lowered his hands and released her.

She had received warmer kisses on her hands from courtiers back in London. Still, the tingle of his touch lingered. She resisted the urge to touch her mouth.

One final blessing by the clergyman, and it was done. She was married. Her problems were solved, neat and tidy. Her parents would be relieved. God approved, too. From this day forward, everything would be smooth as the cream icing on her wedding cake.

A shriek, shrill and jarring as a parakeet squawk, echoed off the stones. Startled, Helena dropped her prayer book.

Lord Ardoch spun toward his youngest child. "Louisa—"

Louisa's red-slippered feet kicked Margaret, who dropped her cousin with a gasp of exaggerated outrage. Louisa fell to her hands and knees, screeching.

"Is she ill?" Helena rushed forward.

"No." Lord Ardoch scooped Louisa into his arms. "What is it, poppet?"

"Get it out!" Louisa's screams reverberated through the sanctuary.

Papa's grumble wasn't loud, but it lifted the hairs at Helena's nape. She didn't need to look up to know every eye fell upon them. All she could do was watch Louisa writhe and howl in her husband's arms. Yet he said she was not ill. Then what sort of problem could explain her behavior? Children knew better than to show such poor deportment. In church. At their father's wedding—

Alexander and Callum—whichever was which— doubled over, hands pressed against their diminutive satin waistcoats, silent laughter escaping their ruddy little faces. Why, they weren't just amused by Louisa's tantrum. No doubt the rascals caused it.

She touched the boys' shoulders. Not hard, but enough for them to spin toward her, their eyes wide.

"What did you do?" She enunciated each syllable.

They glanced at one another. Her eyes narrowed.

"Nothing—"

"'Twas his idea—"

"Dear me," the clergyman lamented, retrieving Helena's prayer book.

Louisa thrashed. Lord Ardoch cupped her golden curls, and below his hand, under Louisa's dress, something *moved*.

Helena's stomach rippled. "Inside her gown."

Her husband's brows lifted. She may not know him well, but it was not difficult to discern his utter befuddlement. With a huff, Helena thrust her hand down the backside of Louisa's lacy bodice and grasped something hot and furry.

She yanked. A thin, hairless tail dangled between her fingers.

A yip, like an angry Pekinese's, escaped her throat and her grip went slack. A gray blur fell from her hand and shot under the pew. The clergyman clutched Helena's flowery prayer book and the boys fell to their knees. Not out of penitence, but to hunt the rodent.

Lord Ardoch held out Louisa to Helena, but Margaret hurried forward and took the sobbing girl, leaving Helena feeling foolish with her arms extended and empty, and half her new family either weeping or crawling about the floor.

Tempted though she was to swoon, she'd never managed to escape in such a convenient fashion, so she fixed another frozen smile on her face.

Lord Ardoch pulled one of the twins to stand. "Enough."

"But he was a good mouse." The boy's lip stuck out.

The lad cared about the mouse more than his sister? No blood or rips marred Louisa's white gown and the child's cries had hushed, but Helena would have to summon a physician to be certain. "Your sister could have been bitten."

"That one never bites." The second twin folded his arms. "He goes about under our waistcoats all the time and all he ever does is tickle."

Gemma and Tavin's ward, Petey, broke from the pew. "I want him in *my* waistcoat."

"Not now." Gemma pulled him back.

"The only creature that beastie will be acquainted with now is the kirk cat, but that is the least of your concerns." Lord Ardoch's brows knit. "Apologize to your *mither* for causing such a scene at her wedding."

Her wedding, and oh, dear, what had he called her? Helena's stomach swirled as the twin's eyes widened. Then narrowed.

"She's not my *mither*!"

Well. Louisa was not the only one with strong lungs in the family.

"I won't call her *mither*, either," the other boy said. At least he wasn't screaming.

"You will not disrespect your m—your st—Lady Ardoch." Emotion bleached a rim of white around her husband's tight mouth. "Apologize now."

The boy's lips twisted, as if he'd been presented with an unappetizing dish. "Sorry, ma'am."

Helena forced yet another smile. "This is a new situation for us all. Perhaps together we might think up a name for you to call me. You cannot call me Lady Ardoch forever." And perhaps they could discuss it later, in private, rather than in front of their assembled wedding guests.

Margaret took the twin's shoulder. "Leave Lady Ardoch alone, Alex. 'Tis *her* wedding day, after all."

"Margaret." Lord Ardoch's snap brought color to the

girl's cheeks. "Your tone leaves much to be desired. Your aunt deserves a better welcome than this."

Margaret hid her face in Louisa's bonnet, but her mumble of "She's not my aunt" was nonetheless audible.

"I apologize." Her new husband looked sincere and poised. Every bit the politician he was, working to pass bills in Parliament.

"None of us has had much time to get used to the idea." Her frozen smile didn't waver. She'd not show how embarrassed the children made her feel.

What had she felt when she'd entered the kirk? Warmth, love? She felt neither anymore, neither in her heart nor radiating from her new family.

Perhaps God had felt the need to punish her further by reminding her that the marriage was as much a sham as the wedding turned out to be. But Helena had been taught that a duke's daughter should exude confidence and poise, so she held her head high as she walked beside him through the kirk door.

Where she was met by shouts and hands. Dozens of them, as children reached out to her.

John withdrew the purse he'd shoved into his pocket for this moment and pulled out a shiny coin. "Will a shilling do, lady wife?"

She didn't take the coin. Instead, her face froze in a detached expression that looked too much like her haughty father's for John's taste. Meanwhile, the village children enclosed them, open-handed and noisy with congratulatory hoots. Why didn't she take the coin? Was she as arrogant as her father, dismissing others below her in rank?

John's jaw set. She was the new Lady Ardoch, and she must comply with tradition before displeasure—and then distrust—grew in the villagers' hearts.

He reached for his bride's hand and pressed the shilling into her palm. He'd been in politics long enough to know how to keep his voice level and diplomatic, but be able to convey a sense of urgency, and he strove to use that tone now. "The first one you saw."

"The first?" Her gaze lifted to his, breaking her emotionless facade.

"Is it not customary for a bride to give a coin to the first child she sees after leaving the kirk on her wedding day?"

"I do not know." Her fingers closed over the coin.

A trickle of shame slid down the back of his neck. He'd judged her as arrogant, like her father, jumping to the conclusion she didn't wish to engage with the villagers, when in truth she'd been ignorant of local customs. He opened his mouth to speak, but she turned away and leaned over a ginger-haired girl in a brown frock. The cooper's daughter. "I saw your smile first. Thank you for your welcome."

"Thank ye, m'lady." The girl bobbed a curtsy.

John emptied the purse of its contents and tossed the handful of dull gray sixpence over the children's heads. While they shrieked and lunged for the coins, he offered her a small smile. Behind them, the children and wedding guests followed them out of the kirk. He waved at the crowd before assisting Helena into the landau they would share to Comraich.

John settled against the squabs beside her as the carriage lurched forward. "You must know how sorry I am about the scene the boys caused. And Margaret, and, well, all of it."

"As I said, it will be a transition for us all." Her expression was polite, which made it impossible to know what she thought.

It occurred to him that his first private words for her as husband and wife were an apology. Half the villagers following after their carriage assumed they were taking advantage of their privacy by murmuring words of affection, maybe even kissing.

Not that he wanted to do such a thing. Never. That one brief kiss he'd pressed on her lips was the only one they'd ever share, and while it had been quick, it had felt important, as if it sealed the vows he made to her—

John blinked. What had they been discussing, before his gaze caught on her lips?

Ah, the children. "My *bairns* know better. It's no consolation, but they've been without a proper governess for some time. A candidate arrives tomorrow, and I'll instruct the housekeeper to hire her."

His bride's brows raised a fraction. "No need. I shall see to the matter."

"You don't mind?"

"'Tis my role now, is it not, my lord?"

"John," he corrected. "You are my wife. Please call me John."

Her lips parted in surprise, breaking her polite mask. Many couples didn't use Christian names, but he didn't think he could stand it if his wife—convenient or not—called him by his title all his days.

"John. And I am Helena, but you know that already." Her head dipped, but then her brows furrowed and she turned to look out the window. "Are they following us?"

The villagers' cheers and the strains of flute and fiddle accompanied the carriage around the bend toward home. "Aye, for the wedding feast."

"The entire village will be there?" Her fingers stilled, but her gaze met his in an apologetic look. "Forgive me. I'd not expected much celebration. My mother said—"

Her lip caught in her teeth, as if she bit back her next words.

"What did she say?" Plenty, no doubt, if she was of the

same mind as her husband. Kelworth certainly thought John uncouth. "Did she think I'd be inhospitable?"

A vibrant flush stained her cheeks, burning away the cool mask she'd affected. "She said naught about you, just my…circumstances. That there was nothing to be celebrated."

John's amusement fled as understanding dawned. His wife expected no festivities because her wedding was no happy union, but a rushed embarrassment, the fruit of her ruin and his desperation.

He'd not known quite what to expect of Lady Helena, beyond Tavin's assurances of her gentility, but he'd learned a few things of her since their first meeting in the ha-ha. She was willing to pay the price for her mistakes, and she was brave to have made the decision to marry him. Most of the time, she wore a mask that made her appear haughty, but beneath it, she was lost, unfamiliar with her new surroundings. And no doubt she felt quite alone.

The carriage rounded onto Comraich's drive. John had but a moment left of privacy while the liveried footman hurried to open the door latch and lower the steps. "Your mother is wrong. There is much to celebrate this happy day."

And it was true. He'd prayed for a wife to help him, and the Lord had sent Helena. Perhaps the tone of their marriage could be set now, with their first steps on his—their—land. "*Comraich* means *welcome*, and it is now your home every bit as it is mine."

"That's a beautiful name." Her smile was small but enough to assure him his words comforted her. John preceded her out of the carriage and assisted her down.

Her head was regal as she met the staff lined in neat rows at the door. She greeted each one, from the lowest of the chambermaids up to the butler, Kerr, the housekeeper,

Mrs. McGill, and his valet, Ritchie. Then the other carriages arrived, followed by villagers, and everyone moved to Comraich's grassy yard, where the aromas of roasting mutton and beef tangled in the air with laughter and strains of music.

After welcoming the guests and nibbling on the roast meat and punch, John and his bride separated. He didn't even glance at his wife until his portly agent, Burgess, stopped midsentence and lifted his brows. "Fetching scene, m'lord."

John turned. His new wife, her white gown billowing in the breeze, linked arms with his niece Margaret as they strolled away from the festivities. Helena's head bent toward Margaret's, and she spoke softly. He couldn't see Margaret's face, but he imagined a smile there.

He expelled a long breath of relief. *Thank You, Lord.* It seemed he'd made a wise decision, after all. Despite the scene at the kirk, Margaret seemed to be regretting her attitude and was now warming to his new wife. Before long, the boys would, too.

He'd had nothing to worry about, after all. Everything would go well from here on out.

At least Margaret didn't try to break free from Helena's loose hold as Helena led her toward the house. "When did you find time to do it?"

"I don't know what you're talking about." Margaret forced a phony-sounding laugh.

Helena's eyes stung from the oversweet tuberose perfume the girl had liberally applied at some point since arriving back from the kirk, but the fragrant fumes weren't all the girl had put on. "I know the effects of Rigge's Liquid Bloom and a rouge crepe paper pressed against a cheek when I see them."

"I didn't do anything."

"You are not the first person I've met to use color and deny it. Even the Prince Regent." Helena glanced about, thankful they stood in the shadow of the house. "I've no wish to embarrass you, but you are far too young for cosmetics."

Although she had a fair idea why Margaret had put them on: that dark-haired schoolboy who'd tugged Margaret's bonnet ribbon. "Who is that young man?"

"Archibald Dunwood, the solicitor's son." Margaret's tone was superior.

Archibald—like every third male she'd met today. "I see. Well, he will still be at the party after we've washed your face."

Margaret's head snapped back, as if she'd been slapped. "I'm not washing my face. I'm not wearing cosmetics."

Really, was she having this argument with a child? At her wedding party? What should she do? Mama would order the nursemaid to see to her punishment and ignore her for several days, dared she behave like this.

But Helena was not Mama. She looked Margaret in the eye, or at least tried to, for the child stared at the house with a mulish expression. "You may not lie to me, Margaret. I know my being here will be a difficult adjustment for us all, but things will go better if we are honest with one another."

That got Margaret to return her gaze, but oh how it crackled, like a log catching fire, sparking and hot. "May I go inside the house to wash my face, Lady Ardoch?"

Helena ignored the sarcastic tone. "By all means. And then we may start again."

But Margaret was already stomping toward the house.

It was a relief when Papa approached, a familiar face among the strangers. Behind him, some sort of dance began, with the fiddle and fife growing louder. Papa would not dance, of course, but the tiniest bit of her wished he would dance with her on her wedding. For one person to be happy. Other than Louisa, that is, who'd been sweet enough once the mouse was out of her dress.

"Papa, isn't this a lovely party?"

"Just so," he said in a tone that implied the opposite as he stared at a toddler attaching himself to her new husband's legs. "Alas, I must take my leave."

"It has been a long day." Helena's feet ached. Or rather, one ached. The other—the one she'd twisted last week—throbbed. And Papa must be exhausted, too. He hadn't been well. "What time shall we expect you to call tomorrow?"

As his head shook, a thin lock of faded blond hair fell over his forehead. "Tomorrow I return to London."

Oh. Her eyes stung, but she'd not allow tears. "When will I see you again?"

If ever? As if on cue, Papa coughed. She reached out but didn't allow herself to touch him. He wouldn't want it.

This spell was blessedly short, however. Within a few moments he took a steadying breath. "I do not know. I'm certain your mother desires a letter from you, once you are settled."

"I shall write to her on the morrow." It would be pleasant if he waited to deliver it himself, but clearly, he had no desire to stay any longer than he'd had to. He hadn't been well, true—

"How could Mrs. Knox permit you to wear that?"

"Wear what?" Was her hem ripped? Did she drip punch on her bodice?

"That gown. 'Tis a good thing no one we know from London can see you—can you imagine what my brother would say?"

"Uncle Cecil?" Papa's younger brother and heir presumptive was a stickler and looked down his nose on others even more than Mama did, and he'd no doubt disapprove of Helena's marriage once he learned of it. But why would he care about her dress?

"If your mother had been here, she would have seen you dressed properly."

"Mama suggested I wear this gown today."

"Then she was rendered daft by grief, for your gown is a disgrace."

The bodice was modest, not at all alluring, as Papa had accused her of dressing after Frederick—after that terrible day. "Is it too showy?"

Papa's lips twisted. "It is too white."

"White is fashionable." The words tumbled out. All unmarried ladies—and many married ones—wore white.

"'Tis also symbolic."

Of course it was. Was the church altar not dressed in white at Easter and Christmas and all the other happy feast days? "White is the color of joy."

"And purity, a quality you lack, so there is little joy today, either. You could have made a dazzling match. Stayed close to us in London. Now you've lost everything." His eyes moistened, which made her eyes sting and her hands tremble to reach out to him, but before she could move, he shook his head. "No, daughter, there is no cause to wear white this day."

With that, he left her alone. A few guests approached, expectant smiles on their faces, forestalling her from fleeing into the house and doing something shameful, like giving in to tears. She forced herself to freeze: smile, posture, proud tilt of her chin.

I am ice. I am ice. And if I am not careful, I will crack.

Chapter Four

Helena ambled onto the grass behind Comraich, the site of yesterday's wedding celebration. All evidence of her nuptial feast had disappeared from the scene, like a dream dissolving at first light. One might well wonder whether it had happened at all.

But the ring on her finger and the children trailing behind her were real. This was her life now.

She cupped the wooden ball in her hands, judging its weight. No heavier than a large apple, it should be perfect for the children. Even Louisa should have no trouble rolling it across the grass for a game of nine pins.

Something whizzed past her ear. Helena spun to where the boys scampered over the grass, swinging rackets. They'd hit the shuttlecock toward her. "Too close, lads."

Alexander—she knew it was him because his coat was darker brown than Callum's today—grinned as he bounced the strings of his racket off his fist. "Accident! Sorry, ma'am."

Callum spun away, his shoulders shaking with laughter.

If it was indeed an accident, the boys thought it a lark of one. Helena's jaw clenched. She wasn't certain how to be a mother, but she'd always wanted to be one. To love a child and be loved in return. Surely God had given women some sort of instinct to care for them, too. Things should get easier once she spent time with them, shouldn't they?

At least she would be hiring the new governess today to help ease things along. She should have asked why the children currently lacked one, but there hadn't been time, with all the wedding guests clamoring for their attention yesterday.

She'd hardly slept in her new chamber—Catriona's chamber, with its heavy, dark draperies that begged to be replaced with lighter fabrics, although she'd not intended to change anything. But it was her room now, separated by a sitting room from John's.

He kept his promise and left her alone, but she hadn't slept anyway. Her ankle pulsated all night, as did her head, with thoughts of Papa and Margaret and white gowns and Frederick until her maid, Barnes, brought her a tray of tea and toast at eight o'clock this morning. She'd forced down a bite and dressed, determined to start being a mother.

Surely Papa would have approved of her primrose yellow gown and matching pelisse. She'd not wear white ever again. Still, her parents frowned at her in her imagination, and her forehead ached.

The smack of the shuttlecock against a tree trunk dragged Helena to the present, where Louisa, held in the nursemaid Agnes's arms, sucked her thumb and gripped a well-loved doll. Beside them, Margaret stared at the clear heavens, a bored expression on her fair, cosmetic-free face.

"Right," Helena said, clutching the ball as if it held her sanity within it. "Who wishes first crack?" She lifted the ball in a gesture of offering.

The children stared at her. *Dear God, help.*

She took a deep breath before trying again. "Please set up the pins, Margaret. That patch there looks flat enough."

The girl slumped off to obey. "Louisa, would you like to go first?"

"Yes!" Louisa's thumb flew from her mouth with a wet pop and she squirmed in Agnes's arms. An exasperated look fluttered over Agnes's thin face as she set the child down and took her by the wrist.

"Are ye sure o' this, milady? She *cannae* play." Agnes shoved a loose tendril of lank brown hair under her white cap.

"Has she never learned? 'Tis not a difficult game."

"O' course *nae*, milady. Because she *cannae* see." Agnes exchanged a glance with Margaret.

How dare she address you in such a manner. Mama's sharp tone resounded in Helena's head. *You must assert your place, or you shall never be respected. Sending the chit off without a reference would send a strong message to the staff—*

Enough of Mama. The children had experienced too much change of late. They did not need to suffer the loss of a nursemaid now, too, but that didn't mean Helena should cower to the staff. After all, she was the lady here now. "I do not see why Louisa cannot try. Come, Louisa."

A grin split Louisa's rosy face, revealing perfect, tiny teeth. Helena took her moist hand and led her to a spot six feet from where Margaret set the pins in three rows of three. Once finished, Margaret stepped back, concern furrowing her brow. "I'm not certain this will work, ma'am."

Margaret's love for her cousin was clear. *Their love for one another is a good place to start.* Helena hoped her smile for Margaret was tender and comforting, especially after having to chide her yesterday. "If she does not enjoy it, we shall cease."

Margaret chewed her lip. "Aye, ma'am."

Helena had better think of something for the children to

call her other than *ma'am* and *my lady* and the occasional *Lady Ardoch*. The terms were appropriate, but they didn't seem at all warm. But *Mother* wasn't acceptable, either. Not after yesterday's scene.

She bent behind Louisa and reached for the doll. It was sticky to her touch. "Let's set Dolly down."

"Tabitha."

"Tabitha, yes. She will sit here on the grass." Helena propped the grimy, wood-headed doll on her cloth haunches. "Now, hold out your hands, as if you're to receive water from a pitcher."

Louisa thrust out her hands and giggled.

Helena set the ball in them, cradling Louisa's hands from below until the child adjusted to the ball's weight. Louisa's thumbs and index fingers rubbed over the ball, and she bent her head down to it. Was she able to see its outline, out here in the bright sunshine?

"The pins are on the grass a short distance from us. Roll the ball, like this." Guiding Louisa's arms, Helena swung them down to the child's knees and back again. "Now let it go."

The ball thudded, landing a foot away.

"You did it," Helena praised. Louisa hopped in place, knocking Helena's chin with the top of her head. Pain sluiced through her jaw and brought tears to her eyes.

"Did it go?" Louisa asked.

"No." Margaret's glare caused a different sort of pain to Helena than the bump to her jaw. "She does not even know where to aim."

The twins paused in their game, staring at Helena as if she had forced Louisa to walk through thistles barefoot.

Her physical pain receding, Helena retrieved the ball. "An excellent first attempt. This time let the ball roll from your fingers."

Louisa released it and it trundled far enough to tap a pin. Louisa's head turned to the side, reminding Helena of a robin scouting for worms. "It hit!"

Warmth coursed through Helena's chest. "Indeed, it did."

"Well done." Margaret's frown twitched upward.

The twins dropped their rackets. "Good show, Louisa."

"Now," Helena said, "it's Margaret's turn with the ball."

Margaret scowled, took up the ball and knocked down eight of the pins. Louisa jumped up and down. "My turn again."

Margaret reset the pins. Louisa's roll missed, but Margaret brought the ball back before jogging to stand beside the pins. "Roll it toward my voice, Louisa."

Again, Louisa cocked her head. As Margaret called to her, she rolled the ball, this time knocking over two pins.

Alexander and Callum abandoned their game to join in, and soon the foursome were cheering and teasing. Helena stepped back to stand beside the nursemaid.

"She seldom knocks the pins *doon*, ma'am." Agnes shook her head.

Mama would send the impertinent Agnes packing before noon, for certain.

Perhaps kindness, shown with firm confidence, would make more difference than dismissing a servant on her first day as the lady of the house. "Louisa enjoys herself. And watch her. When the ball strikes a pin, she aims for the same place the next time. She may never be a champion at nine pins, but then again, neither am I. Yet I still find enjoyment in the exercise."

A huff escaped Agnes's pinched lips, but Helena didn't care. The scene was too pleasant to be ruined by Agnes's insolence. A blue sky banished yesterday's clouds, and the sun's glow lit up the rocky *tor* to the east and warmed her back. The children's cheeks pinked from exertion, and they all clapped for Louisa when she struck a pin.

Something prickled Helena's neck, drawing her gaze. A wheat-colored terrier pranced over the yard, followed by her new husband. He strode across the grass toward them, dressed for riding.

What a dashing figure. Not that she should be thinking such things.

The dog ran to the children, its stub tail wiggling with enthusiasm. "Iona!" The game was forgotten as the children patted the dog.

So they had a pet. She should have guessed.

Louisa hopped in place, a whine escaping her throat, until Agnes hauled her into her arms and carried her to John's side, stopping first to retrieve the dolly, Tabitha.

She'd have to remind Louisa that ladies requested attention with words, not whimpers.

John smiled and placed a hand on each child's head as he greeted them.

"I threw the ball," Louisa announced.

"Did you, now?"

He must have seen it, of course. How kind of him to let Louisa tell of it.

The children spoke over each other, relating the events of their game, and Helena hung back, her hands folded at her waist. These children loved their father. *God, if You forgive me, could some of that childlike, family affection extend to me someday, as well?*

Life was quite long indeed to go through it unloved.

Margaret rose on her tiptoes. "Will you watch us?"

John chucked her under the apple-green bonnet bow, tied at her chin. "Alas, I cannot. It seems we've lost more cattle to theft."

"Who would steal our cows?" Callum's brow scrunched.

"Hungry folk, I fear. I'm also told one of the bulls is causing a stir. He's been separated from his fellows, but I must see what the fuss is about." His gaze found Helena's. "A word, if you please?"

The children pulled faces, except for Alex. "Glad I don't have to ride along this time," he mumbled as he passed Helena.

"You're the heir." Callum shoved his twin's shoulder. "You have to do everything horrible. Don't you wish you were me?"

Helena chewed her lip.

John didn't offer his arm as they walked toward the garden wall, but she didn't need his support over the even grass. He looked down at her with a smile, which was handsome, but it was also restrained. Businesslike.

Just like their arrangement.

"The candidate for governess arrives in a few hours." With the toe of his black Wellington boot, he prodded a clump of sodden leaves, as if testing whether they concealed a rock.

"I shall be ready for her." Helena may be young, but she was no schoolroom miss.

"Hire her and be done with it. They need consistency, something they've lacked since their mother died three years ago. The sooner someone takes charge of the *bairns*, the better." His smile faded. "You've only met the children, but remember Louisa's blindness endangers her. Playing outside like this is not at all wise."

Helena's lips parted with an embarrassing pop. "Agnes and I have kept close watch."

"You cannot watch everything. Believe me. My child lost her sight and my wife her life because some things cannot be predicted. But with proper care, hazards can be avoided."

Helena learned that lesson all too well with Frederick Coles. But this? "Play on grass is not so perilous."

"What if a ball strikes her because she cannot see it hurtling toward her? Or she trips and hits her head on a stone?"

The bite of reproof gnawed at her stomach. "I would never put Louisa in harm's way."

"Not intentionally." A muscle clenched in his strong jaw. "You mean well, but you do not know how things are done here. Catriona instituted rules to protect the children, and I ask you to follow them."

Ask? More like order, when she had done nothing to endanger any of the children. Her hands fisted, but something held her back from arguing further, like a hand of warning on her shoulder. She sucked in a deep, calming breath. John was their father and guardian, and without him, she'd have nothing.

"Very well. Is there a list of these…rules?" Beyond not playing outside?

He smiled that pleasant smile again. Attractive, but the look did not reach his eyes. "Not rules, so much as a system. Agnes knows how things are done here, she can help you. Everything will smooth out soon. I look forward to dining with you this evening, so you may tell me about our new governess."

She nodded her farewell. "Until tonight, then."

He waved to his children and strode the way he had come, leaving the dog behind. Helena watched him go, a mix of frustration and resignation swirling in her chest. How could she be a mother if she had no authority, or if her attempts to better know the children were thwarted by his dead wife's rules—as relayed by a sullen nursery maid?

Besides, John could not possibly expect her to twiddle her thumbs and change nothing but the decor in the drawing room.

Then she sighed and made her way back over the grass.

"Come, children." Her voice sounded flat to her ears. "Time to return to the house."

After seeing to the tenants and the bull, John was met at Comraich's door by Kerr, the butler. "Welcome home, my lord."

"Thank you." John could hardly remember a time at Comraich without Kerr. The upstanding butler's dark hair was now dulled to a leaden hue, but his step was vigorous and his dark eyes shone with wit. "Has the post arrived?"

"It awaits you on the library desk, sir."

"Excellent. I shall adjourn there now. Coffee would be most welcome."

The butler bowed, and John took the main staircase, mulling over the problematic bull he'd just observed. The animal was a valuable sire, a fine specimen with a long red coat, black-tipped horns and thick fringe over the eyes, but the signs of aggression he'd exhibited toward man and beast alike brought up disconcerting questions. As his stewards were well equipped to handle such issues, he did not normally oversee these types of matters, but since the bull was worth a good deal, he'd been consulted about the possibility of putting the creature down.

He'd chosen instead to keep the bull separated for observation. He hoped he wouldn't regret it, but he'd made what he felt was the best choice.

Like marrying Helena.

Despite some difficulties at the start, this marriage would work how they both needed it to. Today, Helena would hire the governess and restore balance to the house. He could return to London trusting the children would thrive in safety and harmony, and his household would be in order.

That, and poor Helena could recover from her dishonor, too.

He entered the library, and his shoulders relaxed. The two-story room was all wood shelves, scarlet wallpaper and leather, his safe haven. He sat at the desk and picked up the post.

Three letters. Lord Carvey, his particular friend in the House of Lords, shared news, while Earl Grey sought his opinion, requiring an immediate reply. When Kerr brought the coffee, John nodded his thanks and picked up the final letter. It rested on the silver tray, addressed in an unfamiliar hand. On the reverse, a dollop of red wax, pressed with a falcon stamp, sealed the paper. With the tug of his letter knife, John broke the seal, unfolded the foolscap and took a large sip of coffee.

The hot beverage burned his throat when he finally managed to swallow it.

So this was what it was like to receive a blackmail letter. John's pulse pounded in his ears and fury ran hot under his skin.

The author—no, the *blackmailer*—knew about Helena entrusting herself to a young man in London without the benefit of marriage, and her marriage to John to disguise her ruin. And, of course, this rogue would hold silent in exchange for money. The large sum was to be deposited with a London metalsmith, Travers & Sons by name, at an address on the fringes of London's better neighborhoods. John had heard goldsmiths could be used for monetary transactions between individuals, but he'd never done such a thing.

Then again, he never imagined he'd be blackmailed.

Helena must never know about this. If the true reason for her hasty marriage to John was made public, her name and honor would be tarnished. So would her family's, but John was far less concerned with the Duke and Duchess of

Kelworth's reputations than about Helena's heart and mind. She'd been through enough.

He'd vowed to protect her yesterday in the kirk, and he was a man of his word. He'd pay the blackmailer, then— tomorrow he'd write to his man of business in London to deposit the demanded amount. He'd also insist his man investigate who picked up the payment, too, although anonymous blackmailers tended to protect their identities rather well.

But he wouldn't tell Helena about this. It would only upset her, and he wouldn't want her to experience a tenth of what he felt now. Instead of subsiding, his anger increased as the realization that someone was willing to hurt Helena sunk deeper into his brain. A fresh surge of anger coursed through his arms and clenched his fists.

His hands were steady when he locked the letter in the ornamental box by the inkwell. But they were cold when he laid his head in them to pray.

Chapter Five

Helena plopped her forehead into her hands and muttered. "Geography. Mathematics. Art." One would think a governess would know a fair bit about such subjects.

Or music. Or manners, something Miss Campbell lacked outright. Oh, she'd not been rude, but once she'd confessed her lack of schooling, she'd wiped her nose on her sleeve and nattered about the benefits of flogging as discipline. Helena's initial misgivings unfurled into certainty.

Miss Campbell was not the governess for the children of Comraich.

Helena rose from the table in the morning room where she had conducted the interview. There was still plenty of time before her scheduled tour with the housekeeper, Mrs. McGill, so she ascended the stairs to the yellow-papered nursery. In the bright central sitting room, the children gathered around a table eating their noonday meal. Agnes and the children, except Louisa, started to stand at her entrance, but Helena indicated that they stay seated. "Pray do not allow me to interrupt your meal."

Sneaking glances at her, they resumed their bites of meat, stewed fruit and a mashed vegetable—well, Callum ate only meat, and Louisa only the vegetable. She leaned forward, her mouth wide like a baby bird's, while Agnes spooned the pureed vegetable into her mouth. Saucy drips of butter trickled down the child's chin.

Helena caught herself chewing her lip, one of Mama's most despised practices—but the sight of Louisa slurping from a spoon was startling. Five-year-olds fed themselves, did they not?

She held back the question. If she asked, Agnes would set her jaw and insist, once again, that Louisa "*cannae* see." Meanwhile, shabby Tabitha lay on the table. The dog sat on its haunches near Callum's feet, begging for a morsel. Mama had never permitted toys on the table. Nor did she allow animals in the nursery. Or the house, come to think of it.

Was Mama unique in her rules? Or were things as Catriona, the previous Lady Ardoch, left them? That was the most important question, for Catriona was still the ruler of Comraich. Helena would have to ask her husband.

For now, she made a show of looking into the bedchambers off the right and left of the sitting room, called them charming, and then eyed the fare on the children's plates. "Callum, did you eat any vegetables?"

"I never do." Callum grimaced. "Just meat."

"I don't like meat," Louisa announced.

"Try a few bites of what you don't like then, each of you."

Callum scowled.

Helena peered down at the dog. It seemed clean and well mannered, at least. "Does the dog always, er, attend you when dining?"

Alex shook his head. "Iona is with Papa much of the time. He calls her his lady."

Did he? Helena gave in to the dog's begging look and

scratched her behind the ears. Ah, silky. Iona's stub tail wagged. "Iona is the name of an island, isn't it?"

"Aye." Alex started to lick a finger, but stopped at her shake of the head. "There were monks on Iona in the auld days and Papa liked their stories. But I don't remember any of them."

"Uncle John says the isle is deceptive. 'Tis small but has greatness about it, like our pup." Margaret set down her fork with a *ping* of finality. "At least, that's what uncle said when he named her. She may be little, but she can be a fierce thing."

Helena patted Iona's sleek belly, which the dog had presented for rubbing. "Well, she keeps her fierceness well hidden in the nursery." If not at all times. The dog was reduced to a puddle of drooling leisure under Helena's strokes.

"Did you come to tell us about our new governess?" Callum leaned back, clearly in need of a serviette to his chin. Helena indicated the linen square and nodded. He made a hasty swipe.

"The candidate did not suit. I didn't hire her." At the children's gaping, a flurry of remorse scuttled through Helena's stomach. "Fear not. I will find another. How long has it been since you last had a governess?"

"Two months." Margaret took a sip from her cup. "It was ever so sudden. Miss McManus left with Mr. Robertson."

Helena blinked. "I beg your pardon?"

"Mr. Robertson. Our music master," Alex explained. "Agnes said they run off together."

"*Ran* off," Helena corrected. It was far more polite than what she wanted to say, which was to repeat Alex's remark in an inelegant balk.

Such a scandal. And it had not been hidden from the children. She brushed dog hair from her hands and stood. She had seen more than a few things that could use improving around here, Catriona's rules or not. She forced her gaze to avoid Agnes's, lest the look sizzle.

"Enjoy your pudding." She crossed to the door.

Her husband had been correct. The sooner she hired a governess, the better. Helena married to atone for her sin, but clearly banishment and marriage to a stranger were not enough to appease God. Yet He had provided a blatant opportunity for her to continue to make amends. The children were in desperate need of stability and wholesome example. Surely God would provide.

With a renewed sense of confidence, she informed one of the footmen—she really must learn their names by the end of the week—to summon Mrs. McGill for their tour. The housekeeper's arrival was prompt, but her mouth pinched shut like a meat pasty.

Perhaps Helena had mistaken their appointed time. She smiled at the plump woman of middle years, who carried with her the fresh smell of rosemary. "Do I take you away from an urgent matter?"

"Not at all, milady."

A fudge if ever Helena had heard one. The housekeeper's sullen expression did not come close to matching her words.

Helena began to open her mouth to ask if another time was more convenient, or question if something had happened to upset the housekeeper.

This staff does not respect you yet. Make them. Mama's words resounded through her mind.

"Then let us begin." Heavens, Mama's voice wasn't just in her head. It was in her mouth, too. But her tone created the desired effect. Mrs. McGill had the grace to blink, although her mouth remained set in a pout.

"Aye, milady. Where should you like to start?"

Helena folded her hands over her waist. She knew how

to run a household. Time to prove it. "Anywhere you wish, so long as I view it all."

Mrs. McGill stepped back, sending the keys on the silver chatelaine pinned to her waist to jingling. Helena passed her through the threshold.

If Mrs. McGill thought to bore her by showing her every last nook and cranny, she was in error. Helena found the stillroom to be clean and organized, perfumed with lavender and rosemary drying from hooks, and she expressed her approval of the supply of tinctures, vinegars and balms prepared by the stillroom maid. She exclaimed over the spotless house, and nodded in appreciation at the well-stocked larders and cupboards. Candles, cheese and meats awaited future use, and a closet fragrant with the sweet scent of dried apples coaxed a pang of hunger from Helena's stomach that was only heightened when they visited the savory-scented kitchen.

She'd eaten so little in the past few weeks, it was a relief to feel hungry again.

At tour's end, she ordered tea delivered to the morning room, along with a small plate to assuage her appetite until dinner.

"Anything else, milady?"

Now it was Helena's turn to frown. No amount of praise could charm a smile from the housekeeper. *So do not praise,* Mama's voice said.

Helena fixed her smile in place. Froze. Prepared to dismiss Mrs. McGill as Mama would.

But I'm not Mama. Nor am I Catriona. Helena could only be herself, and she wanted the housekeeper's affinity. Their duties kept them in one another's spheres, so it was best if they got along.

Helena let her smile crack. "Nothing further, but I'm

grateful for your efforts. Thank you for executing your responsibilities so well."

Mrs. McGill's frown altered into a confused curl.

After the housekeeper curtsied and left, Helena's mouth relaxed. She'd done it, soothed the housekeeper's frown. A rush of triumph shot through her veins.

It had been a rough first day, perhaps, but not all bad. Louisa tossed a ball, the housekeeper defrosted a degree and her husband would be pleased that she'd dismissed the unskilled applicant for the children's governess. All in all, she'd accomplished a great deal on her first day as the Lady Ardoch.

She welcomed the tea's arrival and poured herself a full cup. If one day's success was any indication of the years to come, she'd count herself blissfully married, indeed.

His wife had done *what*?

John set his fork onto the rim of the Wedgwood plate with a soft *chink*. Astounding he hadn't dropped the utensil altogether. "Pardon me, but I didn't quite hear that last bit."

Helena nibbled her food, unable to answer until she swallowed.

Across the gleaming mahogany expanse of the dining table, she made the perfect picture of a lady, all berry-colored silk and proper deportment. Her jeweled combs and pale hair glowed in the candlelight, a glittering contrast to the matte of the marine-blue wall behind her. She looked every bit the daughter of a duke. A *lovely* daughter of a duke.

John retrieved his fork. He'd known she would be fair of face, of course. Her parents were fine in looks, and apples tended to not fall far from the trees on which they sprouted. But perhaps it might have been preferable if Helena had been, well, plain. It seemed rather disrespectful to Catriona to have married such a beautiful woman.

John's grip on the fork tightened. So his new wife was attractive. There was no shame in finding her so. As long as he did not act on an attraction, he would be a man of his word.

Perhaps these…feelings…had more to do with dining in the company of a lady again. He had not done so in a long time. Longer even than the three years Catriona had been gone. Although his conversation with Helena, who detailed her first day as his wife like his man of business listed cattle prices, was nothing like dining with Catriona.

She swallowed, patted her lips with a linen serviette and smiled. "I said the ragout of celery is divine. So is the salmon. What a delicate leek sauce."

Any taste of leeks lingering on John's tongue had disintegrated to sawdust. "Before that. About the governess?"

"*Unsuitable* was the word I used." She forked another bite of salmon.

"How so?" At Helena's furrowed brow, he lifted a hand. "Perhaps you were not aware how desperate the children's need is. Our last governess left without warning."

"I was acquainted with that information." Her mouth turned down in a fair imitation of her father's disapproving grimace. "From the *children*."

How did the *bairns* know about Miss McManus and Mr. Robertson? John's stomach twisted. It seemed the servants had not shown restraint, gossiping in front of his children. Here was yet another reason why he needed a lady in the house to oversee things.

"I share your displeasure over the matter. However, I had expected to remedy the problem of a governess today, as we discussed this morning. Could we have not made this one work?"

"No." She started to chew her lip, then pressed her lips together instead. "What the children require is a governess of character and education. This woman today did not even use a handkerchief. I do not think she owns one."

Was that all? "We provide our servants with handkerchiefs."

"We'd need to provide her more than that before she could teach Margaret anything. She lacked knowledge of globes, French or history." Helena's eyes sparked. "But she knew plenty about flogging. I know it happens at boys' schools, but I never expected to hear of it as a disciplinary option from a governess."

Neither did John. "Are you certain she said *that*? Mayhap you misheard—"

"I did not mishear her."

"But she could be instructed of how things are done at Comraich—"

"You married me for this purpose, and I ask you trust my judgment when I insist the woman is as I said—unsuitable."

John's first response died on his lips. As did his second. Helena was right. Flogging wouldn't be tolerated, and it sounded as if Miss Campbell wasn't qualified. He'd wanted the matter resolved today, but no governess was better than the wrong one. And he must trust Helena to hire another, just as he handled the estate and his political issues. This was, as she said, why he married her.

He sat back in his chair. "So what will you do?"

"I shall make inquiries on the morrow." Her lips twitched into a shy grin, a far different smile from those placid, frozen-into-stillness smiles she wore so much of the time. Her expression was not in the least flirtatious. Nevertheless, her little smile drew him in, and he craved another from her, the way the children hungered after desserts of cream ices and puddings. As if he could ask for *more, please*.

What a ridiculous thing to think, considering their arrangement. He shoved the foolish thought aside. "And in the meantime? Until someone who uses a handkerchief can be found?"

She didn't look up at him, even though he'd used a teasing tone. "I thought I might teach the children."

"You?" The word blurted out before he gave it thought.

"Whyever not?" Her shoulders squared. "I'm proficient at pianoforte and not too terrible with sums."

But she was the high-born Lady Helena. Catriona had never sat down with the *bairns*, not to read or spin a top or play a tune on the pianoforte. He'd not expected this duke's daughter to lower herself to execute the duties of a governess. His surprise faded, replaced by a warm glow of pleasure under his waistcoat.

"I think that would be delightful." His words conjured another of her genuine smiles, the one he liked too much for his own good. He speared a bite of fish.

"How did the candidate for governess come to be recommended to you?" Helena's head tipped to the side. "She said it was not through a service."

The fish stuck in John's throat, even as the plates were cleared. How pathetic he must seem to his new wife, arranging for an interview with an inept governess. But he had thought—oh, never mind. "She is the great-niece of the housekeeper, Mrs. McGill."

Helena's lips twisted. "Now it makes sense."

"What?" He rose when she did.

"Nothing of note."

He didn't believe her. She held something back from him.

Then again, he held something back from her, too. The blackmail letter, locked in the ornamental box upstairs. His secrecy was for her own good, however, not at all like a matter of household staffing. Before he could ask any-thing further about it, though, her brows lifted. "What is your habit after dinner?"

"I bid the children good-night. Yesterday was different, with the wedding and lateness of the celebration. Would you care to join me in the nursery?"

She nodded. Her hand was light on his forearm as he escorted her up the stairs to the nursery. Her closeness filled his senses, from the rustling fabric of her gown to the delicate scent of her perfume. Everything about her emanated femininity.

Then she looked up at him, casting that shy smile. It transformed her entirely. Not that she was not beautiful when she bore that fixed smile, but when her true smile curved her lips, she was no longer like a magnificent art-work, a cold sculpture. She was enchanting.

He did not know how long he had been smiling back, or when he'd patted her tiny hand, resting on his forearm. But her fingers felt so warm and natural there, he left his hand atop hers.

"Papa, at last."

He startled. Dropped Helena's arm. With too much haste, perhaps, but the children—Margaret and Callum, at least—frowned at his hand on Helena's.

Perhaps they were unready to view a sign of affection between him and their stepmother. Perhaps he'd confused Helena by touching her. He'd certainly confused himself. Affection of any sort was not part of their arrangement.

"Ready for bed, I see." He hurried from her side into the main room, where the four children waited in their nightcaps and dressing gowns. Bending away from Mar-garet's glare, he hauled Louisa into his arms. She smelled of milk and soap.

"Papa." She sighed. "I'm sleepy."

"Not me." Alex's dressing gown billowed about his legs as he ran circles around John. "I'm a ship in the sea. Ach, a storm." He flung himself into John's side.

"Time to come ashore." John wrapped an arm about his heir's waist and hauled him off the ground. Alex squealed.

"Me next." Callum jumped on John's back, yanking his neck cloth and almost knocking him off balance. Margaret dashed behind John, and at once Callum's weight lessened. Bless her for boosting her cousin's rump, so he wasn't pulling John backward. But Callum's small hands still held John's neck cloth like a leash.

"My throat, Callum." John's request was gurgled. At once, the pressure moved from his neck to his shoulders. "Enough, monkeys. To bed with you."

"Never," Alex cried. "You can't leave, Papa. No more London."

"You must stay with us." Callum squeezed.

"I'm here for a while yet." But he couldn't ignore the pinch to his conscience.

The boys slid to the ground, and he was left with naught but Louisa in his arms. He kissed her plump cheek, under the ruffle of her nightcap.

"Rest well." Then he bent to Margaret for a kiss, then Alex.

Callum scowled. "No kisses for me."

"Fine, then. Off you go to say your prayers."

The children scattered to their separate rooms.

"Good night, then." The small voice behind him drew his gaze.

Helena lingered inside the threshold, staring at him. He'd forgotten all about her. How thoughtless. Guilt pricked his abdomen and warmed his earlobes.

"Forgive me. Did you wish to kiss the children? I shall

call them back." His tone was apologetic, but even to his ears the offer sounded weak.

"No." Her thumbs fidgeted at her waist and she stepped backward, as if in a terrible hurry to escape him.

Little wonder, the way he'd ignored her. "Helena—"

"Good night, my lord."

"John," he corrected her, but she had disappeared into the darkness of the hall.

One step forward, two steps back. *Lord, help us find ease in this arrangement, before we both come to regret it.*

Chapter Six

*D*o *not run. You are the lady of this house. You are a duke's daughter.* Helena forced her gait to an appropriate speed as she traversed the hall to her suite of rooms, but her legs quivered with the urge to sprint to her bedchamber. To hide.

And maybe not come out again until the children were grown.

What had she expected? That the children and staff would accept her from the moment John brought her here from the kirk? That she would be included? That she would be forgiven enough to be part of a family again?

She shut her chamber door behind her and sank against it. Barnes wasn't here, mercifully. She'd ring for her once she'd recovered herself. Shoving off from the door, she crossed to the window and rested her aching head against the cold pane.

You could have joined in the frolics in the nursery, instead of standing there like an outsider.

But she *was* an outsider. Besides, what could she have done? Climb atop Callum? Ridiculous. She was a lady. *The* lady of the house. When her parents bid her and her sisters a brief, polite good-night, there was no tangling of limbs, no shrieking like urchins.

Besides, no one wanted her. They'd all ignored her.

And it wasn't just the children. The housekeeper, Mrs. McGill, was unfriendly because Helena hadn't hired her niece, that unsuitable Miss Campbell.

A dim light from a handheld lantern bobbed below her window. Helena stepped back. It wouldn't do for one of the servants to see her staring out the window with a baleful expression. Or hanging from her husband and stepchildren laughing, for that matter. Even if it meant she'd feel this alone for the rest of her days.

You deserve it, Helena. You deserve a lonely, empty life. Mama might never have said the words aloud, but her distant silence before Helena married had said enough. Helena was unlovable. She'd thought if she obeyed her parents and married, Papa would approve, Mama might forgive, and Helena would feel cleaner inside somehow, but marrying hadn't changed anything, after all. Why should she have expected who she now was on the outside to change whom she was inside?

I thought You forgive, Lord. Was I wrong? What was that feeling of love at the church yesterday? Was it fancy, or is there more for me there if I return? Could You love me?

Then again, why would God love her? Papa, ill as he was, would probably never see her again, but after the wedding, he couldn't get away from her fast enough.

Helena rubbed her cold arms. Tomorrow she must begin searching for a new governess, and she also had letters to write to her friend Frances Fennelwick and her sisters and Mama, but not her grandmother, who would be furious at Helena once she heard some made-up story from Papa that Helena had become enamored of Tavin's neighbor and there was no stopping her headstrong ways. She would write of her new home, the weather and the village. She'd say nothing of her feelings.

She should sleep, but her emotions continued to churn inside her, making her limbs quiver. She paced to shake them out, but it only seemed to make the matter worse. Should she ring for Barnes and tea? She wasn't thirsty. Mayhap if she had something to read, she'd relax. The library would have something tedious to dull her senses, no doubt. And it was far preferable to fretting over her thoughts. She took up the lone candle sputtering at her bedside and returned to the hall.

It was dark and empty—how long had it been since she'd escaped the nursery? Longer than she thought. Her candle cast grotesque shadows as she tiptoed down the hall and around the corner. Her sisters, Maria and Andromeda, would have clung to Helena had they been here, certain Comraich's dark, damp stones held ghosts. Silly widgeons—

Another pang of loneliness tightened Helena's stomach. Would her sisters ever be allowed to visit her here?

Of course not. There would be excuses based on the distance, but the truth was, her parents wouldn't want the girls influenced by their wayward elder sister.

Did the Bible say anything about being lonesome? Wasn't there a woman in its pages who had been uprooted from her home by marriage? *Whither thou goest, I will go, too*, or something like that? Had the woman's husband loved her? Or had she been as alone as Helena would always be?

Her desire for a musty tome disappeared. Mayhap John had a Bible in his library.

A cry rent the hall's stillness. One of the children.

She hurried to the nursery, where a single lamp cast a comforting, gold glow over the walls. The boys' door was ajar, and Helena rushed inside.

One of the boys sat up in bed, his hands over his mouth. Iona whimpered at his feet, while Agnes patted his shoulder as one might thump the head of a large dog. "Go back to sleep, Master, 'afore you wake the others."

Alex.

Helena had never ministered to a frantic child before. Perhaps she should leave.

Instead she rushed to Alex's bed. "Poor dear." She rested her hand on his miniscule knee. A quick glance assured her Callum slept on in his bed, which was no doubt for the best.

Agnes's fists flew to her hips. "Now look what ye've done, Master, but gone and disturbed 'er ladyship."

"Nonsense, Agnes." Helena perched on Alex's bed, her thumb tracing lazy circles over his kneecap. Did her touch bother him? She only did what she would have wanted done to her, but it was difficult to tell, the way he stared at her, gasping through his fingers.

"Now then. Does something ache? Or was it a bad dream?"

Alex hiccupped and nodded. Helena wiped his eyes with the lace-edged handkerchief she kept tucked up her sleeve.

"What happened in your dream?"

"I was in the water. There was a kee-ask who pulled me *doon* and I could *nae* breathe." He lifted his knees and buried his head between them.

"A what?"

"Kee-ask." Curled as he was, his words were muffled. "I knew I shouldna gone to her, but she looked like *Mither*. When I got closer I saw she was gray with the tail of a salmon and no' like *Mither* anymore. She'd come to take me under the water."

The creature sounded something like a mermaid. A *kee-ask* must be a creature of folklore, then. Poor boy, seeing his mother's face turn into something horrible.

Helena smoothed Alex's nightshirt over his shoulders. "I have nightmares sometimes, too."

He peeked up at her. "What about?"

Frederick Cole's handsome face flashed through her mind. Blue eyes, startling in their contrast to his near-black curls.

"Monsters. Same as you. But I know they cannot hurt me."

"Because they are no' real."

In her case they were, but she smiled anyway.

"I don' want to dream of my monster again." Alex's breath was shuddering and deep, a good sign he had cried himself out.

The sensation she'd experienced in the kirk—of peace and love and yearning—swelled in her bosom, and she cupped Alex's damp cheek with her hand. "I'd pay all the gold and silver I possess to never dream of my monster again, either, and to save you from yours."

Fabric rustled, and she turned to check Callum, but the boy slept on in his bed. Instead, her husband stood against the doorjamb, watching her.

Now it was her turn to cover her mouth with her hand.

John pulled the nursery door shut as softly as he could, glad for Helena's candle to illuminate the hall. "I think Alex should rest well enough now." The poor laddie had been drowsy when they left, with the comfort of Iona curling on the coverlet at his feet.

"I hope so." She held her candle steady, but tension rolled from her. After their awkward parting earlier tonight, it was little wonder.

Mayhap her unease also had to do with the monster she told Alex she dreamed of, but he couldn't ask her about that. Not now, perhaps not ever. Still, he wouldn't ignore the opportunity to get back on even footing with her. "Would you care to join me for a brief moment? I was working in the library, and the fire is still warm in the grate."

The strain eased from her mouth. "I was on my way to the library when I heard Alex."

He released a breath he hadn't realized he'd been holding. After leading her to the library, he indicated his favorite pair of wing chairs beside the fire, where his nightly cup of tea sat, cold and unfinished beside today's letter from his friend Lord Carvey.

Carvey reported an increase in pressure for John to add to the bill he wished to bring before the House of Lords. There were more demands by those who believed he could see it accomplished but did not wish to help him formulate it—except for Carvey, of course.

He didn't mind setting the letter aside for the night. Not at all. He offered Helena a tentative smile. "Alex had a bad dream, I take it?"

"About a kee-ask. What is that?"

"Ceasg." As he spelled it aloud, he bent to poke a wee bit more life from the embers. "A mythical water wraith. I wonder where that came from."

Her tongue snaked out to lick her lips, as if she tasted words she wasn't sure she should speak. Then her head tipped to the side. "He said the head of the creature resembled his mother. I think perhaps my being here brought back memories of grief. I'm sorry, if that is the case."

Of course the children missed their mother. He missed her, too. At least, the way she was at first. He missed the normalcy in his household that he, himself, had helped destroy.

As ever, he was one sorry fool. But there was no need for Helena to apologize. "His nightmare is not your fault."

Her furrowed brow conveyed her disagreement. John

rested his elbow on the arm of the chair and leaned his chin on his hand, the better to study his new wife. Any fool could recognize the pain darkening her eyes. What a dramatic second day she'd had as Lady Ardoch.

And she didn't even know about the blackmail letter.

Was she grieving over her life in London? Her eyes spoke of her losses. Of guilt. She even seemed to feel guilty about Alex's dream.

Perhaps his new wife was the sort of person who felt responsible for everything. He should relieve her mind. "You were good with Alex. I'm glad you'll be here for my children when I'm away in London."

Especially now that she knew Louisa wasn't to go outside. That Catriona's rules were in place for a reason.

She glanced at him. "When do you leave for London?"

Was she so eager for him to leave? He stifled a chuckle. "Not for a few months yet, but it is my habit to return to London before Parliament resumes. 'Tis even more important this session, as I'm actually holding a seat."

Helena's eyes narrowed. "But you sit in the House of Lords, with Papa." And British lords, of course, sat for life.

"Aye. But only sixteen Scottish peers may sit in the House of Lords. We must choose representatives amongst ourselves. The last election was seven years ago, and I was too young to stand then. I'm proud to serve this session, but no matter how well suited I may be to it, I may not serve in the next. We Scots are forbidden to serve consecutive terms, but the Lords Ardoch serve politically whether they sit in Parliament or not, make no mistake."

And the Lords Ardoch served until they died. That was why he was born, wasn't it? To carry on his family name and duty. From the time he was a lad, he'd heard the refrain repeated by his parents, how he must do his duty and train his heir to do so, too.

"I did not realize you were not allowed to sit as Papa does." Helena's gaze was on his hand, and he realized his fingers tapped a slow, pointed beat against the arm of his chair. He stopped the motion.

"I'm not English." He tried to sweeten the bitter words in his throat. "Although Irish peers have less restrictions, and unlike Scots, Irishmen may sit in the House of Commons."

The fire snapped, and something sparked in his brain, too. "What am I doing, keeping you like this?"

"I'm not yet sleepy." For the first time since she'd sat down, she leaned back against the plush gold brocade. Just an inch. "Your work has kept you up late. Is it something you enjoy?"

"Politics?" At her nod, he rubbed at his upper lip, the day's growth of whiskers scratching his forefinger. *Did* he like politics? No one had ever asked him that before. "I know nothing else. 'Tis my duty. But what I truly enjoy is working to improve someone's welfare. I'm excited about implementing ways to improve education, for example. Perhaps that's the path God has set me on."

"That must be a restful feeling, trusting you are on a path of God's design." Her brow furrowed. "Forgive me. The hour is late and I'm rambling nonsense."

"God's with you on your path, as well, Helena." She was here, even if unfortunate circumstances had brought her. God brought good out of all sorts of muddles, didn't He? John hadn't helped her transition tonight, though. "I should have included you better in the nursery. I didn't think. I'm not accustomed to a lady in the house."

She looked up at him. "There's always tomorrow."

"Aye, there is." He'd do a better job of welcoming her. He'd start by learning more about her, this duke's daughter who comforted his son and suffered her own bad dreams.

She rose. "Have you a Bible I might borrow?"

"Borrow? In your own home?" He hopped to his feet and pulled the thick, familiar volume from a shelf near the mahogany desk. "Everything within Comraich is at your disposal. You may keep this one, if you wish."

"But it's yours."

"I have another in my chambers."

"Oh, well, then. Thank you." She took the volume without touching his fingers. "I thought of a verse I heard once, but I've no idea where to find it."

"Perhaps I may help. What is it?"

"'Whither thou goest, I will go, too.'"

"*Ruth*. Beautiful story."

She clutched the Bible to her chest. "Thank you. I shall read it tonight. Good night."

He nodded his farewell and sank back to his chair.

The rosewater smell of her lingered in the room, mingling with the odors of leather and wood smoke. Soon her fragrance and presence would fill the whole house, a subtle but persistent reminder that she belonged here now.

As a mother for the *bairns*. As the lady of his house. And someday, maybe, his friend.

But never more. He'd given his word—to Helena and to his first wife. There would never be anything more than friendship betwixt him and Helena.

And if he started to care for her more than as a friend? If he kept noticing how pretty she was, for instance? He must put a stop to it at once.

Even if it meant leaving for London sooner than he'd planned.

Chapter Seven

"The sooner she leaves us for London, the better we all shall be."

John looked up at Margaret, who stood with her nose in the air and a hand on her hip. It had been three days since John loaned Helena the Bible. Three days of work to create a sense of normalcy at Comraich. And three days of Margaret's complaints about Helena.

His niece had claimed she wished a book when she poked her head into the library, but her gaze scarcely settled upon a single leather spine before it skittered on to another shelf. Margaret's pretense was as transparent as the sheer fichu wrapped about her neck.

John set aside the letter he was writing to the prime minister. "By *she*, you mean Helena, and she has no plans to visit London."

"Not that she's said in so many words." Margaret trailed her finger over the edge of the shelf. "But boredom will no doubt overtake your wife before winter, and she'll leave us—"

"She's not going anywhere!" Panic fluttered in his chest at the idea of it, though. "And her ladyship is not just *my* wife. She is a member of our family."

"Not by blood."

Neither was Margaret, not to him. She was Catriona's niece and came to them at six years old, newly orphaned, a stranger to them since Catriona's sister had married Mr. Allaway and moved far away, but family nonetheless, with all its privileges and duties. Now the child was so comfortable she would confront her uncle on his new wife. "Blood isn't the only tie that binds a family."

"She hates it here."

John's stomach twisted. Helena didn't seem to hate it. It seemed she was settling in, seeking recommendations from Gemma and the clergyman for governesses and in the meantime, teaching the children. She told him all about it each evening, since they'd formed something of a routine: dinner, bidding the children good-night—although only Louisa asked for Helena's kiss before bed—and then sharing the library fire and conversation before they, too, retired to their respective chambers. The past three days had gone quite well, he'd thought.

Except for Margaret's complaints. He pushed his chair back from the mahogany expanse and stood. "What's this about, Margie?"

"Whatever do you mean?" She clutched her fichu with a studied air of surprise.

"You aren't giving Helena much of a chance."

His niece stomped her foot, scattering her pretense. "I cannot help it, uncle. I hate her."

"Not to sound trite, but I hope you never grow to hate anyone. I've seen too much of what it does to a soul to want such a life for you." At her eye roll, he tweaked a stray chestnut curl at her nape. "You dislike the change, 'tis all. In time things will smooth out, after we all grow accustomed to one another."

"Can you not see it? She found fault with the governess

you picked. She is forcing me and the boys to practice sums until she hires someone, who will no doubt be a tyrant. And she taught Louisa to count buttons, and Louisa likes her because she is so *perfect*." The way Margaret wrinkled her nose, it was clear she did not intend it as a compliment.

Louisa could count? How did Helena manage it? Meanwhile, Margaret sniffled, scowling and miserable. His poor, dear girl. "The candidate was not suitable. And it's generous of Helena to instruct you until another governess can be found. As for the rest, you must give Helena time."

"But she wants to visit with Mrs. Knox and those nephews of hers. They're all babies. And she can't tell Alex from Callum, fine stepmother that is." Margaret yanked a book off the shelf without reading its title. "She hates me. Aunt Catriona would never have liked her."

She suddenly looked like Catriona in a fit of temper, set shoulders, narrowed eyes and set jaw. He touched the buttons of his waistcoat, over the spot where a fresh ache pounded at his ribs.

"She doesn't hate you. She's adjusting, as we are. You're the eldest. Set an example for the others."

"Very well, uncle. I shall be the picture of deference, but she is not my real aunt and I shall never love her, so do not ask me to."

"Oh," a soft voice sounded behind them. John didn't need to turn to know who it was. Helena had heard everything.

Helena should have left them alone, but that ridiculous *oh* escaped her throat and now it was too late. They were staring at her.

She froze a smile into place and entered the room, waving the vellum rectangles in her ink-stained fingers. "I wondered if I might add my letters to your post."

"Of course." John flashed his businesslike smile. "How do you fare this morning?"

Margaret swirled to face the bookshelf, hiding her mottled cheeks. It was not a revelation that Margaret disliked her, however. To be truthful, Helena didn't care for the child much, either, especially when she behaved as superior and lofty as an Almack's patroness.

But John acted as if nothing was amiss, so she focused on his face and his courteous question. "I'm well. And you?"

"Well."

Scintillating conversation, polite as ever. They both glanced at Margaret, who'd rooted to the rug. Helena could have sent the letters with a servant, but she'd used them as an excuse to seek out her husband. Speaking to him now about Margaret's behavior wouldn't do, however.

She held out the letters. One to her mother and sisters about the wedding—but not the mouse—and another to her friend Frances Fennelwick of London, inquiring in the postscript about an Edinburgh school the woman had mentioned upon learning Helena was marrying a widower in Scotland, one of whose children was blind. Helena wasn't entirely certain how to best help Louisa. Maybe someone with more knowledge could help.

If John didn't mind. She'd ask him once she heard back from Frances.

John took the letters without touching her fingers. She'd hoped to speak to him, but he seemed distracted, glancing longingly at the pile of papers on his desk.

She'd allow him to work in peace, then. She turned to Margaret. "I thought you, your cousins and I might find amusement together."

John's businesslike smile grew a fraction. "Sounds delightful."

Margaret glanced at him before answering. "Yes, my lady."

"Call me Helena." Mama would declare it overfamiliar, but Helena felt it to be the best course. "Shall we go, then?"

Margaret's eyes narrowed to slits. "Yes, m—Helena."

The girl's eyes widened, however, when Helena stopped their little party in the stone passage between the kitchen and the stillroom. The boys, too, eyed Helena as if she were daft.

No matter. The passage was perfect.

The drafty, chill hallway had been unsettled by the centuries, so now the stillroom lay a few feet lower than the kitchen. At some point, masons added three stairs and a plain, stubby banister. Her papa's estate possessed similar uneven floors, which added character to a house, to Helena's thinking.

And provided a perfect opportunity for Louisa.

"What are we doing here?" Margaret's nose tilted in the air.

"You shall see. Louisa?" Helena took the child from Margaret's arms and set her down. "Give me Tabitha and then take my hand."

Helena propped the sticky doll against the wall. Louisa's hand was equally sticky, perhaps from breakfast or from sucking her fingers. Regardless, Agnes did not clean the child well. With a sigh, Helena patted Louisa's hand against the stone wall. "How does it feel?"

"Cold and wet."

"Yes, it does." The twins darted past her toward the stillroom. Oh, what was the stillroom maid's name? "Boys, Beth will be working. We're not to disturb her."

"Bess," Margaret corrected with a treacle-sweet smile. "And this is her half day."

Helena's teeth clenched. "Thank you, Margaret. Boys?"

One freckled face reappeared in the stillroom doorway, brandishing a bunch of lavender like a sword. Its fresh aroma filled the air as tiny purple petals floated to the ground.

"Put it back," she insisted in a tone she'd never used before, high-pitched and desperate sounding. "Do not touch anything."

A sly grin pulled at the lad's lips. "Sorry, milady. That is, Helena. Don't be blaming Callum, please. 'twas my idea."

So this one was Alex—

"You beast." Red-faced, Callum burst from the stillroom and shoved his brother in the chest. Not hard enough to push Alex against the wall, but enough to send lavender blossoms scattering.

"Enough!" Helena hadn't known she could sound so forceful, but Callum's hands fell. "Callum, we do not call one another names nor do we resort to violence. And Alex, tidy up that mess. The stillroom is not a playroom, and well you should know it."

"Tidy?" Alex's jaw fell into his tiny neck cloth. "We have servants for that."

"The servants were hired to care for a family, not a sty of piglets." If only Helena were gifted with the ability to quirk her brow. "You are the heir. The future caretaker of this estate and these people. Surely you know such behavior is unbecoming. Must I speak to your father?"

Alex's pout eased and then he laughed as he bent to scoop lavender in hasty, inexact handfuls. Oh, dear. These children did not respect her at all. Perhaps she shouldn't have mentioned piglets.

Margaret sighed and Callum glared at her, clenching his fists. At least Louisa liked her.

Back to the purpose of their visit to the corridor. She

squeezed Louisa's clammy hand and placed it on the banister. "There are three steps before us. How many is three?"

"One, two, three!" Louisa stuck her fingers in the air.

"Yes." The child had been quick to learn, and Helena's chest swelled with pride at her accomplishment. "You will count to three again as you go down the stairs, one by one."

Louisa shot up her arms to be lifted.

"No." Helena replaced Louisa's right hand on the banister and took her left hand. "We shall go together, side by side." ₋

"On my feet?" Louisa's face crumpled.

Oh, please do not cry. "I shall hold on to you. You will not fall."

Margaret hopped down the stairs and stood in front of Louisa, glowering at Helena. "Stairs are dangerous. 'Tis against Aunt Catriona's rules."

"I'm certain your aunt would not mind Louisa knowing how to use stairs should the need ever arise."

Margaret did not return Helena's smile. "It won't. She has us to help her."

"Yes, us." One of the twins folded his arms. Oh, dear, she'd already lost which one was Alex and which was Callum. She must insist they dress in contrasting colors.

Meanwhile Louisa hopped and stretched out her leg, tugging Helena off balance. Cold seeped through her thin gown of sprigged muslin as her side smacked into the wall. Perhaps she should offer more instruction first. "Louisa, feel for the edge of the step with your toes."

Louisa pointed her red slipper, patting about until she felt the stair's edge.

"Wonderful. Now lower your foot to the stair below. There."

Louisa grinned. Still, her hands clutched the banister and Helena's hand.

"Now," Helena asked, "how many stairs did I say there were?"

"Three."

"Yes. We've descended one. How many are left?"

Louisa's face scrunched.

"Two," one of the boys said. "Three minus one is two, Louisa."

"Two." Louisa nodded.

Helena squeezed her hand. "Let us count together."

Slowly, feeling with their toes, they descended the stairs. Then they practiced ascending. Louisa's grip on Helena lessened, and at last Helena let her try on her own, so long as she held the banister.

"Again!"

"This is boring," a twin muttered.

"I suppose we have practiced enough for today." And cleaned up the lavender as best as they could. The floor was not spotless, but it was tidy enough. The boys took Louisa and her doll, pulling her ahead. To Helena's surprise, Margaret held back to walk beside her.

"Helena," Margaret said with such exaggerated sweetness that Helena almost regretted inviting the children to use her Christian name. "Callum tricked you, you know. He had the lavender and pretended to be Alex."

Was Margaret the one deceiving her? It wouldn't be surprising. "That makes no sense. Callum still had to clean up the mess he made."

"But if you tell Uncle John, Alex will be the one to receive a scolding." Margaret's tone was almost pitying.

That naughty Callum. *And foolish me.*

The sight of the unenthusiastic Agnes had never been more welcome. "Please have the children ready for lessons in an hour."

She needed a moment to herself. And the Bible. Mayhap some Scripture would comfort her.

She'd read the book of Ruth John had told her about. To her surprise, the verses about *whither thou goest, I will go, too* weren't about a wife with her husband. They were about a foreign woman and her mother-in-law. Still, the story comforted Helena, because even though it wasn't about what she thought it was, she felt kinship with Ruth. She'd gone where John was and chosen to take his people as her own, and realized God cared for her, even when she didn't know Him.

And that made her want to read more.

After fetching the heavy book and ordering tea, she retired to the sun-filled morning room. When the blue-uniformed footman Adam arrived with a pot of fragrant green tea, he also carried a letter on a silver tray.

Post, already? Pleasure swelled in her chest. Someone was thinking of her. The thought was far more effective than tea at reviving the spirits.

But the message was not so unexpected, after all. It was from Gemma, accepting Helena's invitation to visit with the children. A happy thing, but her chest ached with disappointment. She'd been so anxious for a word from home, a scrap of familiarity.

How foolish. It was far too soon to receive a letter from London. Helena had known what she gave up when she agreed to come here to marry. But still, tears stung her eyes.

Helena didn't have many correspondents. The last letter she'd received, back in London, had come from Frederick Coles. Full of passion and promises, it was the sort of letter one locked in a treasure box and brought out on dreary days as a reminder of true love. She'd held the wretched thing to her cheek that day, unaware it was a lure. Passion and promises were naught but a disguise for betrayal and brokenness.

Boot steps sounded in the hall. She wiped her watery eyes with her thumb.

John stepped in the room, seeming to fill it with his height and breadth. His eyes widened when he saw the paper in her hand. "You received a letter from your family already?"

She forced a smile. "Gemma accepted my invitation. I had hoped, however, to alter our plans from a nursery visit to a picnic." At his opening mouth, she held up her hand. "The weather is fine, and the boys so rambunctious. It is against Catriona's rules, I know, but Louisa will be in constant company. I will select an even location, free of stones."

Helena could never compete with the previous Lady Ardoch, nor did she wish to. Yet it was ridiculous to confine the children indoors. The only Agnes-approved exercise they received was running about the nursery or pushing their hoops in the portrait gallery, which stretched the length of a wing and had been cleared of anything that could break or hurt Louisa.

It was difficult not to resent Catriona's years-old rules, which were no doubt placed to protect an infant, not a busy child. But the rules hampered each of the children's play, not just Louisa's, and like her brothers and cousin, Louisa was growing up. She could not be carried or hidden inside forever.

John rubbed his temple, but nodded. "I'll not deny a picnic, as long as Louisa is attended, but even so, we must remain vigilant so she is not injured." The lines furrowing his brow did not ease. "Which is why I'm not sure it was wise to take Louisa on the stairs."

Ah, so that explained his searching her out. Which servant had been the tattle-box?

"I kept Louisa in hand the entire time."

"I know. But her *mither*'s concerns were valid." He nodded, a sort of bow. "I'll leave you to your tea."

She couldn't stomach her tea now if she were parched. "Thank you."

So polite. It seemed they were always trying not to offend each other. How exhausting.

Perhaps he felt so, too, for even his businesslike smile seemed strained. "Until dinner?"

At her nod, he bowed and withdrew, leaving her with fidgeting thumbs and a pot of untouched tea and the first letter she'd received since that terrible note from Frederick Coles back in London—

She should be thinking of the children and John's reluctant permission for the picnic, not Frederick Coles. He was gone now, vanished the night he ruined her.

She was gone, too. So far north he couldn't find her if he ever returned to Britain. But even if she never saw his face or heard his voice again, Frederick Coles would never truly leave her in peace, would he?

Chapter Eight

John poked his head into the nursery one sunny morning a few weeks later. Iona slept beneath the table in the center of the yellow room where the older children sat, writing, while Helena and Louisa curled on the floor with a pile of buttons betwixt them. Louisa counted to eleven before anyone noticed John.

"Oh." Helena scrambled to her feet, her cheeks flushing the shade of her pink dress. The children rushed to him, Margaret guiding Louisa by the hand.

"Is this a bad time?" John ruffled the boys' hair and pulled the girls in for short hugs.

"I wished to speak to you, anyway," Helena said over the children's heads.

She did? They didn't usually spend much time together during the days, but their routine of dinner, bidding the children good-night and sharing light conversation in the library had become well established. John had begun to look forward to chatting with Helena about the children and what they'd read in the Bible that day. A new sense of normalcy was setting in, and even the children seemed to be adjusting. Alex had two more nightmares, but he was quickly soothed. Callum's French had improved. Louisa started making up songs. And Margaret hadn't complained about Helena in almost a week.

But Helena's seeking him out was new. "Is something amiss?"

"On the contrary. I hired a governess this morning. Miss Munro."

At last. "She's a qualified female, I take it? Knows how to use a handkerchief properly?"

"Of course." Helena didn't try to mask her smile. Good. Making her smile was one of John's new favorite things to do. Despite his original insistence that tolerable normalcy was all he wanted from his marriage, John had quickly learned he'd wanted to be friends with his wife. But right now, when she smiled a true smile like this, he realized he wanted one more thing.

He wanted Helena to be happy at Comraich.

She deserved so much more than a bearable existence. John couldn't help thinking God wanted more for her than that, too.

Louisa patted his waistcoat. "Why are you here, Papa?"

"I've come for Alex. Ardoch matters." Years ago, John's father had taken him about the estate and spoken to him of duty. John now saw the importance of such serious talks. Alex must understand that one day it would be his turn to carry on the name and traditions, and seven years of age was not too young to learn of his responsibilities.

Even if he did not look enthusiastic as he joined John. "What about the picnic?"

"Ah, yes. The long-awaited picnic." Although Helena and Gemma Knox had scheduled the luncheon a few weeks ago, it had been postponed when the Knox wards fought summer colds. "We shall return in plenty of time."

Iona joined them outside. First they spoke to Meeker, the land manager, about the crops and animals. A few more head of cattle seemed to be missing, and the problematic bull had been moved to a new pen this morning when it showed renewed signs of aggression. Now that it was finished, they climbed the rise overlooking the Ardoch lands. Father and son. Lord and heir.

He clapped Alex's slim shoulder. "All you see, from Comraich to the crops, will be yours to oversee someday. 'Tis a great duty, but I know you'll do a fine job of it."

Alex stuffed his hands into his coat pockets. Was the lad cold, on this fine, cloudless day? Or mayhap he was overwhelmed. John rubbed the back of his son's neck.

"What if I lose cattle?" Alex's voice was small.

"Meeker will find them."

"Not the stolen ones."

"True." John could only pray the beef filled the bellies of the thieves' hungry children. But if more cattle went missing and the aggressive bull could no longer be used as a sire, John faced a potential revenue problem. But he'd trust the Lord with it and pray for the best. "It pleases me that you ask questions about the way we do things here."

"Because it's mine." It was a statement of fact, not a gloat. "What will Callum be, when I am Lord Ardoch?"

To his shame, John hadn't given the matter much thought. "I do not know yet. I will discuss his options with him."

Alex's boot toed a divot into the grass. "Will they picnic without me?"

The abrupt change of subject drew John's gaze. Children were like that, though. Thinking of fun and games. Ah, well. There'd been enough talk of responsibility today. He wriggled Alex's shoulder in a playful shake. "Of course not, but you're right, the hour is near. Come, Iona." John's shrill whistle summoned the panting dog.

"Will you picnic with us, Papa?"

"Alas, no." There were rumors of political unrest in Manchester, talk of reformation or revolution or sedition, and while there was little he could do, he would write to members of his party, including his friend Carvey, to work on a plan of action. Today he'd also received another letter fastened with a falcon-crested wax seal, demanding more money, and quite a bit of it, too. He glanced down at Alex. "Sometimes being Lord Ardoch means fulfilling difficult obligations."

"Sounds disagreeable to me." Alex skittered off, Iona at his heels.

It was. But John would ensure the matter of the blackmail would be settled long before Alex inherited the estate. Soon enough John's investigator would expose the blackguard responsible for the blackmail, and no one would ever know about it—not the children, and definitely not Helena.

She was starting to be happy, and he'd not do anything to jeopardize it.

Helena restrained herself from throwing up her hands in frustration when John returned with Alex from the nursery, just as Gemma's carriage pulled before the front door.

"What?" John's brows went up. "Why are you looking at me like that?"

"Because they're here and you're late. Alex." She beckoned him, doing her best to smooth down his cowlick while the door knocker sounded.

She must not have given John too stern of a glare, because he grinned at her while he ducked out of the room moments before Gemma and her wards, Petey and Eddie, entered.

After exchanging welcomes, Helena led them outside to the dining table and chairs set up on the lawn under a sycamore tree.

"What a beautiful spot," Gemma exclaimed as they sat down.

It was indeed, boasting a clear view of the rocky *tor*, the pear orchard in full leaf and a grassy meadow spotted with bits of purple heather where the children could play under their watchful eyes. She'd planned a menu of simple, cold dishes suited to the children's palates. Mama would be proud of Helena, for she had thought of everything, and everyone seemed to enjoy the food and setting.

Even Margaret. Her face glowed from the sunshine streaming through the sycamore leaves. "I love bread with black butter."

"Me, too." Louisa smacked her little lips.

Sweet-tart with blackberries, it tasted like summer on a spoon. Helena smeared more onto a fresh slice of bread, took a bite and shut her eyes while the tangy taste filled her mouth. Why, she could almost imagine herself young, basket over her arm, hunting berries with her sisters in the heat of full summer—

"May we play now?" Alex asked, urging Helena's eyes open.

The children's plates were clean, and their eyes were hopeful. She nodded and looked knowingly at Agnes as she scooped Louisa into her arms—John may have agreed to the picnic, but he still didn't want Louisa in danger of falling. Alex bolted from his seat, followed by Petey, Eddie and Callum, who bore a purple streak of black butter on his cheek—

"A moment, Callum." She indicated the lad's linen serviette and then discreetly tapped her cheek.

"I'm not Callum." He swiped the spot. "I'm Alex."

"Then where is the freckle on your right earlobe, Alex?" The boy covered his ear with his hand, and she shook her head. "Do not attempt to fool me again, Callum."

Eyes downcast, Callum nodded.

"You may go."

He ran after his fellows, hollering for them to wait.

"You poor dear." Gemma shifted, as if trying to find a more comfortable position on the wooden chair. "The twins have been tricking you?"

"A time or two. I confess I have spent the past few weeks struggling to find something that differentiates their appearances. Height, build, smile, all the same, down to their cowlicks. The only thing I've discovered that's different is that mole on Alex's earlobe. Oh, dear, did Louisa fall?"

Helena half stood. The footman Adam rushed to pull out her chair, but there was no need and she resumed her seat. "Agnes has her in hand. If she is injured today, I fear it will be a long while before we venture out of doors again. I'm hopeful today will prove once and for all that the previous Lady Ardoch's rules should be adapted now that Louisa is older."

Gemma's brow furrowed. "I didn't know her, but her anxieties must have been severe indeed to cast such a shadow."

"I'm certain she wanted the best for the children. But they are safe and happy for the moment."

High-pitched squeals and shouts floated on the air as the children ran in circles. Per John's request the first day of their marriage, there were no balls that could strike Louisa, just hoops and imaginations. Louisa wriggled to be set down from Agnes's arms, eager to join the fun, but Agnes kept her in hand. Everything was perfect—

Clank. Gemma's fork had fallen from her fingers. Color leached from her face and she stared unseeing at the table.

Helena popped up again, Adam behind her to take the chair. "Gemma."

Gemma's head shook. "A moment—forgive me." Color returned to her face and she took a steadying breath.

Helena chewed her lip. It must be the baby causing such discomfort. Helena knew nothing of these things. She never would, due to the nature of her marriage. But Gemma was a relation by marriage, and Helena was no unmarried miss anymore. Still, one didn't speak of such things, did they? Mama never did.

I'm not Mama. Helena took Gemma's hand. "Is it time?"

"No. They are practice pains."

It sounded awful. "I cannot offer much, but I'm here."

"And I'm glad." Gemma squeezed Helena's fingers. "Thank you for inviting us today. I know I'm supposed to be in my confinement, hidden away at home until the baby arrives, but the boys and I truly needed to be out of the house, amongst friends. Family."

It felt odd and wonderful to be considered part of someone's family again. Maybe God was answering Helena's prayer for a sense of belonging, after all. Mama had said Helena was ruined beyond hope, yet hope was what filled her chest when she opened the Bible John gave her, and when Louisa snuggled against her, and now, when Gemma squeezed her hand. Mama would call it foolishness, but Helena wanted more of this hopeful feeling.

Thank you for this hope, God. For the day, too, with its warm breeze and blue skies. The children's giggles and shouts filled the air while she and Gemma chatted.

A cry rent the warm air. Helena was on her feet before Adam could pull back her chair. "Petey tripped."

Gemma craned her neck, her expression more thoughtful than panicked. Odd, considering Helena's heart hammered her chest. "That is a cry of shock, but I do not think he's hurt."

Sure enough, the crying stopped and Petey dashed after

his brother, appearing no worse for the wear. The nurse-maid to Gemma's wards offered an indulgent chuckle, and Agnes joined in. Helena's heart returned to its proper place, but then it stopped altogether. "Where is Louisa?"

Gemma said something, but the words disintegrated in the breeze as Helena lifted the hem of her gown and hurried toward the children. "Louisa? Louisa!"

Margaret spun. "She is right here."

But she was not.

Helena turned in a circle, searching out Louisa's straw bonnet and white flouncy hem.

"I'll search at once." The footman Adam hastened toward the pear trees.

Helena hastened past the sycamores. How far could the little girl have wandered?

Not all that far—there she was past the sycamores, toddling over the grass, Tabitha in hand, taking sure, firm steps. Alone, except for a great shaggy bull several yards distant.

The creature didn't belong on this part of the property, yet here it was, watching Louisa, pawing its foot.

Chapter Nine

John must have shouted Louisa's name, must have bel-
lowed something because his daughter stopped midstep
and tipped her head. "Papa?"

Helena ran toward Louisa, but he held up his arm. Running could make everything worse. "*Dinnae* move!"

Helena froze, but Louisa hopped up and down. "Papa,
look at me."

"I am, lass. Hold still, now. Still as you can. There's a
bull close to you. I won't let him hurt you, but you must stay
still." His steps were short, slow, steady so as to not agitate
the bull. It was the aggressive one, easy to recognize by the
black tips of its horns and enormous size. *Dear Lord, how
had it escaped its paddock?* "Adam," he shouted behind
him. "Fetch Meeker and men. Now. Mrs. Knox, remove
the children, please."

Helena's head swiveled, checking the movement behind
her. Otherwise she remained still. "John?"

The way she said his name was full of questions. No
doubt one of them was to ask why he was even here. Good
thing he was. It took all his will not to glare at her, but it
was far more important his gaze never leave the bull.

"When I nod, Helena, get back. Far as you can. Understand?"

"Yes." Her voice shook.

The bull's shaggy head twisted, the better to see her. Taking advantage of the bull's distraction, John nodded to Helena. She stepped backward. He doubled his speed toward Louisa and scooped her into his arms. Her shrill scream reverberated in his ear.

"Hush now. I've got you." Although the poor child had been ordered to stillness and then hauled into the air. No wonder she screamed. He was scared, too. The bull didn't charge, but it still moved closer, head bowed. Adam and a passel of men arrived, bearing ropes and rods.

Helena waited with her arms extended, her features contorted into a portrait of grief. John shifted Louisa to Helena, and she folded the little girl against her chest, muffling Louisa's sobs.

"All is well." She spoke in the singsong way his mother had comforted him. "You did nothing wrong. I'm sorry we frightened you."

Bitter as bile, anger filled John's throat. Of course Louisa had done nothing wrong. It was him and Helena who endangered his children. Helena had challenged Catriona's rules, and he'd allowed his desire for her happiness here to cloud his judgment. He'd been foolish to relent and allow the picnic, and while this was as much his fault as Helena's, if she hadn't pressed, this wouldn't have happened.

She had no right to comfort Louisa now, no right to be the one who soothed her with her maternal care. Who did this London-bred girl who knew nothing of his family or his ways think she was?

She is your wife.

John turned away from her and marched toward his men, but they'd already made quick work of roping the bull. For some reason, his inability to help capture the beast increased his ire.

"I'm sorry." Helena chased him, her words rising above Louisa's tears. "Thank God the bull was never close to her."

"You and I do not define *close* the same way." He loosened the noose of his neck cloth. "Have you no idea what could have happened? That bull is separated from the others because he shows aggression."

"Which is why we didn't picnic near the animals. I don't know how the bull got here."

Nevertheless, it had. Life was unpredictable. He'd tried to warn her of that the first day, when she took the children outdoors. "'Tis a good thing I decided to stop in."

"You do not trust me." The skin around Helena's mouth whitened.

The children's chatter increased in volume, reminding John that he and Helena weren't alone. A glance affirmed Mrs. Knox and the children were now within earshot.

Louisa pushed at Helena's neck. "Tabitha!"

The doll lay in a lump several feet away, still too close to the men prodding the bull back toward its paddock. A rescue would have to wait. John patted his daughter's head. "She's on the ground near the bull, Louisa. We'll fetch her in a moment. It is not yet safe."

"He'll eat her," Louisa wailed.

"Cattle do not eat dollies." Helena tucked a stray curl under Louisa's miniature bonnet.

Callum pushed forward. "Goats do. They eat everything."

Gemma Knox's ward Eddie held up a finger. "A goat bit my coattail, but Uncle Tavin pulled me away. The goat had teeth like this." He held his thumbs and forefingers apart at least two inches, forming an exaggerated display.

Gemma shut Eddie's fingers. "I think it's time we returned home, boys. Uncle Tavin will wonder what has become of us."

John forced his fingers to unclench. "Pity the day ended on a sour note."

"Oh, that is not it at all," Gemma probably lied. "The boys require a rest."

Who didn't? John rubbed his forehead.

"Uncle Tavin will want to know about the bull eating Tabitha," Eddie said.

Louisa broke into a fresh round of wails. Helena bounced her in one arm. The other reached for John.

She'd never initiated touching him before. She'd taken his arm when he offered it at church or to escort her into dinner, but she never held out her hand to him. It wasn't that she wanted to touch him, John knew. She wanted his absolution. His comfort. Only he could not spare it for her. Not now. Maybe not ever.

"I must ensure they repair the fence. Pardon me." He stomped after the men, his strides longer than they should be if he wished to do the gentlemanly thing and hide his anger from their guests, from his stranger of a wife.

The fence must be mended now, though, within the hour. There were so many things in his life that were broken beyond repair. Here, at least, was one thing he could fix. He'd have to trust the Lord to see to the rest.

Once the children were comforted and settled—and Tabitha enjoyed a good scrub in the laundress's tub—Helena took a deep breath, prayed God heard her plea for words, pushed down Mama's insistence that Helena was about to behave uncouthly and sought out John. She found him in the library, striding toward the door, Iona at his heels. His eyes widened in surprise, then hardened.

"Pardon me, but I'm heading out." He brushed past her.

"Already?" None of them had been in the house that long.

He took his walking stick from the brass pot by the door. "I require a constitutional to clear my head."

Iona yipped, clearly understanding the word *constitutional*.

He didn't want to talk to her, and the way her heart hammered in her chest, she should take advantage and continue to be a quiet mouse of a wife. But she couldn't. This was too important, so she didn't budge from her position at the door. "We should discuss what happened."

"There is nothing to discuss." He turned back toward his desk, almost tripping over Iona, who circled his feet.

"Sit," he ordered Iona. Iona pranced toward the door, looking back at him with longing.

Helena stepped around the eager dog. "Please, John. This is not easy for me. I'm unaccustomed to conflict, but I imagine you are well versed in it." At his shocked look, heat flooded her cheeks. "You are a politician, after all."

"Conflict in Parliament is one thing." He passed her and replaced his walking stick in the brass pot with a resounding *thunk*. "I'm not accustomed to it at home, however."

"I do not wish to argue." She reached behind him to shut the door with a soft click.

"There will be no need for argument if you accept the rules my late wife laid down."

Iona jumped on his legs, her paws pressing into John's thighs. He pushed her down with more gentleness than he seemed able to extend to Helena.

"We were nowhere near the animals. The bull must have escaped its pen somehow."

"It did. The fence tore and no one saw it wandered free, but that's the problem, Helena. I tried to warn you, that first day when you took them outside with nine pins. Things happen that are no one's fault. That's why Louisa must be protected." He ran a hand through his hair, ruffling it into a disaster. "You do not know the children well enough to know what is best."

Coldness swirled in her stomach. "When will I know them enough? Another month? A year? Or never, because I did not give them life, or because you do not love me?"

His mouth opened, then shut.

"You cannot expect to marry me and for nothing to change. I'm the mistress of this house. To care for the household and the children I must hold authority, yet my decisions are second-guessed and contradicted by Margaret as well as the staff. And by you."

"That's not true. I relented this time, but look what happened. Near disaster." He guided Iona's paws from his legs again. "Sit, Iona."

The dog ignored him and twirled around Helena's feet.

"Iona, sit." Helena pointed at the rug. "Sit."

The dog obeyed. John rolled his eyes and mumbled something about how he'd not roll over so easily.

Well, neither would she. Helena stood tall. "We must ensure the children grow up able to cope with their lots in life."

"We must ensure their safety, or they'll not grow up at all."

"John—"

"You do not know them, Helena." He moved so the desk sat between them, a solid barrier.

"And you do? You are in England more than half a year, and from what I've observed, there are a few things you do *not* know—"

"How dare you accuse me of not knowing my own *bairns*."

Anger mottled his cheeks, but she could not stop. Not now that she'd begun. "Alex—"

"I know my own son—"

"—is petrified by his position as your heir. All he sees ahead is your life, which consists of duty and separation from his family, and it frightens him. I believe that is why he has nightmares. But during the day, he is mischievous because he is trying to have fun before he is forced to grow up."

His hands gripped the desk. "Alex will learn—"

"But Callum is mischievous because he does not have to be responsible for anything. He taunts Alex about his position, which does nothing to improve Alex's anxiety."

John's features morphed, as if he recalled something painful from the past. Then he shook his head. "I regret that it pains Alex. And Callum, too. But their futures are set."

"They can be prepared, however, so they are not anxious. And speaking of preparation, what of Louisa?" She strode around his desk to intercept his gaze. "Have you considered what will happen when she is grown? She must be allowed a sense of independence now, so she will be ready. Today's incident was terrible, but it was an accident."

"Which would not have happened if you had not convinced me to grant permission, something I'll not do again."

"Louisa is no invalid. She cannot see, but she can hear, feel, smell. She must be allowed to live, to know the dignity of doing things for herself. To put a spoon in her hand and eat as a woman someday, not a child."

"Enough." He shut his eyes. Oh, he must hate her. But she could not stop.

"I've learned of a school in Edinburgh devoted to the blind. My friend Frances knows one of its benefactors and mentioned it to me before I left London, when I told her I was marrying you. She wrote to me with more information. It's called the Relief for the Blind."

His lids flew open. The resulting glower almost made

her jaw clamp shut, but she had to keep going. "Perhaps a member of their staff might advise us how to go about helping Louisa."

"Louisa will never be sent away from this house."

"I didn't suggest that. The school is only for males, anyway—but the point stands, she can learn to do things for herself. Frances says—"

"Enough." His voice was dangerous in its lowness.

"Then let us speak of Margaret. She has been allowed to behave as if she runs this household, perhaps because there has been no one to guide her. She is growing up. And she wore cosmetics the day of our wedding."

His eyes narrowed. "You accuse my niece of indecency?"

"Not at all, but no one has taught her about being a young lady. I'm trying, but she will not yet listen to me. She needs you to pay note to her, too. If a young lady does not receive proper attentions from her father, she may one day seek it from another man. I know this better than anyone."

Admitting it stung, like she'd cut open her skin so John might look inside her. He would no doubt find the sight disgusting, but she couldn't allow Margaret to suffer as she had.

He stared at her for the length of several breaths. "I am not your father. And Margaret is not you."

But she could be.

A knock on the door made her jump. Even Iona, who had curled into a ball and dozed off, hopped to her feet.

"Enter." John seemed relieved for the intrusion.

Kerr entered the library, his expression grave as ever. "Pardon, milord. A man claims he has a most urgent message from Lord Carvey."

John's good friend. She'd met the black-haired gentleman once or twice back in London, extending the cool courtesy she showed everyone below her in rank, as Mama had taught her.

"Show him in." John was all business, as if nothing was happening between them.

The moment Kerr turned his back, Helena spun. "But you and I are not finished."

"Carvey is in London, Helena, yet something has occurred to make him send a man on an urgent journey here. You'd have the fellow wait in the kitchen, when we have nothing more to say on the matter?"

She barked a laugh. "You may be done with our conversation, but I am not."

Iona scurried from the room, as if intimidated by Helena's tone, but John folded his arms. How like Papa he was, after all. Dismissive of her. Unwilling to listen. It had taken courage for her to confront him, for her to lay bare her opinions and thoughts. She'd been taught emotional outbursts were unseemly, but despite the twisting of guilt and shame in her stomach for speaking out, she would never regret this.

Kerr reappeared, followed by a brown-coated fellow with a sealed missive in hand. Helena smoothed her face into a mask and nodded to the messenger. "Refreshments await you in the kitchen when you have finished your business with his lordship." She glanced at Kerr, conveying the request.

"Thank you kindly, milady." The messenger tugged a forelock.

"Pray excuse me." She cast a chill smile to her husband.

To her surprise, he held up his hand. "Stay, wife, since we are unfinished, unless this particular matter requires privacy?" His questioning gaze was met by the messenger's shake of the head.

Ah, so he'd offered his own sort of challenge. Very well. She'd stay for whatever boring political tidbit Lord Carvey thought John must know. Some bit of gossip about the Tories like Papa, perhaps.

"I'm to tell you what occurred, milord, as well as deliver this, which says the same." The young man held out a letter. The strong smells of sweat and horse swirled from him.

"What is your message?" John took a knife to the letter's seal.

"A group of agitators assembled Monday on a field in Manchester, milord."

Helena took a seat and John glanced up at the messenger. "Rumors of a gathering to protest their lack of representation in Parliament have churned for weeks, and little wonder. Their voices have gone unheard." John's voice was bitter as too-strong coffee.

"Tens of thousands congregated, so it's said."

"That many?" John's brows rose. Helena's hand went to her throat.

The youth nodded. "Cavalry was called to disperse the crowd, and they did so with sabers drawn."

"Sabers?" Helena shouldn't have intruded, but the question escaped. The way her chest tightened, it was a wonder she'd managed the single word.

The messenger stared at John. "It was a massacre, milord."

Chapter Ten

After excusing herself, Helena hurried to the nursery, drawn as if by an invisible tether. The world—or at least her sheltered understanding of it—had changed to a place of unexpected trouble, protests and massacres, but the nursery would be the same: mischievous boys, sweet Louisa, distrustful Margaret, all comfortingly predictable.

But the scene greeting her at the nursery door was most unexpected. The boys sat at the table, rigid in their chairs, their eyes wide. Someone sobbed in the girls' bedchamber.

"What's wrong?" She touched the children's heads.

"We don't know." Callum's voice was uncharacteristic in its softness. "But it's bad."

"I'm certain all is well." Nevertheless Helena hurried inside.

Margaret huddled in bed. For her part, Louisa curled in her own bed, sucking the fingers of one hand while she clung to the bedclothes with the other, as if they made a substitute for Tabitha while the doll was bathed.

"She won't tell me what's wrong, milady." Agnes's fingers fidgeted against her gray gown. After letting go of Louisa's hand today and losing sight of her, the nursemaid no doubt expected her position in the household to be dubious. "I've tried everything, but she's cryin' like she's dyin'."

"Margaret's dying?" Louisa's cries joined Margaret's.

Helena scooped Louisa and kissed her cheek. "She is not. Agnes, take the others to the long gallery. I'll stay with Margaret."

While Agnes bobbed a curtsy and took Louisa from the room, Helena perched on the side of Margaret's bed, as she did Alex's when he suffered nightmares. Margaret wouldn't want her here, but Helena had to keep trying. *Lord, if you hear me, will you please help us to be friends?* She licked her dry lips. "Will you tell me what's wrong?"

Margaret's head shook. Helena's fingers traced the quilted pattern on the coverlet, but then stilled. Alex hadn't seemed to mind her touch, nor did Louisa. Would Margaret?

With gentle fingers, she brushed the damp tendrils away from Margaret's cheeks. When the child didn't resist, Helena rubbed small circles on Margaret's back. Margaret's sobs slowed, and at last she took a long breath and swiped her eyes.

"Now then," Helena said. "Are you upset about Louisa and the bull?"

"It's my fault." Margaret blinked. "I took her from Agnes. She was with me one minute, and then I wanted to play with the boys—Archibald's right. I'm a baby, too."

Helena's hand stilled and her thoughts tumbled over one another, back to her wedding day. Then her jaw dropped. "The solicitor's son?"

Margaret nodded.

"When have you spoken to him? I've not seen you exchange a word at church—" Helena clamped her mouth shut. She knew quite well how to meet a young man in secret.

"I was being neighborly." Margaret's mouth set in a mulish expression. "You can't punish me for bidding a neighbor *good afternoon* when he's here at Comraich."

"When did he call at Comraich?" They'd had no visitors except the clergyman's wife.

"He didn't." Margaret sniffled. "Not on us, anyway. His father had an appointment with Meeker this afternoon to look at horseflesh—I overheard them discuss it at the kirk Sunday. But everyone was so busy with the bull, I thought I should meet him so he wasn't wondering where everyone had gone."

With numerous outdoor staff, that wasn't likely to happen, but Margaret had grasped the excuse to encounter Archibald. "Did Agnes know where you were?"

"I needed air. If she thought I meant the garden, it isn't my fault. I didn't lie."

"You misled, though." Helena chewed her lip. "What happened next?"

Margaret rolled her tear-reddened eyes. "Archie laughed when he saw me and asked if Uncle John had baby girls in charge of his horseflesh now. A baby! Even though he's no more than a year older than me—" She broke off, flushing. "When Meeker came back, Archie didn't pay attention to me at all. And everyone hates me because I let go of Louisa's hand."

Helena offered poor Margaret the handkerchief she'd tucked in her sleeve. "No one hates you. Watching Louisa was my job, not yours. As for Archibald Dunwood, he's a witless boy to call you names."

"I thought Archie liked me."

Helena understood the feeling. "Sometimes people don't pay attention to how their actions make others feel. But other times, people are cruel." She swallowed hard. "It sounds like Archie is the former, but it is good to remember for the future—we cannot trust our hearts to just anyone. We must wait for a worthy gentleman."

"Like Uncle John."

Precisely like John. "He's a man of his word, isn't he?"

When Margaret nodded without looking away or rolling her eyes, Helena felt something shift in the air, like things were different betwixt her and Margaret now. A little better.

Helena wrapped her arms around Margaret. To her surprise, Margaret didn't pull back.

Pressing his seal into the blob of wax, John sealed the letter to Carvey responding to the news of the massacre and said a prayer. *God in heaven, what a disaster in Manchester. Heal those afflicted.*

He set his head in his hands. Despite his concern for those affected by the massacre, his thoughts kept flitting back to Helena and their conversation an hour ago, before Carvey's messenger arrived.

Had he really so much to learn about his children's lives? While he was in London for months at a time, he received clinical reports on their growth and acquisition of skills. But he'd no idea Alex was concerned about being heir, or how Callum felt about *not* being heir. Was Helena right about Margaret, too? She needed his approval? And were he and Catriona wrong about Louisa? Did she want and deserve more than he imagined for her?

He'd missed those things, but Helena, a stranger to them, had seen it all.

The object of his musings appeared in the library door, her head tilted in a wary pose. Gone was the fervent, insistent woman from an hour ago, when the calm, cool exterior she affected had cracked and she'd passionately demanded he listen to her. Now, she was collected again, her face expressionless, but her eyes were hesitant.

"Forgive me for disturbing you." She'd changed gowns, into something brown and serviceable.

"You aren't disturbing me." It was just as well she'd come. They had a conversation about the children to finish. He rose from the desk and stepped toward her, catching whiffs of her rosewater-and-soap smell.

Her face contorted in confusion. "How could such a thing happen? In Manchester?"

John's brows lifted. He'd not expected her to ask about that. Catriona was never curious about anything beyond the borders of Comraich. "The magistrates attempted to arrest the orator, Henry Hunt. Somehow chaos grew out of it. A dozen dead. It's rumored a child was trampled."

Her hands clutched at her waist. "I will pray for all those affected."

"As will I." He'd already begun, but her intention to pray soothed his frayed nerves like a salve. Ironic, as she had set them on edge before Carvey's man even arrived. He almost smiled.

"Will you leave for London, then?" Her voice didn't sound eager or resigned, just curious.

Duty called, but Helena had reminded him he had another duty, too, to his children. "Not yet, but I expect Parliament to resume earlier than planned. By Christmas, certainly. Before then, however, I'd like to spend more time with the children. Would you care to talk with me now about how I might grow more acquainted with them?"

To his surprise, she shook her head. "I've received a note. Gemma has been brought to bed with the child. Cousin Tavin wonders if I will come now."

"Do you wish to?" From her face, he couldn't tell. He'd be shaking in his boots at the prospect.

"If it is expected. I am a married relative. And I do not wish her to feel alone."

Without doubt, Mrs. Knox had hired a professional accoucheur to deliver the baby, but everyone wanted family
nearby during times of difficulty or change, didn't they?

Even Helena, who had no one but him and the children.
As far as he knew, she hadn't yet received a letter from her
parents or sisters.

"They are family." Hers and now his, through her. "If
you wish to go, you must."

"I may be late tonight, although I think Gemma's pains
began this morning." She flushed, as if mortified she'd
spoken of such intimacies.

"I'll summon the carriage for you. Will you stay the
night?"

"I will, if it is past midnight." She nodded farewell, then
turned at the door. "You should know, Margaret has had a
difficult day. She may be tender."

John puffed out a breath. Weren't they all?

Gemma's grimace of pain rent Helena's heart. The pangs
of childbirth were more severe than she'd imagined. She took
the warm, wet cloth from the basin and dabbed Gemma's
forehead, but the gesture did little to ease Gemma's suffering.

Useless. Helena was useless. She squeezed the cloth so
hard it dripped onto her gown. Why was she here? She had
no knowledge to impart. No experience. Gemma must be
so disappointed by Helena's inability to comfort her.

*Lord, if you hear a sinner like me, please keep Gemma
and the babe safe. And back at home, watch over the children.*

She clutched the damp cloth to her chest. Were the children well? Had Louisa eaten any meat tonight? Had Callum
eaten too much of it? What if Alex had another nightmare
and she was not there to comfort him? How did Margaret
fare after their talk this afternoon?

Home—she'd called Comraich home in her prayer for the children. Even more startling was the realization blossoming in her chest. She loved the children. Louisa and the boys and even Margaret.

And John, too? Her breath stuck in her throat. He'd been so angry with her today, but he hadn't banished her. He'd listened to her, and now sought her opinions on raising his children. And a month ago, he'd rescued her from shame and entrusted his children and home to her. He was as handsome as he was honorable. Any woman would be proud to be his wife—

Did she love him, too? Her heart thumped harder. She couldn't love him, unless it was the way she loved the children, because it would only invite pain and loneliness. They didn't have a real marriage.

Besides, she was ruined, not worthy of being loved. Helena placed the cloth back by the basin, scolding herself. A fine man like John, loving her like *that*? Ridiculous.

It doesn't matter. You do love him.

"Not like that," she said aloud.

Gemma's eyes opened.

"I'm sorry to wake you." Helena fussed with the bedcovers to hide her shaking hands.

"I wasn't asleep." Gemma's head shook an inch.

"What can I do for you? Read the Bible?" At Gemma's nod, Helena read a few Psalms before thumbing to the familiar passage from Ruth she'd read multiple times since taking the Bible from the library at Comraich. "Whither thou goest, I will go; and where thou lodgest, I will lodge: thy people shall be my people, and thy God my God."

She had gone where John was and taken his people as her own. And tonight she'd realized God had heard her prayer. He'd given her love for them, after all.

A soft breeze fluttered the nape of her neck. The windows were open to the twilight to ward off puerperal fever, according to the Glasgow accoucheur, a male midwife Tavin and Gemma had hired to assist with the birth, who now took supper in another room.

"Should I read more Scripture? Or do you wish to talk of mindless things? The castle you and Tavin are restoring looks more like a home every day." When Gemma didn't answer, Helena fumbled with the water pitcher. "Are you thirsty?"

"No water." A high voice drew her gaze. The spindle-legged accoucheur bustled into Gemma's bedchamber from the sitting room. Behind him, a dark head peeked into the room before drawing back. Poor Cousin Tavin, not allowed inside, because gentlemen did not skulk about their wives' bedchambers at such a delicate time. Although Tavin was well acquainted with the art of skulking in his work for the Crown, so perhaps he could not help it.

And something about his persistence struck Helena as sweet and right.

She gladly vacated her seat when the accoucheur shooed her away. "A moment, if you please, Lady Ardoch?"

Helena hurried out to Tavin, whose dark hair was mussed, probably from multiple tugs from his fretful fingers.

"How is she?"

"As expected." At least, she thought so. "Why don't you look at a book whilst you wait?"

"I *cannae* read a word, knowing she's hurting." Tavin's mouth twisted, as if Gemma's pain was too difficult to be borne.

But bear things they all must, tonight. "Your role is to pray and wait. Gemma is busy with hers. Hold fast."

"And are you? Holding fast?"

"For certain." She smiled, but it was her artificial smile.

The one Mama taught her to affix. Real smiles were toothy and vulgar, after all. Especially Helena's.

Tavin's brow arched. "Not just tonight. Ardoch. Did I do wrong sending you to him?" Tavin's gaze penetrated to her bones. She had to look down, lest he see too much in her eyes.

"He is a good man." And someone she loved, but not like *that*. "We are becoming friends."

"I'd hoped love might grow betwixt you someday."

Oh, no. She couldn't discuss this with Tavin. In a spontaneous gesture, she kissed his stubbly cheek. "You are a good man, too."

The accoucheur nodded at her return and indicated she could resume her perch bedside.

Was this what it might have been like for her, had she married John in a traditional sense? Alas, she would never know the pains of childbirth. Nor would she know the anticipation, the joy, the love saturating this room like perfume whenever Tavin poked his disobedient head in the threshold, as he did right now.

Greed crawled over her skin like an itch. All of a sudden, she wanted this, a marriage and family with all the pain and fear and love, every bit of it. Her hands gripped the edge of her chair.

Telling God outright how she felt would be so ungrateful. He'd given her four children to care for, after all. Whether or not they loved her, Helena loved them, and she wouldn't abandon them.

Or Gemma. She took up the warm cloth again. She may not know what to do, but she could be present for Gemma. Just as she would be for John's children. And John, if she could love him enough to be his friend. But no more.

As darkness fell, John and Margaret settled on the terrace to watch the moon rise. Helena's suggestion he didn't know the children churned discomfort in his gut, so he extended Margaret the invitation, and she'd readily agreed.

Margaret gazed up at Orion, looking so much like Catriona a pang of grief and a spark of joy mixed together in a strange muddle in John's chest. She was not his child and yet she was. He couldn't love her more if she'd been born to him.

Birth was on both their minds tonight, with the Knox baby arriving. Margaret shifted. "Do you know what I was like as a baby?"

"You were a beautiful baby." He didn't know for sure, since Margaret was born long before John and Catriona's marriage, but all babies were beautiful. The twins and Louisa certainly had been. "I remember well the day you came to live with us. Six years old, with eyes so big and blue I suspected you held the secrets of the lochs inside your pretty head."

"I do not believe you." But she giggled.

"How could I forget the first moments I beheld any of my four children?"

Margaret's eyes shone suspiciously bright. He squeezed her shoulders, and then tipped his head back. "Orion's belt is much brighter now."

"What happened with the bull today isn't Helena's fault." Her words jarred him from Orion.

"No, it is not." Although Louisa would not have been in danger had Helena—

"I let go of Louisa's hand. We all looked away, so we are all to blame. I'm not saying Helena is a perfect stepmother, but she is new to the task. I suppose we should give her more of a chance."

"Oh?" A slow smile pulled his cheek. "I think so, too."

Something shifted in him, like the stiff, shuddering movement of gears in an old, just-wound clock. It was out of time, unaccustomed to use, clogged with dust and grime, but once wound, the hands moved despite years of neglect.

Helena. His wife. When she dropped that artificial smile of ice, a fire lit her from within, making her eyes spark. She was so beautiful. It wouldn't be hard at all to love her.

He shoved the thoughts away. Helena was never to be more than his friend.

But now that he'd entertained the thought of something more, he couldn't stop thinking about it.

Chapter Eleven

Several hours later, Helena's carriage pulled into the drive at Comraich, and at once, a glowing rectangle of light escaped the front door. Kerr met her on the stone steps. "Welcome, my lady."

In the dim of the lone candelabrum, it almost looked as if Kerr's brows lifted into something like relief. But then the look was gone, and his features returned to their usual stoic state.

She must be weary, indeed. Surely the butler had not fretted over her late return.

"All is well, I trust?"

"Aye, milady. Would you care for tea?"

"No, thank you. Good night." She started up the stairs, her feet aching as if she'd trod all the way home on her own two legs. The downy softness of her pillow beckoned, although sleep might be difficult to attain despite her fatigue. She had witnessed a miracle, and such a thing did not flit from one's mind easily.

Her head lifted like a marionette's, tugged upward by a string.

John stood on the landing, sleeves rolled up to his forearms, his neck cloth abandoned. His index finger tapped on the polished oak of the landing rail, the beat more anxious than frustrated. Had he waited up for her? Was he still angry with her about her confronting him? He did not seem it. He seemed worried.

Pah. John must have indigestion to be up and dressed at this hour. "You're awake."

"You said you'd come home if the child came before midnight. And it is not yet midnight."

She climbed the stairs, her feet no longer aching. "I was ready to return to my own home." To Comraich. This was where her heart lay, where she was safe. This was where John was, and however she loved him, she wanted to be with him now. To share more time with him. "Might I join you in the library?"

"Please. I'm curious about the babe." His half smile made her heart flutter.

They walked in silence to the shadowed library, with its comforting scents of moldering paper and wood smoke. She paused before her usual wing chair and loosened her cloak. Weariness affected her fingers, however, and they fumbled with the bonnet strings under her chin.

"Here." John reached out to loosen the strings. He scarcely touched her—he must have tried hard not to touch her—but the graze of his fingers left shivery trails on her throat.

"Th-thank you."

He smiled, lay her cloak over a chair and set the bonnet on a side table beside a stack of papers. Ah. That was why he stayed awake, because of the events in Manchester. How foolish to think it had anything to do with her.

"Are you certain you don't wish tea?" John must have heard her refuse Kerr's offer.

"There was tea by the bucketful at the Knox household."

Helena couldn't contain her grin. "Gemma is well. So is wee Eugenie Cassandra."

"A girl?" John chuckled as he sat. "Tavin will be besotted."

"He already is." Baby Eugenie was so perfect. Gray, unfocused eyes; the dark hair of her father; ears pink and small as the seashells on Brighton's shore; and a wail that belied the tiny lungs that set it forth. "She's named after her grandmothers."

"Tomorrow we shall toast the good health of Tavin, Gemma and Eugenie Cassandra." His eyes softened. "How did you fare?"

"I was useless." But she said it with a smile. "I had nothing to offer her."

"You offered her love. That's enough."

Was it? Had her presence and care been enough? Was her love enough for God, too?

John's eyes crinkled in concern. "I imagine the evening was difficult for you."

Helena studied her fingers. "I'm sorry we argued."

"That isn't what I meant, but I'm sorry, too."

"I wish us to be friends, John." The admission made her cold. She might as well have cut open her chest and scooped out her heart for his judgment.

"We are."

His response was so quick, she did not believe it. "You were so angry with me."

"I was. And still am, because I do not like to be challenged. Do you?"

"Not in particular," she admitted.

He laughed. "We will work through it tomorrow. Right now there are other things to discuss. You and I may speak plainly, may we not?"

Everything was different, now that she knew she cared

for him. She attempted to disguise her feelings by giving him her most businesslike nod.

"All evening, I couldn't help thinking you might have had your own children if you'd married your, well, the man for whom you felt a *tendre*."

Her hands twisted in her lap. John may be her husband, but he was not her *husband*. And when she'd asked Mama about love in a marriage, Mama had educated her on the inappropriateness of such a discussion.

Telling John about what really happened between her and Frederick Coles would be inappropriate, indeed, because men and women didn't discuss such things, did they?

Mama would disapprove, but Helena wanted to tell John so badly the words clawed each other trying to escape her throat. And John was her friend. Helena lifted her chin.

She met his gaze and almost gasped at the gentleness she saw there. Oh, how kind he was, to care for her, even though they'd argued. To know that she might be sad tonight. *Thank you, Lord, for giving me a husband who doesn't despise me. Who even cares for me a little.*

She moistened her dry lips with her tongue. "As much as I envy the family Tavin and Gemma share, you must never believe I would have experienced such tenderness with Frederick Coles."

John's Adam's apple jerked, perhaps because he knew Frederick. The thought filled her throat with bile.

"Was marrying him out of the question?" John's eyes were dark as coal in the firelight.

"When I first met him, yes. I was taught those below me in society were not worth my notice—including Gemma. I was not warm when I met her, but I followed the example set by my parents. Then I met F-Frederick. He is below me in rank, and Papa had already turned away any suitor he deemed inferior, even a wealthy viscount." She swallowed. "Papa preferred someone loftier. Frederick's uncle, the Duke of Bowden."

John's brows rose. "The man is thrice widowed, and five and sixty if he is a day."

"But he is a well-heeled duke, with daughters but no son yet. Nevertheless, Papa would have gladly married me to Frederick after I was compromised, had he not fled to the continent." Heat flooded her cheeks.

John's hands gripped the arms of his chair. "I was told he could not marry you. I assumed he was wed or—otherwise engaged. Fled?"

"Perhaps he feared Papa's wrath, since I was not a willing participant. But Frederick needn't have fretted, because my parents would have seen me marry him to cover my ruin. Swift action was best, according to Papa."

In one swift motion, John quit his chair and dropped to his knees before her. A muscle clenched in his jaw. "You were not a *willing participant*?"

A tremor of shame sent a spasm through her. Maybe she had been wrong to speak of this to him. Maybe Mama was right and she should never speak of it again. Ever.

But the fatigue of the evening and the desire to tell John everything loosened her tongue. She would no doubt regret it tomorrow, because John might well hate her for her weakness, as Mama and Papa had, but she couldn't stop. The truth wanted out. She looked down again.

"Mama says I enticed him. She is probably right. I remember the first time he touched my arm. Just a light touch, almost an accident. But I had not been touched in so long, beyond gloved-hands greetings, or a servant combing and pinning my hair. Any moment he could steal, Frederick caressed my cheek, and I allowed it."

Her swallow pained her throat. "I thought his touch meant he loved me. I told my parents I wouldn't marry

Bowden, but they refused to hear it, so I disobeyed them and every rule of conduct I was taught by sneaking off to meet Frederick at every opportunity for a few stolen kisses and words of endearment. It was wrong and selfish, and I thought only of myself, not of how my actions might cause scandal or hasten Papa's demise. Did you note Papa's cough, when he was here? It was actually an improvement on what he's suffered for a several weeks. His own father died of a lung inflammation, and no one has said it, but he's probably dying of the same disease—yet I cared only about myself. So can you see how even though I did not give Frederick my assent for anything more than a kiss, I deserved what happened to me? I caused grief and scandal. I made Papa worse."

Tingling shot through her jaw as his fingers gently touched her chin, guided it so her head lifted and she was forced to look at him. With his kneeling, his eyes were level with hers.

"I regard you too highly to allow you to believe that." His voice was firm, but gentle. Like the hard muscles of his arm under the soft, fine wool of his coat sleeve. Strength within tenderness. "You are not responsible for your father's illness. I didn't know he was that sick, truly. But another thing I never knew? That you were not willing. That Frederick Coles assaulted you."

She shook her head, breaking free of his kind fingers. "I think he did, but in truth, I don't remember." She enunciated each syllable. "It was at a house party at the Duke of Bowden's Chelsea estate. Frederick sent me a note, inviting me to meet behind the dovecote. I went willingly." He had to understand.

His clear eyes revealed no judgment. Only patience as she paused.

"We'd met in secret before. Normally our meetings were

brief, no more than a minute or two. This time, he had a picnic, with bread and cheese and mulled cider. I took a sip. Then I felt ill. After that, I remember nothing until I came to my senses. Alone behind the dovecote."

Something snapped. An ember in the fire. Or John's knuckle, cracking as he gripped the arm of her chair. The muscle in his jaw worked again.

"What—" His voice was harsh. He cleared his throat. "What happened after that?"

She looked down, trying not to think of her parents' accusations, then silence, those horrible first days afterward. "Frederick was gone. He'd told the Duke of Bowden he'd been summoned to London for some urgent matter, but he wasn't there. To avoid the hint of scandal, Papa let the matter go. He didn't even seek the assistance of Frederick's brother, Baron Shawe, to locate him, because he feared the baron would gossip. Papa would never expose our family to the shame of a criminal investigation or trial. He deemed it best to begin discreetly hunting for a husband for me in case I was with child. Tavin knew of someone who needed a wife. You. And now I am here."

John laid his large hand atop her head. For some reason, the gesture resonated, sweet and warm, all the way to her marrow. Tears stung her eyes.

"I didn't tell my grandmother or Uncle Cecil's family goodbye, because of appearances. Mama said she'd tell everyone Papa and I took a brief trip to see Tavin. She has by now invented a story about me meeting you and insisting I marry you. Papa's sister, Tavin's mother, eloped, and was snubbed by the family for the rest of her life, as I will probably be." She tried to laugh, but it didn't work. "None of this would have happened had I not snuck out to meet Frederick."

"Nothing you did deserved what Frederick Coles did to

you." His voice was calm, but insistent. "The blackguard drugged and assaulted you."

"I know he gave me some sort of sleeping draught, but I was so susceptible to his charms, what if I told him yes and can't remember it?"

"I doubt you were sensible enough to speak at all."

Her parents had not wanted to hear that. When Helena told them the same things she had told John, they sent her to her chamber. "That is kind of you to say."

"There is no kindness in it. It is the truth." John's hand disappeared from her head.

"Why do you take my part?"

"You are my wife. I will always take your part." He leveled her with his gaze. "I may not always agree with you, as you experienced earlier today, but I will stand beside you. No matter what. Now tell me, have you any recollection of the cider? It was mulled, you say?"

She blinked. He believed her. He truly believed her.

"With strange spices. I remember thinking how odd it was to see saffron floating in it, all gold, but he told me the recipe was Indian or some such fustian."

"Saffron." He tasted the word. "A known inducer of sleep, but not in such a small quantity. However, I suspect he used several powerfully flavored herbs in his so-called mulling spices, the better to mask the laudanum."

Her brow furrowed. "It did not taste like laudanum."

"I know something the methods people use to disguise its taste. Catriona was quite fond of it, you see."

What did he mean by that?

"Helena, I must say this again, because by your look I don't think you believe me." He dipped his head to meet her gaze. "You didn't deserve this. No woman deserves such an assault."

"I know. But I—am still disgraced. Papa was astonished

I wore white at our wedding because he said it is a color of joy and purity and—"

She couldn't finish.

"You may wear whatever you like. It means nothing. What is important is you. I don't want you living in this mire of guilt, nor does the Lord. You are precious and lovely in His eyes."

"Someday, perhaps if I'm good enough. My parents brought us to church because it is the thing to do, but they do not believe God cares much what we do. At some point, though, I realized God does care, and He was disappointed in me. I thought if I married, and was obedient at last, God would forgive me, but I don't think He has. He's answered some of my prayers, but not that one."

"First of all, you did not need to marry to be forgiven. God's desire to forgive and renew you is not based on your actions, except for your willingness to ask and accept. He delights in you."

Impossible. No one delighted in her, ever. They tolerated her at best—

John rose and pulled her to stand. In a gentle motion, he wrapped his arms around her, even though he had promised never to do that, even though she had sworn she would never let him. He left a proper distance between them, as if they were about to waltz, but this was nothing like a dance.

This was an embrace. A true, real clasp of his arms around her back.

She shut her eyes. He smelled of starch and wood smoke and soap, so wonderful, she'd bottle the scent if she could and sprinkle it on everything she owned.

She shouldn't prove to him how weak she was, but she let her arms go 'round him, too. Her hands fisted, though. She'd not be so wanton as to splay her fingers on his shoulder blades.

His breath expelled, whether exasperated or resigned to endure her touch or—Oh! He laid his jaw atop the crown of her head.

"'Tis all right." His voice was mild, as if he spoke to Louisa. "You are safe. He'll not harm you again."

"I know." It was true. "Thank you."

He didn't let her go. Instead his thumb traced lazy ovals on her shoulder.

There was nothing sensual in his touch, but it was addictive, and she would crave the comfort and closeness of it again, as she had with Frederick. She should pull away before John thought her reckless.

"I don't mean to frighten you," he said against her hair, as if reading her thoughts. "But there is nothing wrong with touch. Appropriate touch, of course. The children need it. So do you. And perhaps I wished for comfort as much as I wished to comfort you."

He needed a hug? Something glowed under her rib cage, light and warm. With that, her head dipped against his chest.

God, is John right about You? Do You love me as I am now, without my earning it? Is my loving You enough of a place to start?

It made little sense, considering she'd done nothing to earn God's love.

Nevertheless, she chose to believe it.

Warmth suffused her, crown to toe. God loved her. She didn't deserve it, couldn't earn it by any effort other than believing Him. And suddenly, her perspective shifted. She was not the same person she was a month ago, or a minute ago. She was someone entirely new.

God granted her a gift in this moment—the recognition of His love while she was held in John's arms. She memorized it to treasure later: the warmth in her heart from the Lord, the knowledge she was part of God's family, the line of John's jawbone against her head, the breadth of his torso between her arms, the calm spreading through her limbs. He swallowed, and she felt it above her ear, heard its echo. Had she ever been so close to another human being in her life?

John was so good to her. She didn't deserve this any more than she deserved God's love.

But they were here, anyway.

Then, as slowly as John had drawn her to him, he pulled away. It was cold without his nearness. But his smile warmed her to her toes.

"It's late," he said, "and you know the children will be eager to hear of Baby Eugenie come dawn."

Louisa would hop up and down when she heard the news. Helena nodded at the stack of his correspondence on the side table. "May I suggest you take to your bed, as well? Your business will wait until the morn."

"Business? Oh. Yes." He sounded surprised.

Hadn't he stayed awake to work? He certainly wouldn't have waited up for her.

"Good night." She paused at the threshold. "Thank you. For believing me, even though we argued."

"Why would our argument inhibit my belief?" His smile once again sent heat through her veins. "You can tell me anything, you know."

Not everything. Not how her regard of him had changed and how even now, she wasn't at all certain if she might be starting to love him like *that*. Instead, she nodded. "I'm glad we are friends, John."

"Always. Though we will no doubt continue our heated debate about my parenting come morning." He joked, when she'd thought he'd never forgive her.

Mirroring his smile, she glided down the hall as if in

a dance. For the first time in a long while, she felt happy. Her love for Gemma had been enough for tonight. Maybe her new love for God was enough of a place to start, too.

So this was what peace felt like.

For having prayed, John had no peace.

His fingers gripped the back of his chair, resisting the urge to break it apart since he could not snap the limbs off the *Honorable* Frederick Coles.

God, grant me calm. He breathed, in, out, counted to ten, but tranquility eluded him. He paced, his boots smacking the oak planks. After a while he dropped to his chair, gripped the fireplace poker and smacked the graying logs to ash.

Helena. Gazing into her wide, vulnerable eyes 'twas all he could do not to crush her in his arms. As it was, he'd held her, a dangerous risk when all he wanted to convey was safety and comfort—something she'd clearly been denied by her parents.

She blamed herself, and without question, her parents had validated her guilt. It was not a shock the Duke of Kelworth refrained from seeking justice for Helena, since society judged the victims of such attacks harshly, wrong though it was, and justice would have come at a harsh, cold price for her.

But her parents hadn't defended her, either.

John resumed pacing. He'd never been so angry. Not at Catriona, when she withdrew to her dream world of laudanum when Louisa first got sick. Not even at himself, when he had caused Catriona pain.

But this marriage was nothing like his first. Helena had been brave to share with him, and he'd not allow her to regret it by mishandling their relationship now.

No matter how John felt, this was about her. Not about

a man's need for justice or revenge or honor. John must do something to help her.

He hastened to the desk and dug for fresh foolscap. The scent of ink permeated the room as he scrawled.

The inquiry must be ready to post at first light. This was an act of faith for Helena, and he'd not delay.

Chapter Twelve

Considering her confession about Frederick, Helena had feared John would treat her differently by morning's light, but he greeted her the next morning with a wide smile and his usual friendliness when they met in the nursery to tell the children about Baby Eugenie. Afterward, he pulled her aside.

"Have you a moment, Helena?"

"Of course." A nervous flutter trembled in her stomach as she followed him into the hall.

"I sent a letter this morning."

To Papa? To hunt down Frederick Coles? "Oh?"

"To The Relief for the Blind, that school in Edinburgh your friend Miss Fennelwick wrote to you about. I thought we might visit, discern if there's something more we might do for Louisa." He looked at her with such tenderness, such expectation at her response, her heart swelled, pushing the breath right out of her lungs.

"Truly?"

"We know next to nothing about this school, and I make no promises to apply any of their methods, but I heard what you said about me not knowing my children as well as I might, and needing to help them grow up. So will you go with me?"

Like partners.

Words didn't form, but her enthusiastic nod made John laugh. He didn't touch her, though. He'd needed a hug last night and known she did, too. If they made a habit of it, though, she might become greedy for more embraces.

The next ten days were busy for Helena, welcoming the new governess, a tall, slender reed of a woman named Miss Munro, taking the children to visit Baby Eugenie, and preparing for the overnight trip to Edinburgh Helena and John would undertake. At last, the day of their voyage finally arrived, and Barnes's cool fingers tied Helena's bonnet ribbons under her chin. "Your heart is racing, milady. Excitement at seeing Edinburgh, I'm sure."

"It will be an adventure for you and me both, seeing a new place, will it not?" Helena smiled at the lady's maid, but the truth was more complicated. After her admission about Frederick and his gentle response, her feelings for her husband grew more pronounced. It was growing far more difficult to not love him beyond friendship. Her stomach fluttered at the thought of sitting alone in the carriage with John, all the way to Edinburgh, and all the way back.

"Anything more, milady?" Barnes folded her hands at her waist.

"Thank you, no." Helena hurried to the nursery. Iona lounged on the rug with the playing children. The remnants of breakfast had not been cleared from the table, and the scent of bacon lingered in the air. Agnes and Miss Munro bobbed curtsies. Helena greeted them, dismissed them to their team and hastened to the children, touching each in greeting.

"How long will you be gone?" Alex peered up at her.

"One night in Edinburgh is all," she told them for the hundredth time.

"Why may we not come?" Alex folded his arms. "Why are you going alone?"

Callum rubbed Iona's ears. "They aren't going alone. They are taking Barnes and Ritchie with them."

"They are servants," Margaret chided.

"But we're their children." Louisa's protest brought up Helena short. It was the first time one of the children mentioned her with ownership.

She bit back her smile. "Our business would be of little interest to you. We are visiting a school to observe their teaching methods."

"You mean Uncle John is observing for the bill he'd like to propose at Westminster, and you will shop." Margaret's tone held a tinge of envy.

Helena wouldn't correct her misunderstanding. "Perhaps you and I can shop sometime soon." Things between her and Margaret were still tenuous. Finding common ground seemed to help. If Margaret liked shopping, then Helena would oblige. "A visit to the linen draper's would be most welcome."

"That's boring. I like pastry shops." Callum grinned. "Let us come to Edinburgh, please?"

"Please?" Louisa curled her dolly, Tabitha, to her chest.

"Not this time." Helena sighed. "We shall miss you terribly, though."

"We are accustomed to having no parent in residence." Margaret's voice was sharp, resembling its old, tart tone.

Helena could understand Margaret's frustration, however. John would be leaving for London in a few weeks for his parliamentary duties. The thought unsettled her, too. She wrapped her arm around Margaret's slim shoulder and squeezed, even though she knew Margaret still wouldn't respond. At least Margaret didn't move away. "I shall bring you all something."

Louisa hopped like a robin. "What will you bring me?"

"I do not yet know." Helena's mama used to bring her rosewater after trips.

"I should like a sword," Alex offered.

"She won't buy you a sword, ninny." Margaret slipped outside the semicircle of Margaret's arm. "You'd hack off your own foot."

Callum leaped at Alex, wielding a spoon from the table as a weapon. Iona joined the fray, barking and jumping on the boys' legs.

"I want a sword, too!" Louisa scuttled toward her shuffling brothers.

"No fighting, play or otherwise." Helena took the spoon. "Not in such close quarters."

Iona kept jumping. "What a rambunctious lot you are." Helena pushed the dog's paws off her legs, hoping Iona didn't soil her primrose traveling gown. The yellow fabric would easily show dirt or oil—

Or jam, which Louisa now unknowingly spread on her knee. Helena would have to change her ensemble.

Margaret screeched. "Mouse!"

A shudder of disgust slithered up Helena's legs. Rodents lived in walls and under floorboards, of course, but knowing one was in the room set her knees to wobbling. "Are you certain?"

"It's gray and loathsome," Margaret insisted, pointing to the cupboard by the girls' bedchamber. No gray fluff was evident, but Iona investigated the area.

Helena cleared a wide berth of the cupboard on the way to the bell pull, praying a member of the staff would respond with astounding promptness. "This is your doing, lads?" She'd not forgotten the disaster at her wedding.

"No, we promise." Callum's nostrils didn't flare, so chances were good he was being truthful.

Alex rushed to the cupboard, gently pushing Iona aside. "But I want this one since we lost the old one."

"Oh, no. There will be no more mice in waistcoats in this house." Helena's breakfast crept up her throat.

Margaret shrieked as Iona, and presumably the mouse, dashed into the girls' bedchamber. "Get it out before it gives birth in my bed!"

"Will there be mouse babies in my bed?" Louisa's eyes welled with tears.

Helena hoisted her into her arms. "No."

"I do hope so," Alex said at the same time.

Of course John entered the nursery *now*, when the room was in utter chaos.

Her face burned. She was probably as scarlet as the jam stain on her gown. He lifted Louisa from her arms. "What's all this?"

"There's a mouse and Alex hopes it has babies in my bed and they can all live in his waistcoat." Louisa sniffed. "What will you bring me from Edinburgh, Papa?"

Ah, to be young and able to dash from disaster with such ease.

"Something fetching." His lips twitched, then curved into a frown. "Is that blood, lady wife?"

Her blush heated further, like a warm kettle put farther into the fire. Really, he shouldn't call her *lady wife*. Especially in such a sweet tone. "Strawberry jam."

He set Louisa down. "Callum, help Alex with the dog and remove her from the nursery. Ah." At the arrival of Adam the footman, he issued instructions like a military general. "Summon Miss Munro, Agnes, a cage or two, and some cheese."

"We're to trap her? I'd rather have a pet cat." Margaret hopped on tiptoe.

"No cat. Don't kill her, Papa," one of the boys shouted.

"Or him," Helena clarified. Or worse—them. All this talk of baby mice was most unsettling.

"Pet cat or no, mice cannot live as pets in the nursery," John insisted.

The boys groaned. Margaret sat at the table with a look of triumph.

The way John took control was delightful. Helena could have sighed with pleasure, but then, she wouldn't wish him to mistake it for appreciation of how fine a figure he cut in his deep blue coat and fawn pantaloons.

Miss Munro hastened in, apologetic and fussing. She gasped at the sight of Helena's pelisse. "Forgive me, my lady."

"Nonsense."

"Our departure will await you making any necessary changes." John nodded at her. "No need to hasten."

"I shall indeed make haste. I do not wish to be late for our appointment."

She returned a few minutes later, donned in a dirt-concealing moss-green ensemble. The children and John gathered around the nursery table, regaling Agnes and Miss Munro with their versions of the events.

"I want to keep the mousie." Alex frowned.

"And it wants to be free. Preferably out of doors." John smiled.

Helena adjusted her gloves. "Has it been caught?"

"Not in all this noise." Then John took each child in an embrace and dotted swift kisses on their brows. "Take care of Iona, now. Listen to Miss Munro and Agnes."

Helena followed behind, embracing the children. Margaret, again, neither responded nor pulled away. The boys squirmed under her kisses, but Louisa snuggled close. "We shall see you on the morrow."

"With presents." Louisa patted Helena's cheek and then kissed it. The child smelled of jam and soap.

"With presents," she agreed. And hopefully something more for Louisa, as well. A plan for her future.

It was a fine day to travel, dry and bright, not so warm the carriage grew stuffy, not so cool they required lap robes. John had offered one to Helena anyway, but she'd refused, and they'd spent the past four hours in light conversation, comfortable but superficial.

"Have you already decided on presents for the children, then?" he asked.

"Not exactly." Her smile was the genuine one he liked so well. He'd seen more of it these past ten days than he had in the first month of their marriage, as if their conversation about Frederick Coles had in some small way been healing for her, and the real woman beneath the beautiful but stoic mask was emerging through the facade.

As she talked about ideas for toys for the children, her eyes shone, and he sat back against the plush carriage squabs and watched her, allowing himself to forget he had no business liking her smile or her voice or her nearness. Only for a moment, though. He may be her husband, but he had promised Helena—and Catriona—he would not behave like one.

Even if he was starting to wish everything had been much, much different.

He'd asked God to submerge the rising feelings he held for Helena, and even now repeated his silent petition.

Her delicate hand waved. "I was thinking we might purchase doll clothes for Louisa. Something with texture and ribbons. She should learn to tie a bow."

John nodded. "Doll clothes it is, then." Although Louisa might never tie the wide bow of a bonnet under her own chin, much less slender ribbons on doll clothes.

Helena twisted toward him. "You don't think she can accomplish it."

"I said nothing of the sort." He tried to look affronted, but his smile won out.

"Where is your faith?" The tone was light, but the words struck his gut.

John had not offered to make the trip because he had faith they'd find true help at the Relief for the Blind. He came to offer Helena a gift, to prove he listened to her. Perhaps he should have included faith in God in his equation.

"My faith, or lack thereof, is about to be reckoned with, for it appears we are near our destination." He tapped the window beside him. Nicolson Street, if he was not mistaken.

Helena leaned toward him to look out his side of the coach, filling his nostrils with her rosewater scent. "I haven't paid any mind to the scenery at all."

"Because my conversation was so scintillating."

She looked about to tease a response, but then the carriage lurched to a stop before a wide house. The Edinburgh Asylum for the Relief of the Indigent and Industrious Blind. Helena's gulp was audible.

A slither of anxiety shot up John's spine. "Ready?"

She nodded, but her smile fell into an artificial mask. When he took her hand and assisted her from the carriage, he squeezed.

Her head tipped up and she met his gaze. "You are a kind man."

Something raw and honest in her eyes struck him in the chest like a flame-tipped arrow, spreading heat to his limbs. It was too much and not enough all at once. He wanted to kiss her.

No. He'd promised Helena and Catriona he'd never—and why was he thinking such things on a public street, anyway? He took Helena's arm. "Kind, eh? Let us hope you still think so in five minutes."

Within moments, they were ushered inside a clean but dimly lit study with the gentleman in charge, Mr. Holme, a small-boned man in his thirties with ash-brown hair and a wary expression. He was probably unaccustomed to being in the presence of a lord and lady. John smiled to set the fellow at ease.

"Thank you for accommodating us. We have come as a matter of curiosity. As I wrote in my letter, my daughter is blind."

Holme's head dipped. "So I recall, my lord."

"Naturally I'm interested in donating to charitable organizations devoted to assisting the blind." At John's remark, Helena spun to look at him.

"You'll not find many such places, if I may say so, my lord." Holme shook his head. "The Relief for the Blind is one of a few in Europe, besides Paris and Liverpool. Our goals were set forth near thirty years ago, and remain unchanged. To promote for our residents' welfare, and to provide education and training in an industry."

"How do you do this?" John sat forward.

"With patience, my lord."

"And care?" Helena spoke for the first time.

"We see to the physical and spiritual needs of our residents." Holme's face cracked into a smile. "Perhaps the best way to illustrate how we teach is by showing you. Would you like to meet some of our residents?"

"Yes," John blurted. He offered his arm to Helena, and she eagerly took it.

The sound of singing met them in the hall. Helena tilted her head. "What fine voices."

Holme grinned. "Our residents have no limitations placed upon their tongues, nor their hands."

They entered a large, open chamber. More than a dozen men in neat clothing sat on the oak-planked floor beside bowls of tools and sundry materials. Each held a wooden board on his lap.

"They make brushes today." Pride tinged Holme's tone. "They also make other handcrafts, such as baskets or mattresses. When they leave us, they should find gainful employment."

"They will support themselves?" John blinked.

"Aye, my lord."

If these men could weave baskets, form mattresses, Louisa could do many things, too. She would be able to tie the bow Helena wanted to teach her, mayhap sew a seam, even though her eyes might never view her stitches. *Lord, is this possible for Louisa?*

John wished to speak to the men, yet at the same time he'd no idea what he'd ask. The questions running through his brain all related to how he and Catriona chose to raise Louisa. *Do you walk outside? Are you fed or do you hold your own spoon?*

The men found pegs and tiny hammers and measured bristles without the benefit of sight. Clearly they could manage a fork at table. How stupid he had been. Stupid and afraid.

A young man with freckles spattered over his thin nose stopped his work and singing at John's approach. He tipped his head, like Louisa when she heard a noise.

John cleared his throat. "Your work is well done."

"Thank you, sir." How old was this lad? Twenty?

John asked about the youth's history before moving to

the next man, and then the next. He inquired as to their names and villages and expressed appreciation. Behind him, Helena did the same.

Although it felt like a betrayal to acknowledge it, Catriona would never have spoken as Helena did. Catriona would never have even entered the building.

After John and Helena circled the group, Holme held out his arm. "Would you care to return to my office?" As John and Helena followed, he kept up a steady stream of information. "Our first home was smaller. This residence affords us greater space. As yet, however, we have no facility for women."

"Pity. I wish for everyone, male and female, to learn and fulfill their potential." John had such a plan ready to propose to Parliament for impoverished children, but in his ignorance, he'd forgotten about children like Louisa.

"That is our hope, as well." Mr. Holme smiled. "There are more interested in living here than we can accommodate. Some are born blind, although one of our residents was struck by a branch last winter. His life changed in an instant."

"My Louisa had sight during early infancy." His words came out in a rush. He hadn't spoken of it in so long, there was no stopping the flow once begun. "Her first smile— she looked me in the eye when she was a few weeks old and she smiled at me. But she got sick and when she recovered, her gaze didn't follow the direction of her smiles. Clouds covered her eyes."

Helena brushed a tear from her lashes.

Holme's brow rose. "Was she examined?"

"Yes, by the family physician, but there was nothing he could do." Not for Louisa, at any rate. But Catriona had needed a great deal of attention afterward. She'd been impossible to calm since Louisa grew ill, and from then on, she demanded a steady dose of laudanum.

John swallowed hard, aching his throat. "I attended university with a fellow whose sister was born blind. They treated her like a doll, not a person. When the physician said we must protect Louisa, I never questioned it."

"You never consulted anyone with particular knowledge of the eye?"

A chill pricked John's skin. "Is there someone with such expertise?"

"Aye, there are a few. Seems providential, your coming."

"Could her sight be restored?" John never dared hope something could be done for Louisa beyond keeping her safe and comfortable.

"She'd require an exam, of course."

"Then I shall bring her here."

"What about London?" Helena's hand clutched her armrest. "You are soon to leave."

The massacre in Manchester on Saint Peter's Field necessitated his return to London in a few weeks. His duty, however, was not just to king and country. It was time he proved it. "There is no finer place for medical training than Edinburgh. If there's someone here who knows the working of the eye, I'd like Louisa to be examined."

"Are you certain?" Her love for Louisa glowed on her face. His hand moved without his thinking about it and took her fingers in a gentle touch of reassurance, but he felt it to his boots.

Helena's pupils dilated. He didn't breathe, didn't think, until Holme's cough jarred him to the present.

"The best doctors are Scottish, that's true. But there's one I think you should see who *isn't* here in Edinburgh."

"Where is he?" John would go anywhere, anytime.

Holme smiled, crimping his eyes to half-moons. "You'd

best prepare for a trip south, because the doctor in question is teaching in London."

"Perfect. I'll take Louisa to London with me."

Surely, Helena would be as delighted as he. He turned to her, but her face had frozen into that all-too-familiar mask of ice.

Chapter Thirteen

Helena fixed her calm smile in place and kept it there as they thanked Mr. Holme, stopped to buy the children presents and made their way to the inn. She'd forced the smile throughout a supper she could barely taste, and kept smiling while they retired to the sitting room they shared. John sat at the small desk, writing to his friend Carvey in London, while she sat by the fire stitching embellishments on an altar cloth.

If she unfroze her face, it would dissolve into tears, because now when John left for London in a few weeks, Helena would lose him and Louisa, too.

The thought pricked at her, as if she stitched her skin instead of the cloth spread over her lap. The white-on-white sheaves of wheat looked as untidy as her sentiments, but she kept stitching. Needle down, John leaves for London. Needle up, he's taking Louisa with him.

The pain threatened to crack her in half.

She would miss Louisa's growth. Loose teeth, perhaps. And Louisa would be lonely without the boys and Margaret. She may even miss Helena, and Helena would be hundreds of miles away.

But this was Louisa's best chance to perhaps see again. *God, what do you have in store for her?*

With a rustle of paper, John folded his letter into a precise rectangle. "Done. Are you unwell? You scarcely ate, and I daresay you're pale as your embroidery canvas."

She glanced up. "I'm overwhelmed after all we learned at Mr. Holme's office."

"I was overwhelmed, too." He dropped the letter onto the edge of the desk. "To think I doubted this trip would bear any fruit. I'm sorry, Helena."

"No need to be sorry. And I'm glad you don't think the trip was in vain." If nothing else came from their venture to Edinburgh, Holme's Relief for the Blind received a substantial donation from her generous husband, but it seemed John wouldn't fight her in teaching Louisa more skills now. "Do we leave after breakfast? I'm anxious to return home."

"The children will be delighted to see their presents." A smile tugging at his lips, he settled into the chair to her left, as if they were in the library at home. "And us, of course."

Then why take Louisa from Helena?

He seemed ignorant of what his edict had done to her. On the contrary, he'd behaved like a different man altogether at the toy shop when they shopped for the children's presents. Lighthearted and playful, touching the puppets and mechanical toys like Callum and Alex would. She'd wanted to join in his childlike spirit, but she'd felt as if she were petrifying inside.

Still, the gifts she and John had chosen for the children seemed perfect. For Margaret, a new type of board game, Virtue Rewarded and Vice Punished. For the boys, toy ships to sail in the creek, breaking one of Catriona's rules, of course, but John seemed to have forgotten. And for Louisa, simple dolly frocks for Tabitha.

"How long do you suppose you will keep Louisa with you in London?"

John stretched his legs before the fire. "I thought to bring all the children, not just Louisa. They've never been to London."

The altar cloth slipped off Helena's lap. "All four?" Without her?

"All six of us, unless you'd rather not, but I think Louisa would be comforted by your presence during the examination." His soft smile twisted as he studied her face. "Did you presume I meant to leave you behind?"

A lie rushed to her lips. Instead she scooped up the cloth from the floor. "I wasn't certain."

"I'd like you to come, if you wish. For a month or two, at least. Perhaps your father's health has improved. You can visit your family."

Could she? Mama, Papa, her sisters…perhaps even the family she'd not been able to bid farewell, her grandmother and Uncle Cecil, whose wife Mama abhorred for her lower station. After so long a separation, Helena would be delighted to see any one of them.

But especially Papa. The chance to spend time with him, ill as he was, seemed like a gift. And the thought of being together with John and the children for the holiday was better than any trapping of Christmas: plum pudding or mummers or wassail or packages or playing in the snow. She'd appreciate the holiday in a new way, too, now she'd begun to place her trust in the Baby whose birth they celebrated.

John's brow was lifted as he awaited her answer. "So we'll all go to London, together?"

She could not repress her smile. "I should like it very much."

John grinned back.

It would be the best Christmas of her life.

* * *

The next two weeks passed in a flurry of preparations for the trip to London. John was grateful for the busyness of it all, since it kept his mind distracted from the feelings stirring in his chest for his wife.

Far better to be occupied with making arrangements for the London town house to be opened and handling the flood of correspondence regarding the massacre in Manchester— Peterloo, as some were calling it, referencing the Battle of Waterloo. Another blackmail letter arrived, too, with a falcon imprint in the seal, demanding money. He locked it into the treasure box with its loathsome brothers.

He'd see to putting an end to the blackmail once he arrived in London.

The journey proceeded as schedule, and continued, smooth and uneventful, aside from the disturbing effect prompted by sitting near his wife in the carriage. He spent too much time admiring her eyes, laughing at her little jokes with the children, enjoying being a family with her and itching for more than they agreed to. After two days of such torture, he decided to ride his horse alongside the carriage.

The boys joined him part of each day, and it turned out to be a rich time with them. They spoke of their toy soldiers, the mice they'd kept as pets and the estate, but he was sure to include Callum in the conversations on running Comraich, and Alex didn't have a single nightmare over the journey.

The afternoon of their arrival, London was dressed for autumn in hues of gray and brown. A light wind blew off the Thames, carrying a tangy odor that followed them into his town house on Saint James's Square.

"What is that smell?" Callum grimaced.

"London." John exchanged a glance with Helena. She was smiling.

After they divested their outer garments and greeted the staff, John beckoned Helena upstairs. The boys followed them up, but then ran down again, as if stairs were a novelty. Well, these particular stairs were. Iona kept pace with the boys, a doggy smile on her face. John peeked back. Someone had better be mindful of Louisa.

Margaret had her in hand, and they counted the stairs as they ascended.

John led Helena to the sitting room between their bedchambers. Weak autumn sunlight spilled between heavy green brocade curtains and over the faded furniture, some of it a hundred years old, which made it both charming and uncomfortable to sit on, to John's thinking. He gestured around the room. "I've not seen the need to update anything. Not when it was just me living here. Not when it has *always* been just me."

"You said the children have never been here, but Catriona never came with you, either?" Her dainty hand landed on the back of a bulky brown chair.

His head shook. "Mother seldom came to London, either. I thought you might want to change the room to suit your tastes. All the rooms, here and at Comraich, too. Our marriage might not be conventional, but I don't wish you to feel as if everything you have is secondhand. They're your rooms, Helena. I want them to be new for you."

She didn't say anything. The only sounds in the house were the children's whoops and the scrapes of servants unloading trunks outside. Did she understand what he was saying? It had less to do with interior design and replacing moth-eaten draperies than it did with wanting her to be happy and comfortable. She needed to know this was her home as much as it was his.

And because he had feelings for her. Warm feelings, despite his efforts to keep Helena from taking over his heart.

The tiniest corner of her lip curled. "Do you like blue?"

His shoulders relaxed. "It depends upon the shade and where you mean to drape it. Cerulean is fine for walls but not my pantaloons."

Her jaw dropped in mock despair. "I had meant to surprise you with cerulean pantaloons. Pity. They were to go with the scarlet silk coat I planned for your Christmas."

"I'll not wear scarlet for you, woman."

Her laugh was like little bells. "'Tis well, I suppose. I like you in green. It brings out your eyes." Then she flushed. "Thank you, John. I should enjoy this project. Something pastel, to allow in the light?"

"Splendid, yes." Pastel, stripes, puce, he didn't care. He looked well in green?

Barnes bustled past the doorway between the sitting room and Helena's bedchamber. Spying her, Helena moved to join her lady's maid, but turned her head back to smile at him. "I shall start on the morrow, then. Shall we entertain soon? My family, your friends, whomever you like."

It was an ordinary expectation for one of her station in society. "Of course. Let us start small. With your family. I shall see enough of Carvey at Westminster."

Her grin warmed his bones. She was at home in London. And if she was happy, it would be enough to sustain him through the rest of their marriage.

Chapter Fourteen

It was not the happy Christmas John had hoped for his wife.

Oh, it had been festive and loud and fun at their town house on Saint James's Square, where the children reveled in their gifts and nibbled candies before breaking their fasts. Helena had a gift for him, too: a gold stickpin for his neck cloth, not a scarlet coat, as she'd teased. He'd given her a shawl trimmed with scarlet ribbon, because of that teasing. They'd both laughed, and he'd been warmed to his bones to share in a joke with her.

Although the library had grown rather frigid when Adam brought in yet another blackmail letter with a falcon-imprinted wax seal. This time, the blackguard did not want money. He wanted John's vote for Sidmouth's Six Acts, in particular the one prohibiting political assembly of more than three individuals. Much as John did not like the law, it would pass. So why did someone want his vote when it wouldn't even matter?

Power. Someone would manipulate him for the sport of it, and sent the note of blackmail today of all days in order to ruin his Christmas.

John had refused to let it, but he should have known Helena's family would ruin hers.

At the appointed hour, they'd bundled the children into their coats and ventured to the grand town house Helena had lived in before she married. John had never been there before, nor had he met the blonde duchess, their two unwed daughters and the dowager, a tiny, sharp-eyed woman who examined him through a bejeweled quizzing glass. He wasn't certain whether to feel offended or amused, but chose the latter and flashed her a saucy smile.

Her brows rose, but it also seemed as if the tiniest corner of her lips twitched.

After quick introductions, the duchess sent his children upstairs, including Margaret, who was of age with Helena's sister Andromeda. Margaret's cheeks had flushed with indignation. "Why—"

"You'll have more fun," John whispered to her. Miss Munro and Agnes would no doubt organize games and amusements, and they'd enjoy their dinner together.

After pleasantries, John followed the small family party into an elegant, gold-papered dining room for the Christmas feast.

"Helena," his mother-in-law said the moment grace was spoken and they filled their plates with a savory dinner of roast goose, root vegetables, buttered fish and jewel-colored jellies. Her smile was precisely like the one Helena wore when she applied her stoic mask, but otherwise, she did not look much like her daughter, although she was a beauty. "You will never guess who attended the Fairburns' ball last Thursday. The Duke of Bowden."

Bowden had been their intended husband for Helena, rich and old enough to be her grandfather. Not only that, he was the uncle of the man who'd assaulted her, Frederick

Coles. Did the duchess realize how much pain she was inflicting right now by broaching the subject? John scowled.

Helena's gaze dropped to her plate. "He is well, I hope."

"He is to wed. Banns will be posted soon. I think you know the young lady. Viscount Ralston's daughter. The match is so far above her, she is reveling in her success."

And Helena's match was so far beneath her—John caught the duchess's subtext. Helena had confessed she'd looked down on those beneath her in rank before her marriage, including her cousin's wife, Gemma. It was clear where Helena had learned to hold such a high attitude of herself. Were her sisters the same?

John leaned to his left, where the middle sister, Maria, poked at her food. "Helena says you will come out in society this spring."

Maria watched her mother, as if waiting for permission before responding. "Yes," she said at last, turning back to her food with such focus he had no choice but to end that conversation.

Andromeda sat on his other side, looking like a rounder, younger version of Helena.

John smiled at her. "Andromeda, did you make a wish on the Christmas pudding?"

"Wishing on pudding?" the duchess interrupted before Andromeda could speak. "How charming." Her tone implied she thought it anything but.

"It is, Mama," Helena inserted. "We had a wonderful time together. Everyone in our house takes turns stirring the pudding and then makes a wish."

"From the lord to the chambermaids." John sliced into a portion of goose.

Kelworth skewered him with a pointed gaze. "Did you wish for a petition for education for all? It would be most predictable of you."

His bite of goose didn't go down easily.

"Enough politics," the duchess said with a long sigh. "We are at the table."

Helena's grandmother cackled. "Christmas is not Christmas unless someone is upset."

"I'm not upset." Helena flinched, as if speaking had taken great effort. It probably had. *Brava, my dear.* "I'm happy. To see you all after so long an absence."

The silence stretched too long before Kelworth nodded. "Yes, well, yes. It surprised us to learn you'd come to town. So soon after the, er, wedding."

The goose sat in a lump in John's gullet. "We travel as a family. The children are attached to Helena, as she is to them."

"You're staying through the social season, then?" Maria didn't sound pleased. Was she afraid Helena and her lower-born husband would somehow affect her debutante season?

"No." Helena toyed with her food. "The children and I will return north in a month or thereabouts, leaving John to concentrate on his work. But we came to spend Christmas together, and for a special appointment. We are to take Louisa to a physician in two days."

"Louisa?"

"The youngest. She is five and she—"

"Oh, yes." The duchess investigated the carrots.

"I say, Ardoch, what think you of this weather?" Kelworth sliced into his goose. "Colder than it has been for a few winters."

John blinked at the abrupt change of subject. What was wrong with these people? Scornful, rude, unwelcoming. They hadn't seen Helena in months. Now she looked at each of them like a penitent pup, scolded for stealing a sock.

His grip tensed on his fork.

They should rise from the table and leave, prove to them

all how ill-mannered he was and give them something new to discuss. But Helena wanted connection to her family, so he'd endure more of it for her. Although he'd far prefer to tell the lot of them what he thought of them.

Instead he stared at the duke. "Yes, it's cold."

And he didn't just mean outside.

The dowager, the duchess and Helena's sisters all remarked on the snow. He and Helena need not be at the table at all, the way they were ignored.

It was a relief when the ladies finished and withdrew to the drawing room, although it left him alone with Kelworth to endure talk of politics and thinly disguised slights. John sat back and, in the spirit of Christmas, let his father-in-law speak. It allowed him to think.

Tonight made something clear. Helena's family hadn't given her the care she'd needed and deserved while she was growing up. His family had had its own issues, but he'd known he was cared for more than Helena had. Little wonder she'd responded to Frederick Coles's displays of affection.

So few in Helena's life loved her back, and she'd hid her wounds beneath a wall of ice. Such a barrier would not disappear in the course of a conversation. Or a half year of marriage with him. But with time and his full support, perhaps she would heal.

How could he help her?

The shawl he'd given her for Christmas was a token, a trifle. But his real gift to her would be a loving home, the companionship and affection she'd been denied under this roof.

He'd be her champion, her friend, and he'd see her happy, God willing.

"Why are you smiling like that?" Kelworth's brow furrowed.

Was he? John didn't attempt to smother it. "Just thinking of your daughter. How glad I am to have married her."

Kelworth's head snapped back. He probably thought 'twas bad enough John had married his daughter, but it was downright distasteful that John and Helena might be happy about their marriage.

For some reason, that made John smile even wider. "As you were saying?"

This was what Helena had anticipated most of all since returning to London: time with her sisters. She followed Maria to the green-papered drawing room, intent to sit beside her on the cream velvet settee. Mama took that seat, however, leaving no room for Helena. Andromeda curled at Mama's feet with an issue of *La Belle Assemblée* while the dowager settled into the plushest chair by the fire.

Helena perched on the chair closest to Maria. "You must tell me everything I've missed in London."

"Is Scotland so removed you receive no newspapers?" Maria didn't meet her gaze.

"I meant what I've missed of you. I imagine you are preparing for your presentation at court." They used to daydream of their special court dresses, chatting about lace and feathers and managing the dresses' long trains. "What will your gown be like?"

Maria examined her buffed nails. "White."

All come-outs wore white. "Yes, but what fabric?"

"Gauze with satin sprig. And accent of Clarence blue." Maria's chin tilted. "It is anticipated to be one of the most popular colors this season."

Mama rapped her fan on Maria's arm. "Take pity on Helena, dear. She has likely not seen a fashion magazine since her marriage."

"Would you like to see this one?" Andromeda lifted the issue of *La Belle Assemblée*.

Helena took the periodical and beckoned her little sister closer. "Show me your favorites."

Andromeda shook her head. "Keep it. I'm finished."

"Perhaps this year's fashions will arrive in Perthshire by next year." Mama perused Helena's emerald silk gown with a critical eye. "You wore that last winter."

"Excellent memory, Mama." Her voice trembled. Mama wasn't remembering old times. She was judging Helena's being out of fashion. Helena used to do the same, before she fell from grace and learned a woman's worth had naught to do with her gown.

"Is there no decent mantua-maker in your village?" Her grandmother spoke for the first time, her gray brows lifting under the brim of her rose satin toque.

Helena dropped the magazine atop the table. She didn't want it anymore. "I have been busy with the children and as yet have had no need of one."

"Ah, yes, you are a mother now." She tapped a gnarled finger against the armrest. "To all those children."

"There are but four, Your Grace." She'd never been allowed to call her *Grandmother*.

"But one of them blind." She whispered the last word as if it were a secret. "Why did you not leave them behind?"

Helena blinked. She'd explained why in her letters. "We brought her to London to consult a doctor."

"No, not to London. I refer to bringing her here, tonight."

"It is Christmas." How foolish she'd been to think it mattered. "I thought you might wish to meet my new family."

"Whyever would you think that? They're not even your children," Mama said, blinking. Then she reached for the magazine. "Show me what you found, Andromeda. You will require something spectacular made up for Easter."

Maria pointed to the first page. "What an admirable flounce."

Something altered within Helena, as if a flickering candle sputtered out. She'd hoped her family missed her, hoped they would be glad to see her. Hoped they would accept the children, but they didn't care about her or her new family at all. Fixing in place the smile her mother had taught her, Helena excused herself and strode from the room.

Once cleared of the threshold, however, she covered her mouth with her hands and rushed to the alcove near the staircase, where she could hide and control herself. Much as she wanted to return to Saint James's Square at once, the children shouldn't see her like this, with foolish tears streaking her cheeks.

No one loved her.

Not her family, who seemed to scarcely tolerate her. She was no longer part of their fold.

Not Frederick Coles, who could have married her for her money if not for love, but he must have so despised her he preferred to have his way and abandon her.

Not the children, who might be growing used to her, but they did not love her.

And certainly not John.

God loves you. Have you already forgotten?

Helena's lips mashed. She'd learned a great deal about Him and His ways these past few months, but sometimes, her old questions and fears sprouted like fungi before her, seemingly out of nothing.

Your love alone is sufficient, isn't it, God? Then why does this ache to my soul?

She swiped her wet face with the back of her hand. The problem was her, after all, wasn't it? She was selfish, wanting love for her own sake. She should have prayed to love John's children so she could better serve them, so she could give them what they needed. Whether or not they loved her back was inconsequential.

Same with her family. And, too, with John.

She took a ragged, calming breath. John must never know how drawn to him she'd become. She could hide her feelings for five weeks until she and the children returned to Scotland, couldn't she? Once there, she'd have distance and time to recover from her fanciful emotions, time to focus on the children and care for them as they deserved.

Resolved, she stepped from the alcove as John, handsome in his bottle-green coat, came down the hall.

His eyes widened when he saw her. "You've been crying. What's happened?"

Her lips parted, but then her eyes moistened again and she shook her head. When he guided her back into the alcove, she went willingly.

"Your mother said you were in the nursery." He withdrew a linen handkerchief from his waistcoat pocket and dabbed her eyes. "I hoped to join you. Have you been tucked in here this whole time?"

She started to answer, but no words came out.

He opened his arms.

Despite her determination not to want her husband, she needed this, needed him, one last time. She curled into him and let her arms go around his back, feeling weak and grateful all at once. And so comfortable with her cheek against his waistcoat. Warmth suffused her forehead where his lips rested. "What happened?"

"The evening has not gone as I had hoped," she understated.

"I hoped for a merrier gathering, too."

She sniffed. "I'm sorry."

"'Tis not your fault." His breath was hot over her lashes, her brow.

A watery chuckle escaped her throat. "We always speak the same things to one another. I tell you I'm sorry, and then you are gracious and say I'm not at fault."

"Perhaps we shall assume those words said from now on and spare ourselves the trouble." She could tell his lips stretched into a smile.

And then they were not. He dotted a kiss on her forehead, warm and gentle. Her fingers unfurled and rested against the soft wool of his coat. Moved down a fraction, to a more comfortable position on his back.

His lips moved down, too.

They pressed the corner of her eye where tears lingered on her lashes. Touched upon her cheekbone. Soft, brief, laced with his compassion for her distress. Kind kisses, no more—they could not be more, surely.

He drew back, no more than an inch. Their breath mingled, tinged with tea and sugar. His clear gaze locked on her, and for the briefest of moments, she expected him to pull away.

Instead he dipped his head again and kissed her lips.

The kiss was as tender as those he'd pressed on her brow and cheek, but this time a shock jolted from her lips to her toes, sparking something in the dry tinder of her heart along its path. She was aware of the faint stubble tickling her lip, the cedar smell of him, how this kiss was like the first bite of a nectarine, sweet and bursting with the promise of summer.

And then, parting her lips to return the kiss, she stopped thinking at all.

Chapter Fifteen

John's pulse beat fast in his throat as his hand cupped the silken skin of her jaw, gently tilting her head up so he could better kiss her—

What was he doing? Ruining everything, that's what. His hands fell, and he pulled back as if she scorched him.

He had tried to offer comfort, offer tenderness, show he cared for her with a small kiss on her brow, but he'd had such little control of himself he'd kissed her, really kissed her, like a husband kissed his wife.

"Forgive me. I never should have—I promised you I wouldn't."

"I promised the same."

But she'd not returned the kiss. Her lips had moved against his and in the moment, he'd assumed she was responding, but she was probably about to reprimand him.

How could he have been so stupid? Not ten minutes ago he'd determined to be her friend and champion, nothing more. He thought hugging her would demonstrate care to her, and maybe a friendly kiss on the brow wouldn't hurt.

If only he'd stopped there.

"I'm sorry," he said again. To her, to God, to himself. "I don't know what got into me."

Well, he did know. She was beautiful and he was drawn to her, but to cross this boundary? "So can you find it in your heart to forgive me?"

"There's nothing to forgive." As if to prove it, she met his gaze.

"I assured you that you could trust me, and I've betrayed that trust. I should never—"

A loud knock rapped the front door, followed by footsteps striking the stone floor as a servant rushed to answer. By the murmured voices and sounds of the shuffling as the servants collected coats and hats, it sounded like a small party had entered.

And John and Helena were hiding in an alcove off the foyer.

She tugged him flush against the wall, the better to stay concealed.

He shook his head. They weren't children, to be caught in such inappropriate circumstances. Better if they stepped out—

Her head shook with more vehemence. *Uncle Cecil*, she mouthed.

It didn't matter who it was, but fine. He'd play it her way. Quiet as a cat, he sidled closer to her, hopefully out of sight when the guests passed the alcove into the drawing room.

Meanwhile, she still clutched his hand. He squeezed back.

The party passed them—two men and a woman—and once they were gone, Helena expelled a huge breath.

John tipped his head down toward her. "Relieved they didn't see us?"

"Shocked, actually," she whispered back. "We are right here—but more than that, Uncle Cecil brought Young Cecil. And his *wife*."

"What's wrong with his wife?"

"Aunt Davinia and Mama loathe each other."

Helena's mother didn't seem to like much of anyone. John almost smiled.

"It's quiet out there now." John tugged her hand. "Are we safe to go out? And go home?"

The moment he spoke, footsteps rapped the stone floor of the hall again. A servant bearing silver cups walked past the alcove, then spied them, pausing half a second to peek at them before resuming his trajectory.

Helena watched after him. "They must be preparing to toast the day with lamb's wool punch. 'Tis a longstanding tradition. We can't leave now without greeting my aunt and uncle, anyway."

"Are you certain?" Her family was rather beastly, but then again, John had behaved poorly, too, kissing her. "If my inexcusable actions didn't give you a headache, then I'm certain sipping punch in the drawing room with the lot of them will. I can tell them you are indisposed."

Her fingers fidgeted at her sides. "I'll not lie. Nor will I let them think me hen-hearted."

If he had not known it before, he surely knew it now. Helena was amazing. "You are the bravest female I know. No one would dare call you coward, my valiant lady wife."

Her smile warmed him to his stockings. "We shall toast. *Then* take our leave."

"Perfect." He took her arm and led her out.

At once, she tugged him to a stop. "What you said in the alcove? I do trust you, John. More than I trust anyone."

She forgave him, then. His heart lightened considerably, and he was almost smiling when he escorted her into the drawing room.

The temperature seemed to fall several degrees as they entered the room, among a frosty tableau. Everyone looked at them, but none of them spoke, much less smiled. The blond, thin fellow who must be Lord Cecil actually sneered.

Little wonder Helena's cousin Tavin Knox had little to do with this family, and his mother escaped them by eloping.

Helena adopted her icy, artificial smile and made the introductions. If her Uncle Cecil, round, dark-haired Aunt Davinia and gangly brown-haired cousin of fifteen or so, referred to as Young Cecil, were pleased to make John's acquaintance, they hid it well.

"Yours was a hasty marriage?" Lord Cecil's superior tone insinuated he didn't approve.

The smile playing at John's lips stretched into a grin. "Our betrothal was short, yes, but we knew the moment we first saw one another we would wed. Is that not so, Helena?"

It wasn't a lie, although it took her a moment to catch on. "'Tis true."

"That sounds romantic." Lady Davinia smiled at her husband. "We knew the same when we met."

Her son rolled his eyes.

Lord Cecil frowned. "But our betrothal was lengthy enough for preparations to be made. Our families were invited, even if they didn't all attend."

A nervous-sounding laugh escaped Helena's mother's throat. So she hadn't gone to the wedding, then? Helena had said her mother didn't like Lady Davinia.

Eyes narrowed, the dowager duchess peered at John. "We all wondered at the news of such hasty nuptials, but yes, I see it now."

See what?

Helena tipped her head in exact imitation of her arrogant mother's. She took a cup of lamb's wool punch from the footman's tray. John followed suit, catching a whiff of the apple cider.

Kelworth reached for a cup, only to succumb to a racking cough. The poor man's face reddened as he bent over, but not a single member of his family near him moved to assist him. So John did, Helena a half step behind him.

"Your Grace, come, sit."

Kelworth shook off John's arm as the cough receded. "I'm well."

"Don't be a fool, Arthur. Sit." Lord Cecil shook his head.

"Your brother is right, dearest. Listen to Cecil." The duchess smiled, to John's surprise. She hadn't smiled at anyone tonight.

Lord Cecil eyed his brother. "You know what happened to Father when he was plagued by coughs—"

"I said I'm well." The dark color leached from Kelworth's face.

Helena's hand reached out. "Papa?"

Ignoring her, he turned, taking a cup of punch and lifting it in a toast. "Happy Christmas."

"Happy Christmas," the chorus responded, rather flatly.

"And a prosperous New Year." Kelworth drained his cup.

John toasted his wife in silence. She bore her artificial, frozen smile again, but for the first time since they'd met, the frigid turn of her lips didn't bother him a whit. He understood it now.

She'd been taught to don that frozen smile by her mother, but she also bore it as a measure of protection. It was her armor, hiding the hurt she felt over her family and the fear she had for her father's health.

The look would defrost when they returned to their town house on Saint James's Square, when she didn't need it as a shield anymore, where she was safe and cared for. He'd do his best to comfort her, with his words and prayers and maybe a hug. Maybe one more kiss—

John almost choked on his punch. No more of that. Kissing, or wanting it.

* * *

Two mornings later, cold nipped Helena's goose-fleshed skin as she stood outside the town house at Saint James's Square, although her thick woolen gown, cloak, muffler and gloves provided admirable defense against the chill weather, if not the cold in her heart.

John's Christmas kiss was forefront in her thoughts. As was her reaction to it.

For a moment in that alcove, Helena thought something was changing between them, that he felt drawn to her, too, to kiss her like that.

But clearly, she was wrong. While he'd been considerate and caring since their moment in the alcove, he was true to his word and he hadn't touched her again.

A friendly relationship was what they'd agreed upon—what she'd wanted, after all, after Frederick—but she wasn't so sure she wanted that anymore, other than to return that kiss of John's. Since the moment he pulled back and apologized, rejection's cold spikes pricked her flesh.

So, now, did the winter wind. She drew her cloak tighter about her shoulders.

John, wrapped in a caped gray greatcoat, scooped Louisa into his arms and hoisted her into the waiting carriage as Agnes joined Bill Coachman up top.

"I'll place the warmer of hot coals under your feet in a moment." John's words to Louisa were spoken with such tenderness, Helena's heart swelled. His love for his children was one of her favorite things about him.

"I don't want a warmer," Louisa called. "It will hurt my patterns."

"*Pattens*," Helena corrected as she prepared to enter the coach. "And the warmer will not hurt them." The metal rings on the soles of her own pattens, strapped over her boots to provide more traction on the snow, clinked on the coach step.

"Pity," a cheerful female voice resounded behind her. "I chose a most inopportune moment to call."

Helena spun and hopped off the step. "Frances! How delightful to see you!"

Miss Frances Fennelwick resembled a frost maiden, blue-eyed and pale-haired with snow dusting her pale blue bonnet and cloak. The maid shadowing her at a respectable distance likewise wore a smile and a gray cloak dusted with snow. Helena presented Frances to John and Louisa, who remained in the carriage.

"Lord Ardoch." Frances dipped her head and then peeked into the coach. "Good afternoon, Miss Louisa. My, what a pretty doll."

"Tabitha." Louisa extended the wooden-headed toy out the door for inspection.

After oohing, Frances returned her gaze to Helena and John. "I mustn't keep you standing outside, in this weather."

"I'm Scottish. We do not fear snow." John grinned, bringing out his dimples.

"The Thames is frozen as far south as Kew." Although she smiled, Frances spoke with the dry authority of a governess. "A pretty sight, although it has put a damper on several holiday festivities. With Parliament in, Town is full of society, but hardly anyone attended the rout at Lord Gillings's, and Lady Bulthwaite caught chill and was forced to cancel her ball last night."

"How dreadful." Helena hadn't been invited to either event, but she didn't much mind. Last year she would have been mortified to be overlooked for an invitation. To be considered beneath someone's touch. She was a duke's daughter, after all.

Back then, she thought Gemma Knox, as well as Gemma's friend Frances, to be beneath her. Neither of them was as highborn as she, which Mama had taught her was utmost. But Helena had been wrong to judge them, for Gemma had shown her nothing but kindness. Several months ago, Gemma had introduced Helena to her closest friend, Frances, and Frances had been Helena's only London acquaintance to write to her since her marriage.

Her old friends really weren't true ones after all, which made seeing Frances now all the sweeter.

The urge to embrace Frances tensed the muscles in her arms. Helena might have begun to understand there was nothing wrong with a hug, but she couldn't bring herself to show such a display on the street. Instead, she smiled. "We are to visit a physician recommended to us by Mr. Holme at the Edinburgh Relief for the Blind. It is thanks to you we learned of this expert."

Frances's gloved hands made a muffled sound when she clapped, an overt display that would have made the Helena of yesteryear cringe. "Wonderful. I shall pray for a successful visit."

That was Frances. To the point, open about her prayerfulness, without artifice or guile. She probably did not know how pretty she was.

John glanced at the horses, a subtle signal they should be on their way. Helena smiled at Frances. "May I call upon you?"

"Any day." Another difference between Frances and Helena, or at least Helena's fashionable mama, who received callers only on Tuesdays. "Papa's health is recovered, and we would enjoy your visit."

"Later this week, then." After bidding Frances farewell, Helena was up in the coach, the warming box at her feet and a lap robe over her thighs. She tucked the robe tighter around Louisa while John climbed into the coach and took the seat across from them.

Louisa's prattles about her *patterns* and Tabitha kept Helena and John from speaking much. A good thing, since Helena started to grow more anxious about the doctor visit the closer they came to it. Was there hope for Louisa's sight? Would the examination hurt Louisa? Her innards knotted like tangled embroidery threads.

She'd never felt like this before, so frightened she was almost sick. Oh, she was scared when she woke from whatever Frederick had done to her. Afraid to go to Scotland and meet John. But this was entirely different. Louisa chatted away in blissful ignorance, so innocent, so sweet, but Helena couldn't help but worry for her and her future.

Without a word, John reached across the coach and took her hand. It was the first time he'd touched her since the kiss. She couldn't feel his skin through their gloves, but the pressure around her fingers was a comfort. Did it mean he didn't completely reject her, after all?

Regardless, she was grateful for his compassion and she held John's hand until the coach slowed to a stop on a cramped, busy street. The coach jostled as Bill Coachman and Agnes climbed down, and with a scrape, Bill lowered the step and opened the door, admitting a rush of brisk air.

"Do not carry me." Louisa shirked from John's touch, preferring to take each step as an independent miss. "My *patterns* want to be on the snow."

"Of course, but I should like to hand you out of the carriage, as a gentleman helps a lady." John winked at Helena.

"And we must let your father take our arms, else he should look ill-mannered." Helena smiled.

Louisa sniffed, but allowed John to take her hand. Helena took John's other arm, and they entered the narrow building.

There was not a thing unsavory about Dr. Morse, the balding, plump gentleman whom Dr. Holme claimed was an expert on the eye, but Helena chafed at being left in a sitting room during his examination of Louisa in another chamber. She perched on the edge of a too-hard chair. "What if she needs us?"

"She'll be fine." John's pacing belied his confident words, however.

"This is taking so long."

"It has been but five minutes. I imagine she is still telling him about Christmas and her new pattens."

"Her feet are growing. So are Callum's, but not Alex's. I'd assumed identical boys grew at the same rate." She was nattering on, but speaking prevented her from dwelling on what Dr. Morse might be doing to Louisa, poking or prodding with questions and instruments.

"Quite." John paced.

The opening door brought her to stand. John stopped midstride. Dr. Morse smiled and bade them sit. "I took the liberty of calling your nursemaid to sit with your daughter while we speak."

So Louisa was not alone. Helena resumed her uncomfortable seat, but this time, John sat beside her. He cleared his throat. "Have you news?"

"She is a charming child, my lord. Quick-witted and kind."

But what of her eyes? Helena almost growled.

"Thank you." John leaned forward an inch. "And the examination?"

His smile slipped a fraction. "Alas, I do not believe her vision will return. It occurred after a bout with measles, did it not?"

"Yes." John's swallow was audible.

Helena's stomach plummeted while the doctor droned

on about the limits of the examination and the nature of Louisa's blindness. Her attention returned when he spoke her name. "Lady Ardoch, I commend you for allowing her a sense of independence. Her strong spirit will serve her well as she grows."

"Thank you, Dr. Morse." They collected Louisa and returned home with her childish chatter filling the coach as it trudged over the new-fallen snow. John did not take Helena's hand, but once they were inside the house and divested of their cloaks, he followed her to their sitting room. Before her tears slipped past her chin, she was in his arms, bonnet and all.

"I'm sorry." Helena had pushed for this. Pushed for change. "I raised our hopes."

John crushed her against his chest. "You were right to pursue this. I should have had her examined years ago, but I didn't know such a thing was possible. It is best to know she won't see again, even though it isn't the outcome we'd hoped for."

It did not feel best. Noisy sobs escaped her throat and racked her chest. She had never cried like this before, but she couldn't stop. She tried to escape John's strong arms, to free him from the embarrassment she was making of herself, but he clung on.

"Don't send me away from your grief. You love her with a mother's love. And I'm so grateful."

But it wasn't just her love for Louisa pouring out of her. It felt like everything spilled out. Her family's coldness. Papa's horrible cough that meant he was dying, like his father had. And Frederick Coles. Oh, that was a bitter, dark grief.

But worst of all was John holding her. His comfort was like its own anguish. She could too easily grow accustomed to his closeness, but she would never have his love.

Everyone she ever loved did not love her back.

Except God. He'd reminded her of that two days ago when she hid in her parents' alcove.

Helena sniffed. The tears slowed, and one of John's arms let go as he produced a handkerchief from his pocket.

"You are a good man." She swiped her cheeks.

John shook his head. "No."

"Yes." She untied her bonnet and set it on the table. "A good father. A good husband."

"I haven't been a good father. I've been gone from the children more than with them, as you've reminded me. And I was not the best husband to Catriona."

What did that mean?

His hand reached out, palm up in invitation. "You should know about my first marriage."

Foreboding slithered up her arm, but she took his warm fingers anyway. He hadn't judged her when she'd told him the bad things she'd done, like being willing to secretly meet with Frederick Coles. Had she the right to judge him? She gave his fingers a small squeeze. "What happened?"

"Our marriage was arranged by our parents. Quite early, too. You see, my siblings all died young, one after another in their cribs. My parents' grief manifested in reminding me of my duty as heir—advising me to have as many children as I could so Ardoch would continue despite potential loss or hardship. Catriona and I were young when we wed, and we didn't love each other, but we had the boys, and then Margaret came to live with us. And then Louisa arrived."

He led her to the settee, and they sat. "When Louisa grew ill, Catriona did, too, from worry, she said. I tried to help her, but she wanted nothing to do with the children. Or me." He tried to smile, but there was a sad turn about his lips. "She spent the next two years shut away in her chambers with naught to comfort her but laudanum and misery."

He'd said something about laudanum the night she told

him about Frederick. Now it made sense. "How sad. For all of you."

"Even before that, we weren't close. She was happier when I was in London. But when she chose laudanum over her family, over me, I nevertheless grew desolate."

So many remarks she could make. So many questions. But only one rose to her lips. "What did you do?"

"I confronted her about the laudanum and vowed to help her wean from it, but she refused. It was—difficult. Then she grew ill. The physician said she had a growth." He absently touched his stomach. What a horrible time it must have been. Helena kept silent, praying for him as he gathered the words to continue.

"I kept vigil by her bedside, though she didn't respond to me. Then one evening she grew frenzied, shouting and issuing instructions to be followed after her death. She begged me to never replace her in my heart. I said I wouldn't of course. A week later she died. And here I am, having broken my word to a dying woman by marrying again."

"You did not break your word." Helena's chest ached for him. "You did not marry for love."

His lips twisted in a mirthless smile. "That's what I told myself when I married you. The children and I needed someone. The past three years, my duties in London pulled me away, the children have suffered instability with multiple governesses, and I didn't know what else to do. The children and the house needed someone in charge of them. Catriona was deep under laudanum's influence when she begged me. She may not even have remembered the next morning. But I still feel guilty."

No wonder he'd had such difficulty going against Catriona's wishes with the children. His guilt was woven into the fabric of his being.

Somewhat like hers.

"I'm certain Catriona would understand. She knew you cared for her and always will, and you married me to help look after the children and Comraich."

"True." He looked as if he wished to say more, but then he shook his head. "Even though she wasn't involved with the children, or me, she didn't want anything in the house to change from the way she left things. But they have. Louisa's not the same." He met her gaze. "I'm not the same, either."

To lighten the mood and ease his guilt, she smiled. "I'm not the same person who fell into the ha-ha and hurt my ankle."

"We've both changed since we married. I think for the better." His gaze fixed on hers, deep and fathomless, and she wondered what he was thinking, wondered if he minded their hands were still joined, wondered if she'd been in the middle of breathing out or in when he started looking at her like this because she hadn't breathed since that moment—

"Now you are a mother, Helena, and you're quite good at it." He tucked a damp tendril of her hair behind her ear, and her breath left her in a whoosh.

Then John's hands fell away and he stood. "I should—"

"Yes." She stood, too. "There's much to do."

With what, she couldn't say. But there was always something to see to in a busy house. And she'd jump into the distraction.

He wouldn't kiss her again, and now she better understood why. He hadn't just promised Helena a friendly marriage. He'd made a promise to Catriona, too, and John was a man who kept his promises. It was one of the things she admired most about him.

But it was also the one thing that would always keep them apart.

Chapter Sixteen

❧

That afternoon, Helena couldn't bear being cooped up in the house with her thoughts. Miss Munro, the governess, enjoyed an afternoon off, so Helena gathered the children for an outing to Hookham's circulating library. The children expressed excitement to get out, but within five minutes only Margaret showed interest, wandering off to peruse Minerva Press titles. Helena stood before a shelf with the other three children. The twins bore matching skeptical looks and Louisa cuddled Tabitha to her chest.

"There's nothing here that sounds good." Callum's tone was almost a whine.

"What about this one?" Helena held out Godwin's translation of *Swiss Family Robinson*.

Alex eyed the book with a suspicious glint. "What's interesting about them?"

Helena bit back a smile. "A shipwreck and a tropical island."

"I say, a shipwreck? It might be all right enough, then." Callum took the book.

"I want *Cinderella*," Louisa insisted.

"You have it at home." Alex folded his arms.

Helena patted Louisa's shoulder. "We shall read it again

later." The story of the cinder-maiden was all Louisa wished to hear. Everyone in the family knew it by heart, even John. Helena bit back a smile at the recollection of John with Louisa curled on his lap this past Sunday afternoon, one of the few days he was not occupied with political matters until so late at night she'd formed the habit of retiring without waiting up for him. The massacre at Saint Peter's Field had caused no small amount of debate as to how the government should handle it.

Perhaps tonight's meetings would not go on so long. If John were home after dinner, he could read *Cinderella* to Louisa. The thought brought a smile to Helena's lips.

A soft thud sounded from Margaret's direction. Margaret and the footman Adam both bent to retrieve a dropped book, but a nearby gentleman was far quicker to reach it and hand it to Margaret. He doffed his fashionable beaver hat, allowing a familiar dark-as-chocolate curl to fall over his brow.

Frederick Coles.

Helena rushed forward, inserting her body between Margaret and Frederick. Her gaze flickered to the footman's, but only for a moment. "Adam, see about the books and take the children to the carriage. Now, please."

"Yes, milady." Adam must have caught the urgency in her tone, for he hastened to the children.

Margaret hesitated. Just once it would be delightful for the child to do what Helena asked of her without argument. Helena glanced at Margaret, forcing a smile. "I shall be along in a minute. Help Louisa, please."

Margaret spun away. Helena swallowed down the bile burning the back of her throat. "Frederick Coles, what are you doing here?"

No preamble. No well-mannered nod of the head. No swift kick to his shin, as he deserved.

"Good afternoon, Lady Ardoch." To think that smile once weakened her knees. Now it only weakened her resolve to refrain from violence. "I'm searching for a gift."

"I meant in England."

"What becoming children. And you, well, you make quite a maternal picture." His bright blue eyes dared glance at her midsection, as if judging whether her cloak covered a figure rounded by pregnancy.

"Have you no shame?" Her fingers itched with the desire to slap his handsome face. *God help me.*

"Steady your hand, Helena, or we'll be fodder for the gossipmongers."

She hadn't realized she'd clenched her fingers. But he was right. She shouldn't even be speaking to him. She stepped back, but he held up a hand.

"Have cheer, Helena. Our dalliance turned out well enough. You are wed, although I'm surprised you didn't marry better."

"My husband is a fine gentleman, and don't you dare call what you did to me a *dalliance*. You attacked me."

"You've no proof. Even if you did, if you sought to prosecute me, you'd only shame yourself. And your family." His hand ran over the cover of a novel. The same hand that had fed her a narcotic and rendered her senseless. "Look at it with a fresh perspective. You're free from Bowden, thanks to me."

"No thanks to you, you mean." She should leave. Run. But she couldn't quite move yet.

His smile seemed as boyish as the twins', but far more practiced. How had she ever succumbed to its allure? "I'd heard talk of you long before we met. Did you know of your reputation? Cold, unfeeling, too good for anyone else. You were so glacial in your manner, one of my friends thought you an impossible icicle to thaw. I took it as a challenge.

I'd make you like me. So I ensured we were introduced. It was all rather fun."

"You—did it for sport." Her skin slithered, as if it would grow legs and crawl off her bones.

His lips twitched. "Oh, dear, I see I have shocked you. You must have truly cared for me, then. Perhaps you thought we'd marry? How foolish. Your father would never have allowed it. Had we defied him and eloped, we'd have had no money, no friends, nowhere to go. I have no hope of a title until my useless brother dies. The allowance he provides me is such a pittance, I only have one servant, can you credit it? A man must eat and drink and get one's coats tailored by Weston, but such things are expensive. I've learned there are ways to get by. Making my own fun, of course, but secrets are a valuable currency all their own."

Did he threaten to blackmail her? "You are a black-guard."

"Haven't you heard? I'm a hero."

"Deceiver, liar. Those are better names for you."

He laughed. "So you haven't heard. You will. In any case, take comfort in knowing you were not the only one who fell prey to my charms."

"I fell prey, but not to your charms. You assaulted me." The urge to vomit on his shoes rose up her throat. "Stay away from me.

She spun on her heel and hurried out to the carriage. How she'd manage to walk when her knees shook like saplings in a storm, she'd never guess.

"Who is your friend?" Callum waved *Swiss Family Robinson* in the air.

"No one of consequence." Yet her voice quavered. So did her fingers when she settled the lap robe over Louisa.

"You might have introduced us." Margaret's observation was a reprimand.

At last, she could look Margaret full in the eye. The girl should be able to read the warning in her gaze. "You shall never be introduced to him. If you see him again, you must turn the opposite way."

"But he was so kind, gathering my book." Margaret flopped against the seat. "He said he was honored, like a knight finding his lady's handkerchief."

"Just like *Cinderella*." Louisa held up Tabitha.

"There's no handkerchief in *Cinderella*." Alex sniffed.

"Every lady has a hanker-cheef," Louisa countered.

"Let us see if the *Swiss Family Robinson* has any handkerchiefs." It sounded stupid even to Helena, but it was the best she could think up on the spot to change the subject. "When we arrive home, we may begin on our reading. We shall dazzle Miss Munro with all we've accomplished on her afternoon off."

As if it were a normal day, when everything inside her quaked with fear. If only John might return soon from Westminster. *Please, Lord, may things not go late tonight so I won't be alone.*

She blinked. Even if John didn't return home until late, she wouldn't be alone. God was with her, a comforting companion and strength even if she couldn't see Him. Or—with her heart skittering with terror at seeing Frederick again—feel God with her.

Her spine straightened. How far she had come, trusting God would care for her and be with her, even if she didn't *feel* his presence in a physical way, like she had when she first walked into the stone kirk on her wedding day.

God had been changing her, little by little, as slowly and surely as spring flowers pushing up through thawing ground after a long, cold winter.

It was a hopeful thing that God's work wasn't finished yet. She would continue to grow in His love.

And maybe someday, with God's help, she might even pity Frederick Coles instead of loathing him.

Tugging his coat collar tighter about his neck, John pitied anyone sleeping on the streets this icy night. He and his close friend Carvey had ridden to Westminster Palace this morning, which had seemed a capital idea when they both thought they'd finish at a suitable hour. But discussions had gone late, and now they rode home through frigid blasts of wind when they could have been carried home in coaches like their far more intelligent peers.

John cast Carvey a mock-glare his friend probably couldn't see in the light of the waning moon. "Riding would give us time to clear our heads before returning home, you said. Fresh air. The peaceful sound of the horses' hooves crunching frost underfoot. But all I hear is the chattering of your teeth."

Laughing, Carvey adjusted his hat farther down over his ears. "Spare me a shred of your famous compassion, man. You abound with it for every voiceless villager and child you represent in Parliament."

John's horse snorted, echoing his thoughts. "There is compassion, but one must also acknowledge facts, and the fact is we are cretins for dragging our horses and out in this cold."

"Speaking of cold, Kelworth's snubbing you tonight was unforgiveable." Carvey muttered under his breath, no doubt calling Helena's father a choice name. "How you manage with him as a father-in-law, I cannot fathom, unless it is—"

"Compassion," they said together.

John laughed, but Kelworth's turning away during John's speech still galled. They didn't have to agree on everything, but they could be polite to one another.

What was almost worse, however, was Kelworth's rebuff when John attempted to greet his father-in-law after the session. The affront stung, not for his sake, but Helena's. She deserved better than to have her family disapprove of her husband.

They might never like him, but for Helena's sake—and out of obedience to God—John would never cease trying to extend grace to them.

"I say, have we reached the square already?" Carvey came to a stop. John turned to gaze at the familiar-looking stoop. While light spilled from the ground-floor windows, the upstairs chambers appeared dark. Of course Helena would have gone to bed by this hour. A shaft of disappointment speared his stomach, but it was for the best she didn't wait up for him. He was worn to a farthing.

Still, he wanted to see her, something work had prevented him from doing much of these past few days. Despite their lack of time together, he felt closer to her, probably from having told her about Catriona.

But he still hadn't told her everything. Like the fact he was being blackmailed. A twinge of guilt twisted in his gut.

I've wanted to protect her, Lord. Is that so wrong?

Protecting her was as vital to him as protecting the children. His lovely Helena—

"I said *good night*, old man. Has the cold affected your hearing?" Carvey snickered. "Or by the dazzled look on your face, are you thinking of your wife?"

"Good night, Carvey. See you on the morrow." He waved at his laughing friend. In minutes, the gelding was on its way to the cozy mews and John crossed the threshold to his house, soaking in the warmth of the vestibule while he removed his hat and ice-specked coat. A few minutes by the library fire would warm his hands and toes.

But the library was occupied. Helena stood at his entrance. She was still dressed for dinner in a pale blue gown, wide-eyed, her mouth small and unsmiling.

"What's wrong?" He should have greeted her first, but the way her hands gripped the crimson shawl he'd given her, it was evident something was off. "Is it the children?"

Her head shook a tiny bit. "He's in London. F-Frederick Coles."

The fire snapped in the grate as the blood drained from his head to his boots.

"Are you certain?"

"We spoke."

John was before her in a moment. "Did he touch you?" Which was what John did now. Her cheeks were hot under his cold hands. "How did he find you?"

"He didn't touch me. Or call here. He was at Hookham's."

Out in public like an innocent citizen. "He should be locked in Newgate Prison."

"We can't seek justice in the courts without scandal." Her head shook with such vehemence the blond curls at her temples bobbed against her cheeks.

How wrong it was a woman was violated and punished for it, while her attacker slithered the streets. Something was truly amiss in society for this to be standard. John stroked her cheeks with his thumbs. "I would never allow you to be shamed."

"Not me. You. I don't wish to embarrass you or the children. Please, let it lie."

"I don't know if I can." There had to be some justice. *Please, God.* "I will speak to him."

He didn't do as good a job keeping a growl from his throat as he'd hoped. Helena leaned back, eyes wide. "Confronting him will only make it worse."

Probably, and John might not be able to control his temper. Or his fists. But he shoved his anger down so as not to frighten Helena. "I will find a way to stop him. I do not know how, but I pray God grants us justice."

"I don't think he'll hurt me again." She looked at the floor. "He said he only did it as a challenge. Because I was considered haughty and cold."

A challenge. John's vision tinged scarlet. His fingers fisted and bitter bile filled his throat.

God help me, but I don't know what I'd do if Coles was here before me.

Nothing good.

But that didn't mean John wouldn't do all he could to seek justice for Helena, somehow. He swallowed back the bile and rage. "He is the vilest of blackguards."

"He said he'd done it before to others. What if he does it again to someone else?"

John's hands still trembled with the desire to do violence, but he willed himself to calm as he pulled her into his embrace, praying for peace all the while. "We shall pray God intervenes. Shows us what to do. Executes justice."

"I know Frederick is a rogue, but I can't help but keep thinking about what he said people thought of me." Her voice was small against his chest. "That I was so awful and cold I deserved to be brought low. That I deserved that fate."

"Never. You are lovely and kind and gentle. They are villains and you did not deserve this."

Did she believe him? Much as he wanted to hunt down Frederick Coles and throttle him and whoever had said such things about Helena, her sense of value was far more crucial right now, in this moment. "Your worth cannot be measured in coin, or jewels or anything else of this world. You are precious, Helena."

"I'm trying to remember that. But seeing him again—"

She didn't finish, so he hugged her tighter. Her forehead

rested on his shoulder. His head dipped so his lips brushed her ear. "I'll protect you. I promise."

Just let Coles try to touch her. John's fingers twitched.

She pulled back, leaving his arms empty and cold, swiping her eyes. "He said something about secrets having value that made me think he might blackmail us."

Then he would have to stand in the back of the queue. Unless the falcon-seal letters were Coles's work, as well—

"What if he does?" She frowned. "Blackmail us, I mean?"

Was Coles the owner of the falcon seal? John set the idea aside, for now. "We shall face it, should it come."

Guilt filled his chest, though. Since they were on the topic of blackmail, should he tell her about the notes he'd been receiving?

Not now. Not when she was so raw with pain and fear. He'd only upset her more.

But that didn't mean John had no intention of acting on her behalf. "If there is a way to bring him to justice without sullying your name, to prevent him from hurting others as he did to you, I shall do all I can to achieve it, sweetheart."

Her eyes flashed at the endearment—in warning, not warming. Maybe calling her that was as bad as kissing her had been. He'd only wanted to extend comfort and care, but clearly he'd overstepped.

He took a deep breath. "In the meantime, you must know you're safe now."

She nodded. "I know. I never go out without one of the footmen, at any rate."

"And you have me."

Something passed over her features, like grief, but then it was smoothed as she donned the icy mask with the tiny smile. "I should let you retire."

"Helena." What had happened? As she moved past the

mantel clock, John sighed. It was indeed late. Helena was tired. She'd received a brutal shock today. Tomorrow, they'd discuss things further.

She took up a candlestick and moved toward the door, pausing at the threshold. "Thank you, John."

"I've not done anything." If he could, he'd go back in time to protect her from Frederick Coles.

"You've done far more than you know."

Then she was gone, her figure swallowed by the dark in the hall.

John might be tired, but anger surged through his veins, warming him more thoroughly than the fire burning in the grate. Ideas of how to put an end to Frederick Coles's freedom bandied through his head, all of them ridiculous, only making him angrier.

He slumped in the chair to pray, the one thing he should have done the moment Helena left him.

After several minutes of conversation with God, John had more peace, if not answers. He sat back, his gaze touching on the post awaiting him on the desk.

The post was the last thing he wished to review now, but he could use the distraction, so he ambled to the silver tray on the desk. Two items. Something from his solicitor. And a vellum rectangle with thick, bold script. He didn't need to turn it over to know a falcon stamp pressed into the wax seal.

He took the foul, falcon-sealed letter, shoved his finger beneath the seal, and yanked. "Is this from you, Coles?"

It was the same sort of drivel. Vote a certain way and send money or Helena's story would be exposed for public consumption. John flung the offensive page to the floor.

If the blackmailer wanted money alone, then it would be in keeping with what Helena had said of Coles. But this particular rogue toyed with John, demanding John's votes in the House of Lords, which remained a ridiculous request. Likewise, the money demanded was not so extravagant as to drain his coffers.

Power motivated this blackmailer, not desperation.

He bent to scoop up the letter. He'd need it for evidence. If Coles was indeed the blackmailer, he'd be brought to justice.

For that crime, at least.

Chapter Seventeen

A few mornings after the new year, Helena took breakfast in her chamber. She picked up a slice of buttered toast and opened the morning paper. At once her gaze fell upon an article that made her drop her food.

Hand over her mouth, Helena hopped to her feet. If only John was home—but she'd watched him from her chamber window as he left a short time ago. Had he read the newspaper first? He'd be as angry as she was, no doubt.

They'd not had much opportunity to speak since she saw Frederick at Hookham's last week. The morning after that wretched encounter, she awoke with a sore throat, as did Callum, but hers turned into a nasty cold. John had granted her a privacy to recover she wasn't certain she wanted, but she'd forced herself to remember the nature of their marriage.

They might be friends, but they'd never be more.

Still, she wanted to talk with him about this article— this foul, ridiculous, astonishing article lauding Frederick as a hero.

She had to talk to someone.

So once she ensured the children were settled with Miss

Munro, she donned a cloak and bonnet, stepped out into the frigid winter morning and called on Mama.

As she arrived, a tall, well-dressed gentleman with prematurely graying hair exited the house. Her footsteps slowed, and when he spied her, she offered a tentative smile. "Lord Holliver?"

"Lady Ardoch." They'd met several times, although he'd made no lasting impression on her. She'd had no idea he intended to ask Papa for her hand in marriage. Not until after it was done and Papa had soundly rejected Viscount Holliver in favor of the wealthier Duke of Bowden.

Considering his failed proposal, seeing him now was somewhat awkward. He seemed to feel it, too, forcing a smile and staring at her as if he had questions he couldn't politely ask.

No surprise. She'd expected curiosity about her sudden marriage to a gentleman her father clearly didn't adore. Let everyone wonder. But why was he here? He and Papa weren't friends.

And propriety didn't allow her to ask, so she nodded and made to pass him.

"I am hosting a musical evening in a fortnight." His rushed words drew her around. "I should be honored if you and Lord Ardoch could attend."

"How kind." Mama taught her never to accept or reject an invitation like this at once, but she wanted to accept, despite the awkwardness of the encounter. A social gathering! It had been so long!

"I shall have my secretary send 'round an invitation."

She nodded, a sign of thanks as well as farewell. Her thoughts projected ahead to the party. The prospect of an evening out was almost enough to distract her from what she'd read in the *Morning Post*.

Almost. Her hands were clenched when she entered the

house and the butler showed her into the morning room. Mama rose from an embroidery project but didn't embrace her, bidding her to sit across from her. "Paying calls so early in the day?"

"I am not the only one. I saw Lord Holliver."

"A personal invitation to a gathering."

Strange. But Helena had more pressing matters. "Have you seen today's *Morning Post*?"

"If you mean the article about Frederick Coles, yes." Mama bent to search out something from her embroidery bag. "You must put that nasty business behind you."

"But he is in London. And he's being extolled as a hero? He is no such thing."

"Yet there it is, in print." Mama dropped pale blue floss onto the table between them. "Lord Bridgewell was robbed of a diamond stickpin and three rings during a supper party. Mr. Coles, upon his exit from the party, caught sight of a flash under a window and discovered the jewels before Bridgewell even knew they were missing. The burglar must have been frightened and dropped them when he made his escape, but a ruby ring is still missing. Bridgewell's grandest, too."

"I cannot believe it."

"The robbery, or the quality of the ring? Because it is exquisite. The ruby is unlike any I've seen."

Not those. "Frederick Coles as a hero, Mama. The thought is repugnant."

Mama's blond brow arched. "We cannot deny he did something gallant. Society will forever behold him as an ethical personage, despite his less-than-perfect behavior outside the public eye."

Helena snorted. "He is not to be trusted."

"I did not say I trust him. But my friends do. Lord Holliver was saying Coles is a decent gentleman, one of his closest friends. I cannot contradict him without providing cause. And if you do not wish the truth out, you should not either. If it bothers you so, return to Scotland, because here you will ever be reminded of him."

"I'm reminded of him wherever I go. You know what he did to me."

Mama scowled. "Such an outburst. If you cannot control your emotions better, you will embarrass us all, more than you already have by marrying so far beneath you."

At once, Helena was a child again, unable to speak or defend herself. Her lips pressed shut, and she allowed the ice to freeze her expression and work its way into her marrow.

But she was different now. A new creation, since she'd allowed God to thaw her heart. Mama might be more concerned with status, but Helena knew better.

The ice inside her thawed a fraction.

"My husband is noble in every way that counts." She stood. "Before I take my leave, I must ask about Papa's health."

Mama examined her buffed fingernails. "You know how he is. Struggling to breathe. Coughing. Fatigued. It is much as his father's illness was. There is no use speaking of it."

There was every use, if Papa was going to die from this disease.

Did he love her? Did he know she loved him, despite his sending her away? As much as her heart ached to know the answers to those questions before he passed on, she'd be content to never know if she was confident in one last thing. Did Papa know God?

Tears stung Helena's eyes. She could pray. God had changed her. He was certainly capable of helping her family see the truth about Himself.

If only they'd open their eyes.

Right now, however, Mama wasn't even looking at her.

There was nothing to do but curtsy. "Give my regards to Papa and the girls."

Mama's hummed farewell followed her on her way from the room.

Out in the frost-tinged air, Adam handed her up into the coach and they returned home. Bill Coachman had to park the coach in front of the neighbor's, however. Helena peered out the window. A familiar curricle waited by the front stoop.

John was home. Her pulse quickened. Was this good or ill?

"There you are." John's grin was wide when she entered the vestibule. "You must be feeling better, to be up and paying calls."

Despite her qualms, the sight of him knocked the breath out of her, and it was no good blaming it on her cold.

She busied herself with removing her gloves so he wouldn't see her admiration for him in her eyes. "Quite so. Enough to call on my mother, at any rate."

"Brave of you." His brow arched. "I'm stopping in between errands. Do you have a minute to join me in the library?"

She nodded and once there, she waited for him to shut the door. "Have you read the *Post* yet?"

He grimaced. "Only just. I wish I'd seen it before I left so I could warn you. I'm sorry."

"Mama says I must accept Frederick is a hero or return to Perthshire."

"Your mama, forgive me, is in error."

It was easy to return his smile. "Where were you so early this morning?"

"Tattersall's, assessing horseflesh with Carvey. For him, not for me. Last night you were still indisposed from your illness, so I didn't wish to disturb you with my plans. Forgive me if I worried you."

Her head shook. She wasn't worried, she'd…missed him. Wanted his comfort when she saw that horrible article. "I hope it was an enjoyable time."

"It was, and I thought I'd take the boys with us tomorrow when Carvey makes a final selection."

Her hands clasped to her warming chest. "They'll love the idea. Have you told them?"

"No, and I can't yet. I've another obligation this morning. Carvey is waiting for me. Tell them, if you wish, or I'll inform them this afternoon." By the way he avoided her gaze when he spoke, she couldn't help feeling he was hiding something from her. Like he didn't want her to know where he was going.

She shook her head at herself. What foolishness, to have suspicious thoughts about her husband! Her nerves were still raw from visiting Mama and the article about Frederick, that was all. "Will we speak more about Frederick later?"

His smile was sad. "We will, Helena. I'm sorry I cannot now. I'm overdue. But please do not forget, you are safe now."

She nodded, and he moved closer until he stood inches from her, looming over her, capturing her gaze. Fire burned behind the jade screens of his eyes, like he restrained the fervor of his feelings behind tender words.

Like he might kiss her again.

Breathing, swallowing, words, all were lost as she stared back at him.

"I mean it, Helena." John's hand slowly, slowly reached to cup her cheek. "I will never let him touch you again. I will protect you with my life."

His life. He'd already given her his name, his home, the

care of his children. She could not ask for anything more than he'd already given her.

But as his hand fell and he stepped away, greed crawled over her skin like an itch. She wanted more than a brief touch of his hand on her cheek. She wanted him to pull her into his arms again. To kiss her, despite their agreement.

"Until later." John's smile was gentle as he left.

"Yes," was all she could manage. Not even a proper farewell, but her heart was beating so hard and fast she couldn't think straight.

She wanted him to stay. She wanted him to love her—

This is not about being loved, remember? But about loving.

And she had people to love, given to her by God. Four of them were upstairs at their lessons right now, and come what may with Frederick Coles or her parents or even John, she had a duty and privilege to love the four children upstairs.

Helena's footfalls landed heavier than was ladylike on the stairs, but she couldn't help but hurry. The children should be done with lessons shortly. And not a one of them would be able to resist her offer to shop for toys.

"Where does she think you are?" Carvey pulled the reddish-brown fur collar of his coat higher up his neck as he and John strode up the snowy street toward the fringes of Mayfair.

A chill trickled down John's spine, but not from the wind whistling between the narrow gaps between the buildings they passed. "I told Helena I had an errand. Not a lie."

"Omission is a lie. I say you tell your wife the truth and be done with it."

He'd told himself the same thing, over and over, but kept

arriving at the same conclusion. "The timing isn't right. I'd not worsen her day with this, not after that bit in the *Post*—"

"What bit?" Carvey's tone rose as they trudged up the snowy street. "Was she mentioned in it? I didn't see her name mentioned."

John stifled a groan. "No. Pay no mind—she's been ill, you know. But speaking of the *Post*, did you read the article on Frederick Coles? Do you know him?"

Carvey grimaced. "He's not my friend, if that's what you're asking."

"What are your impressions?"

"Do you want the truth, or the polite answer I'm supposed to give?"

"I think you've said enough to shed light on your opinion."

"Why do you ask?" Carvey slowed as they approached a street vendor. The scent of meat pasties swirled in the frosty air, and Carvey patted his stomach.

John waited while Carvey exchanged a coin for the small pie. When they'd resumed walking and Carvey's mouth was full, John glanced up and down the street. No one he knew lingered about. No one passed close enough to overhear.

He couldn't tell Carvey what happened to Helena, not without her consent. But he could enlist his friend's help. "I'm suspicious of Coles stumbling across some of the items stolen from a party he attended, which happened to be left on the snow?"

Carvey swallowed his bite. "Ridiculous, isn't it? My mother was at a house party with him last summer—hosted by her close friend, otherwise Mother wouldn't have heard this tidbit, but a quantity of silver was stolen during the party."

"Coin?"

"Forks. Teaspoons. The butler noted them gone from set

tables, much to his horror. He and the housekeeper were in arms, blaming footmen, accusing half the house, as it turns out, but one of the maids insisted she spied Coles poking about the dining room the day a spoon or some such disappeared. No one believed her, of course." Carvey took a large bite of pasty.

Poor maid had probably been dismissed. But what if she'd spoken true? "Coles could be desperate enough for money to steal teaspoons and fence them."

"Pah. He's Bowden's nephew, isn't he? What would he need with the proceeds of selling teaspoons to a metal-smith? If it was him, I'd say he did it on a lark. Some nobs pinch things for the thrill of it."

"I wonder."

"It is rather curious." Carvey finished off his pie.

John glanced around again. "Tell me if you hear anything more about him, will you?"

"I doubt I shall hear anything more like I heard from my mother. Below-stairs matters tend to stay below stairs, and few would wish to broadcast they are losing cutlery." He started to laugh, but it died when he caught John's gaze. "This is about more than filched trinkets. This is about Coles."

John exhaled. "I cannot explain. I ask only you to trust me."

"Of course I trust you." Carvey shoved a lock of thin black hair off his brow. "If you say Coles is a rotter, I believe you."

"I didn't say he's a rotter." Although the description was apt.

"But it's clear you don't think he stumbled upon missing jewels at that party. If that's the case, and he's a thief, shouldn't we leave it to Bow Street to handle?"

"Not at this point. I require evidence to present to the magistrate first."

"You have an investigator already," Carvey said with a nod. "Although he's found nothing about the identity of your, er, *correspondent*."

A nice way to say blackmailer. John had told him about the letters, but not divulged that Helena was the reason for them. And Carvey, true friend that he was, never asked.

"I won't give up. Not until whoever is responsible is revealed."

Carvey's dark brows rose. "Do you think Coles is the blackmailer? Is that why you're asking about him?"

John chose his words carefully. "I don't know what to think."

"Your wife has no idea how devoted to her you are, does she?"

"What?" John's boots almost slid on the snow.

"I'm not daft, man. This blackmail is about your wife. If it were over anything else, you'd never pay. But you're meeting the demands to protect her, and keeping it from her so as to not upset her. And she doesn't even know the lengths you're going through to do so."

And here he'd been thinking Carvey was too good a friend to poke his nose into John's business. Then again, John had invited him into this mess when he'd asked for his help hiring an investigator. That didn't mean he was free to discuss it, either. "The reason for the blackmail is not what you think—whatever it is you're thinking—"

"I'm certain Lady Ardoch is everything honorable, and this blackmail springs from a twisted misrepresentation of her character or something else that's none of my affair. I don't care about that. I do care about my oldest friend, though, and this is a side of you I've never seen."

John glanced at him before they crossed the street. "I've no idea what you mean."

"Don't deny it. I've known you since university, and you've changed since this marriage."

John snorted, the steam of his breath curling in the air. "I'm the same."

"No, you're not." Carvey's expression lost its amusement. "Your children are with you here in London and you can't wait to get back to them at the end of the day. And when I mention your wife, you get a calf-eyed look on your face for a half second before you recover your composure. The gossips claimed your hasty marriage was a love match, and while I had my doubts when you first wrote of marrying *Kelworth's* daughter, I see they were right. You love her."

No, he didn't—

Did he? Panic pooled in his gut.

He couldn't love Helena. He was attracted to her, but that was not love.

He certainly cared for her, and he'd continue to champion her and be steadfast for her, as her friend, with all his heart and strength, just as he'd determined to do at Christmas.

He'd kissed her—yes, but he'd intended comfort. And gotten carried away.

She hadn't pushed him away after that, so she must have understood he made a mistake. She was kind not to hold it against him.

Carvey was wrong. John didn't love Helena. Nothing was changing.

Except John certainly felt happier than he had before his marriage. Not necessarily in his circumstances, what with the blackmail and Frederick Coles and the struggles in Parliament and his plan for educating children being thwarted at every turn.

But there was a deeper happiness within him. Spending time with the children, seeing to their needs, helping them grow into the people God made them to be. Growing closer to Helena. Those things had made him happy.

So he was changing, after all.

"I've stunned you to silence." Carvey brushed pastry crumbs from his gloves. "I don't care to get maudlin on you, chap. Just wanted you to know I'm glad you've found happiness, that's all. I know what it's like to be where you are. Don't squander it."

John stifled a groan of frustration at himself. It was January. A date he shouldn't forget. How could he be so thickheaded? "Today's the day, isn't it?"

Carvey nodded, staring at nothing, his thoughts clearly fixed on the memory of his fiancée, Lydia, who'd succumbed to a fever four years ago today. Afterward, Carvey had crawled into a dark place of grief, and he still mourned Lydia's loss, but when John's first wife passed away, Carvey had been a staunch source of support and comfort.

John opened his mouth to offer comfort in return now, but Carvey shook his head. "All this is to say you mustn't waste the time you've got. And I'm happy for you and I'll do what I can to help you. If you think Coles is worth watching because he's got his finger in a bad pie, you go on and speak to the metalsmith and I'll visit some of the places Coles is known to frequent. Perhaps I'll learn a thing or two."

"Thank you, friend."

"It's time I had adventure. Lydia would've wanted that for me, don't you think?" Carvey's lips twisted into a boyish smile as he turned to go back the way they'd come.

"She would have," John called to Carvey's retreating form.

But Carvey was wrong about one thing. John hadn't married Helena out of love.

That didn't mean he couldn't care for her by doing all he could to protect her, though. That's why he was out right now, to put the ugly matter of the blackmail to rest. Or at least make a solid attempt.

John turned up the collar of his coat and hastened onward. Although his investigator had turned up little about the blackmailer, John determined to keep searching. Which was why he'd decided to meet the latest demand in person, at the metalsmith of Travers & Sons.

And ask a long list of questions about the person collecting the payments.

For Helena's sake. So they could put their troubles behind them.

And as Carvey said, time was a luxury he couldn't afford to waste.

Chapter Eighteen

"The promise of toys can settle all manner of disputes," Frances said with a sly wink at Helena as they stood inside one of the toy vendors at the shopping bazaar. "Not five minutes ago they fought over the mechanical bear, and now they are sharing the toy soldiers."

"For now." Helena chuckled as the twins examined a set of lead soldiers on display. Alex and Callum weighed the figures in their hands and stood them end to end, their rapid speech expressing their approval. "I suspect within five minutes, they'll be arguing over which of them can pretend to be the Duke of Wellington at Waterloo. Neither likes taking the part of Napoleon."

"No surprise there." Frances shrugged. "Perhaps one can pretend to be the Prussians. Although they do not wear scarlet, like the toys do."

"The boys' imaginations can easily overcome such a trifle." Helena glanced over at Margaret, who lingered beside a grand paperboard theater. Louisa held Margaret's hand, her head cocked as she listened to Margaret's descriptions of the red paper curtains and little board dolls who performed on the stage.

The movement of the pock-cheeked toy vendor drew

her gaze back to the boys. He gathered one of the toy soldiers, running his index finger down the soldier's painted front. "See the brass buttons? Quality to detail and a reasonable price."

"May we get them, please?" Alex was at her sleeve in an instant.

"Please?" Callum echoed.

Margaret approached in a swish of apple-green cloak. "You have soldiers already. Enough to trip us as we cross the floor."

"That is true." Helena tipped her head, considering.

"But these are a new regiment." Callum's voice rose in pitch.

"Margaret found a script and paper characters for *Cinderella*," Louisa announced.

"And *Hamlet*." Margaret held out sheaves of paper. "For the paper theater."

"My," Frances exclaimed. "I had a marvelous time producing *Hamlet* in my own toy theater. I drew costumes and set pieces with my cousins. What happy days."

How fun—Helena had created paper dolls, although she'd never had a theater for them. Neither did the children. "What about a theater?"

Margaret grinned. "We have one, at Comraich. We didn't play with it for a while, so it was put in the attic until we missed it."

"We miss it," Louisa insisted. It was difficult not to laugh, because Louisa's insistence probably had more to do with acquiring something about *Cinderella* than any memories she might have of the theater.

"I want to play, too. But not *Cinderella*." Alex's mouth pursed. "Are there soldiers in *Hamlet*?"

"Yes, but, is *Hamlet* not, er, too dark?" Helena could not dismiss the image of Yorick's skull from her thoughts.

Margaret tipped her head. "Miss Munro says Shakespeare is essential."

"She is quite right." Frances nodded.

"*Hamlet* and *Cinderella* it is, then, and while we're in London, you may use a table as a stage. Boys, will you look for scripts? One each. We shall save the soldiers for another day."

Once the boys selected *Don Quixote* and *The Miller and His Men*, as well as the two-pence colored paperboard characters for each story, Helena's stomach made an embarrassing growl. "Adam," she beckoned the ever-faithful footman. "Take our purchases to the carriage, if you please. I think it time for cakes and tea."

"Cakes!" Callum's eyes glowed.

They had multiple confectioners to choose from. The covered bazaar on the edge of their Mayfair neighborhood boasted a colorful array of shops and dealers selling interesting wares, from shawls and books to caged birds and a black-and-white monkey. Vendors hawked bready Yorkshire cakes, fruit tarts and Dutch biscuits, aromatic with ginger, but Helena chose a quiet pastry shop with a table and chairs.

"Isn't this bazaar more fun than the Burlington Arcade?" Frances said once the tea arrived.

Helena nodded. The bazaar was a delight, but it was also less fashionable than the arcade, so Helena hadn't been here before. Nor had she spied another soul she knew—leaving her free to relax with the children and Frances, with no worry of stumbling into her family or Frederick.

All were quiet while they enjoyed their treats. Helena's heart swelled within her chest, however, when she gazed on Louisa, scooping cake into her rosy mouth with a spoon and then, like the little lady she was, taking a sip of milky-sweet tea.

Thank you for how far Louisa has come, God. And for Gemma introducing me to Frances. She's a dear friend, but she's also helped out family. Without her friend's letter about the blind school, Louisa might not be feeding herself today.

Outside the tea shop window, a gentleman passed through the bazaar. His back was to Helena, but the height, the hat, the breadth of his shoulders beneath his blue coat and the way he walked—

"Helena? Is something amiss?" Frances set down her cup with a *chink*.

Helena's gaze swung back to Frances, who stared at her with unabashed curiosity. "Forgive me. I thought I saw something."

A tall man who looked enough like John from the back that her heart started galloping in her chest.

How ridiculous. She was so drawn to him, she was imagining him. *God, will You prune back my affections for John to love for a dear friend? Will you change me, so I will be content with what You've given me?*

"Things take time," Frances was saying to Margaret, drawing Helena's attention. "Winter is cold indeed this year, but spring will come. The ground will thaw and new things will grow."

"I know, but I'm weary of the cold."

"So is Tabitha." Louisa held up her doll.

"Not me," Callum protested. "Alex and I built a snow fort in the garden."

Their conversation was about the weather, not Helena. It didn't even include her. But she couldn't help feeling it spoke to her briefly uttered prayer, like God was answering her in some small way by reminding her to wait on Him. He changed things in His time.

Even her.

Parts of her had thawed. New things sprouted within her heart, like love for her family. Faith and trust in God.

And Helena heard Mama's scolding voice in her head less and less.

Helena drained her teacup. God had given her so many people to love. Smiling at her family and friend, she resolved anew to enjoy them and the joy they'd brought into her life.

Frances glanced at everyone's plates. "It looks as if we are all finished with our cakes. Is there something else we should like to see before returning home?"

"The monkey again," Alex exclaimed.

"And the man with the birds. He said we could feed the parrot." Margaret's eyes sparkled.

"Will it bite?" Louisa rubbed her fingers over her chin instead of her napkin.

Helena tucked the white linen square between Louisa's fingers. "I will be certain to ask before I let your little fingers anywhere near it, poppet."

After donning their gloves and mufflers again, they sought out the monkey. Immediately, the children were caught in its antics, and she bent to describe the creature to Louisa. Behind them, Frances laughed. Margaret—

Where was she? Panic shooting through her veins, Helena rose, but she spied Margaret at once. She hadn't wandered far. Just to the dealer selling exotic birds, who handed her what looked like a seed. Margaret tentatively extended her hand toward the vibrant green parrot on the perch. A gentleman sidled alongside, encouragement on his handsome face. So gallant, so handsome in an ash-gray caped greatcoat and tall hat.

Frederick Coles.

Helena handed Louisa to Frances and rushed to Margaret. Margaret spun, eyes round as coins. Frederick laughed, not sounding at all surprised. "Lady Ardoch, how pleasant to see you."

"I cannot say the same."

A large presence in the blue Ardoch livery appeared at her elbow. Adam the footman looked to her, his brow furrowed in concern. "My lady, may I assist?"

She nodded. "We are leaving. Now."

Helena did not look back, but passed a man whose thinning black hair reminded her of John's friend Carvey. Mercy, everyone's double was at the bazaar today. As well as the most undesirable of persons. How foolish she'd been to think she'd not see anyone she knew here.

Margaret's lips pressed tight until they dropped Frances home and were alone in the carriage. Then she turned a look of hatred on Helena. "How could you embarrass me like that? In front of Mr. Coles?"

"How do you know his name?"

"Everyone knows of him. He's a hero. When we were playing in the square this morning, my friend Kitty told me about him finding stolen gems, and she was jealous when I told her I'd encountered him in the bookstore."

Ah, the neighbor Kitty, who'd no doubt heard about Coles from her parents. "Nevertheless, I don't wish you to speak to him."

"Why?"

"Enough." Her voice held a metallic tone that startled all four children into gaping. "There will be no more discussion of it."

Margaret flopped in a heap against the seat. "I'm not your daughter."

"I know." Still, the words ached. The pain relieved a little when, an hour later, a servant brought her a hastily scrawled note from Frances.

Brava, Lady Ardoch. Mr. Coles is no hero, despite the

tale making its way about town. Should you require my assistance in any matter in his regard, even as a listening ear, consider me a willing servant. F.F.

It shouldn't have made her cry, but it did. She had a friend in Frances, who didn't even know what Frederick did to her last summer at the dovecote. Frances supported her anyway.

John did, too, and she would need him now. Because Frederick Coles wasn't staying away from her or their family. He was goading them, gloating in their inability to prosecute him without bringing scandal to themselves and her family.

What had Frances said about things taking time?

Lord, grant us protection and justice. But please hasten.

Knowing Frederick was free to hurt anyone, flaunt his violence in Helena's face, speak to her children…

It was almost too much to be borne.

Chapter Nineteen

"Frederick Coles is a blackguard," John blurted when Helena told him about the bazaar that evening in the library. Rage roiled in his gut and made his fingers fist. "Time for me to do what I should have done long ago."

"Pray do not call on him. It won't help."

"I won't call on him." He stomped to the rosewood desk, sending Iona hurrying out of his way. He yanked a piece of foolscap from the stack, smacked it onto the blotter and thrust a pen into the inkwell. "I'm challenging him to a duel."

"Do not be absurd." Helena moved to his elbow. "Stop writing to Frederick."

"I'm writing to Carvey." With decent penmanship considering the anger flooding his veins. Every fiber of his being seemed sharper, pounding power. "He'll agree to be my second."

"You cannot be serious. I doubt you own dueling pistols."

"Every gentleman owns dueling pistols." But—

They were at Comraich, a never-used possession of his grandfather's. No matter. He'd buy new ones.

Was that a sigh escaping Helena? "Enough of this foolishness."

He blotted the page, then made a mess of folding it. "I'm not joking."

"You would break the law." Shouldn't she sound frightened, rather than disbelieving?

The way his heart pumped liquid fire and his head seemed detached from his body, yes. "Twice now he's approached Margaret. Twice now he's attempted to intimidate and frighten you and revive the horrid memories of what he did to you. Enough. I must protect you, can you not see that? Has no one protected you before?"

Her breath hitched—there was no disputing the sound—but then she looked down, hiding her eyes.

"An invitation to duel isn't protection." Helena's tone was matter-of-fact, as if she explained the alphabet to Louisa. "And as much as I appreciate your efforts, as much as I wish to string Frederick up by his boots for taunting us by speaking to Margaret, we must be sensible. A duel is not only illegal, but rather dramatic, is it not?"

It was, wasn't it?

Thankfully God had sent Helena to talk some sense into him. He must be calming down, because it sounded funny now. A little. "I'm a good shot, you know. Of venison and pheasant. Iona can attest."

The dog looked up at his mention of her name. Helena chuckled. "I'm certain you are, John. But that isn't the point."

No, it wasn't. He moved closer to her. "Look how you saved me from a terrible decision. The Lord sent you to be a North Star to me and keep me on the proper path."

And that was what she was. The ice-bright light that drew his eye and beckoned him home to his children.

'She rolled her eyes. "You'd have come to your senses in a moment or two without me."

"I'm not so certain." God help him. "I'm unaccustomed to such rage as I feel, but he's provoking us. And you deserve justice. Perhaps if I spoke to a barrister, in hypotheticals—"

"The truth would come out. These things always do."

And despite the lack of justice in it, the victims of crimes such as Helena's were not treated kindly. Right or wrong, it was the truth.

That didn't mean he had to like it. "There must be a way to stop such a fiend."

She made a humming sound his first wife sometimes used when she meant *I know something you do not*. Even the dog looked at her with curiosity.

"What?"

"Nothing. I'm hopeful you are right." She took his note to Carvey from his fingers, turning to toss it into the fire crackling in the hearth. "Now that you are calmer, I would appreciate advice on another matter."

A change of subject? Probably for the best. "Anything."

Her gaze fixed on his letter to Carvey smoking on the grate. The edges curled and blackened, and then it caught fire. "Margaret discovered Frederick's identity somehow. The girl next door told her Frederick is a jewel-finding hero, and Margaret was excited to see him again today. Naturally she doesn't understand why I…dislike him. I must find a way to speak to her about it without telling the entire truth."

"Can't you tell her he is not appropriate in our family and be done with it?"

Helena turned from the fire to skewer him with a disbelieving look. "I have."

"Yet you wish to prolong this unpleasant conversation with her?"

"She reminds me I am not in authority over her, as a real aunt or mother would be. Sometimes I think she warms to me, and then—" Her eyes bugged and her hands waved. "She explodes like a firework. I know she is of an age, but her continued opposition pains me."

John's gut tightened, like he'd been kicked. Was part of this his fault? In truth, he probably wanted Helena to handle matters with the children, freeing him to work and to participate only in the pleasant times.

He'd been ignorant to leave it all at Helena's feet. She'd handled the tasks of bringing the staff and children into line, but it might have been smoother for her had he supported her with his presence and words, rather than fighting her when she challenged Catriona's boundaries.

It was too late to go back, but he could start now. "Let's speak to Margaret together."

Something he should have done when he first wed Helena, presenting a united front. He rang the bell pull, summoned Margaret from the nursery and took the seat beside Helena while they waited. "I have failed to tell you what an admirable job you've done with the *bairns*."

Her head shook. "I cannot take credit. They are your children."

"They're flourishing, and not because of me. Alex hasn't had a single nightmare since we arrived. Callum isn't ribbing him about being the heir. Margaret smiles on occasion. And Louisa, well, look at her. She is growing more independent by the day."

Warmth flashed in her eyes. She loved his children, that much was clear.

And he was so grateful for it.

Margaret appeared in the doorway, a defiant tilt to her head. She looked less like Catriona then, her air resembling the old Helena's far more. It was impossible to stifle a smile. John beckoned her. "Lass, come sit with us."

His niece obeyed, perching on a Chippendale chair. "Yes, uncle?"

Her choice not to include Helena irked. "I hear you were speaking with a man to whom you have not been introduced."

Margaret's eyes flashed betrayal at Helena. "We were not really speaking, so I did not think I required an introduction. Besides, he is a famous hero, and it's clear he and Helena are acquainted."

Cheeky lass.

"He is not my friend." Helena's voice was flat.

"So you have said." Margaret echoed Helena's tone.

"Enough." John held Margaret's angry gaze. "You know your manners far better than that, Margie. Helena was in the right today. A lady doesn't speak to anyone who has not been properly introduced to her. It is the way of the world. And as for knowing him, well, Mr. Coles is not fit for our family's friendship."

"But Helena says we should extend the hand of friendship to all, no matter his or her station." Margaret's supercilious tone might have made him laugh, under different circumstances.

"I do not refer to his station. I refer to his actions."

Margaret's gaze sought out Helena's. "What did he do?"

He opened his mouth, but Helena stayed him with her hand. "I'm not your blood, Margaret, but I pray you know I hold your best interests at heart. Will you not trust me to tell you when you are old enough to understand? And believe me when I say Mr. Coles is not suitable?"

John leaned forward, resting his elbows on his knees. "She is right, Margie. And I expect you to obey your aunt in this and in all things."

The girl had no choice but to nod, but John prayed she meant it. Especially when Helena cupped Margaret's cheek. How good it would be if Margaret truly looked at Helena as an aunt, if they could be like a real family. Even if such a thing was impossible, due to the nature of their marriage. But he prayed, nonetheless.

The moment was heavy until Helena dropped her hand and smiled. "What are the four of you doing upstairs? I heard giggles earlier."

Margaret's shoulders relaxed. "We are reading through the script of *Cinderella* for Louisa. She is making Tabitha flop around the room instead of the board character."

"I should like to see this."

"As should I," John said. "But I have meetings. Forgive me, poppet. Perhaps tomorrow."

"Yes." Margaret's shoulders sank. "Tomorrow."

Once Margaret adjourned, John glanced at the clock ticking on the mantel. He'd be late for parliamentary duties if he didn't leave now, but he didn't want to go. "I glanced at the post. We've been invited to a musical evening at Lord Holliver's next week. I scarcely know the fellow, so he won't mind us sending our regrets."

"Actually, I should like to go. If that's well with you. I can go alone, if you prefer."

"No, if you wish to go, we shall go together, as we shall handle Margaret and everything else together. I will make more of an effort to support you in front of the children."

The tiniest twitch of her lips was the only clue she was pleased. But it warmed his chest and kept him company as he headed back out into the frosty air.

Until he remembered Frederick Coles again. Nothing would please John more than if Coles turned out to be the blackmailer with the falcon seal, for then the ne'er-do-well would find himself in shackles, as he deserved.

Then Helena could be free from fear. Coles couldn't hurt anyone else. And with justice of a sort served, John could focus on his plans for educational reform. Since his visit to the Relief for the Blind in Edinburgh, he'd had all sorts of notions swirling through his head about how to improve schooling for all children. Without distraction, he'd be free to put those ideas into action.

Actually, work was its own sort of distraction—from Helena.

He hadn't been able to ignore the idea Carvey put in his head about his being in love with Helena. Ridiculous, but the truth of it was, he thought of her far more often than he should. He should be thinking instead of his promise to Catriona never to replace her in his heart.

No, he could not fall in love with Helena.

He must not.

He shoved his hands deeper into his pockets and quickened his step.

Helena's hands trembled slightly a week later when the dainty linen draper's assistant offered a bolt of silk for her inspection.

Helena wanted to cringe, but it wasn't the assistant's fault the fabric resembled that of her wedding dress, the gown that made Papa look on her with disgust. She forced a smile. "Nothing white."

Frances, her companion for the afternoon, tipped her head. "No? You look becoming in white. I always thought so."

Still bruised from Papa's words about her lacking purity and her marriage being nothing to be joyful about, Helena shook her head. She wouldn't be wearing white again for some time, if ever. "The embroidery pattern is pretty. You should buy it."

"I wish stark white didn't make me look ill. Usually I do not care a jot for the fancies of fashion, but I am relieved colored bodices are becoming popular for ball gowns. You should get it for the skirt."

Helena chuckled. "I don't think I will require many ball gowns in Perthshire."

"For an evening gown, then. Styles are changing, waist-lines dropping." Frances exchanged nods with the tiny assistant, who set aside the silk for her. "I'm sure you have something new to wear to the party tonight at Lord Holliver's."

"Alas, no." Helena's tone was light. "I will wear something from last season."

"Dreadful." Frances tut-tutted like she was chucking a cat under the chin.

Meeting one another's gazes, they burst into laughter. Mama would be mortified if she saw it.

"Oh, how good it is to hear your laugh." Frances fingered a length of sprigged muslin. "You've seemed preoccupied today."

"Forgive me—I am." With the children. Frederick Coles. And with her husband.

He'd been occupied with work this past week, but he'd made time for the children, taking the boys to Hyde Park, listening to readings of both *Cinderella* and *Don Quixote* multiple times, and enjoying a dainty tea with Louisa and Tabitha. He'd walked Iona with Margaret and promised to teach her how to drive the pony cart this summer when the House of Lords prorogued. Sunday after church, they'd dined all together, but he'd excused himself afterward, claiming too much work to sit with her that evening.

She'd sought him out twice. Once, to remind him about Lord Holliver's invitation. He'd grimaced and questioned the wisdom of it, should Frederick be in attendance, but remained adamant that he'd go with her. A second time, when she'd searched out Iona, he'd shown her a new article on Frederick, whom the newspaper had dubbed Frederick "The Finder" Coles after he'd "discovered" an emerald-tipped stickpin on the floor of his party host, Mr. Covell, who'd thought it safely tucked into a drawer upstairs.

Half of London thought Frederick's "heroism" astonishing. Helena wanted to screech whenever his name came up, and though John tried to hide it, his fingers fisted, too—

"Helena?" Frances's query drew Helena to the present, where the tiny assistant stood holding a bolt of yolk-yellow silk. "What of this?"

"Perhaps something paler." She turned to examine spools of trim. Purchasing fabrics to take back to Scotland with her in a few weeks might be unnecessary, but she'd thought an outing with Frances would offer a chance to speak about the note Frances had sent her about Frederick Coles.

It was a successful shopping trip, too. She'd found several things she liked, in every color but white, from blues similar to those she'd chosen to remake her rooms at Comraich to black bombazine, a necessary purchase to have on hand should it be required for mourning attire. Word was the king grew more ill by the day.

The assistant returned with fabric of medium-yellow hue, embroidered with flowers. "Evening primrose, milady?"

"Yes, set that aside." But not for her. The girls would look lovely in it.

While the assistant dashed away, Frances leaned close. "When you wrote inviting me to shop 'and discuss Frederick Coles,' I wondered what you thought of my note last week."

"I dared not reply in writing, and I hesitate to discuss

among others' hearing." She glanced about and found the shop empty, for the moment. "How well do you know him?"

"He called on me three seasons past, but not because he sought my friendship." Frances shuddered. "His handsome face masks a foul intent."

Was Frances one of the others Frederick had referred to, one of the women he'd attacked as a challenge? Could Helena confide in Frances what Frederick had done to her?

The earnest look in Frances's blue eyes made the decision easy. Helena took her friend's hand. "I thought he was my friend, too. But he wasn't."

Frances's eyes filled with tears. "Oh, darling friend, did he—"

Helena nodded.

"I shall never tell anyone, but you must know you are not to blame for his wrongdoing. I narrowly avoided such a fate because we were discovered, but I have often wondered if he behaved so villainously with another. I've borne guilt for not speaking, but the disgrace of such a thing as he does is—well, I see you understand." She squeezed Helena's hand, and looked at her with compassion, not judgment. "Suffice to say, I was horrified to read in the *Post* this morning about Frederick 'Finder' Coles thwarting yet another attack by the so-called Thief of Mayfair."

Helena forced a laugh. "He has become quite the hero. First he recovers Bridgewater's jewels, and now stumbles upon Mr. Covell's emerald stickpin."

"Mr. Covell lost a small sum that night, I've heard. As at Lord Bridgewater's, the thief managed to dash away with something of value while leaving a thing or two behind." Frances leaned closer. "I have no proof but shall say it outright—he is not The Finder but the thief. I am convinced he needs funds."

"He is a blackguard."

Frances scowled. "I pray he is caught, in some way or another, before he harms someone else."

"Precisely." Helena strove to keep her voice down. "That's what I wished to speak to you about. How do you catch a thief—"

The assistant's return stopped her speech. She smiled and issued instructions settling the account and sending the purchases to the town house before turning to Frances. "I've an idea to share with you."

Once they were seated in the carriage, Helena spun on the plush seat to face Frances. "I'm hoping Frederick Coles will attend Lord Holliver's musicale tonight."

"I do not. It would quite ruin the evening."

"I shall amend then—I'm hoping Frederick, the Thief of Mayfair, strikes tonight. And I'd like to catch him when he does. If he cannot be punished for what he did to me—and others—then he will at least go to prison for thievery."

Frances's blue eyes widened. Then she grinned. "Tell me more."

Chapter Twenty

The next evening, John's gaze closely followed his wife as she sailed about Holliver's salon, where the guests milled after listening to a soprano. She greeted acquaintances, fluttering this way and that like thistle down on a breeze.

She was beautiful, a vision in her gown of pale pink, but her loveliness wasn't why he kept close watch on her.

Coles was here, and John wouldn't let the blackguard within three feet of her. How could Helena stand being in the same room with him? Since their marriage, she'd been in turns furious and afraid over what Coles did to her—rightly so—but now she glided through the room, unwilling to go home, as if Coles's presence didn't bother her in the least.

Except—yes, there was a subtle working of a muscle in her jaw. She was not happy about Coles's being here, but she was a better actor than he. John might be schooled at hiding his emotions in the most heated of debates at Westminster, but the desire to draw and quarter Frederick Coles was proving much harder to conceal.

John craned his neck as Helena disappeared behind a group of gentlemen. Ah, there was a flash of pink—

"Your wife is a vision, isn't she?"

John's molars ground together as Frederick Coles drew alongside, reeking of bergamot cologne and arrogance. "Brave of you to speak to me in public, Coles. Do you have the courage to meet me outside?"

Coles's eyes flashed with something like fear, but he quickly hid it behind a grin. "Calm yourself, Lord Ardoch. I wasn't sure she'd told you about us—"

John gripped Coles's arm. He didn't care who saw. He didn't care if he left bruises on the villain's skin. "Leave her be, am I clear? Better yet, leave London."

"Unhand me, before someone wonders why you are so cross and guesses how well I know Helena." Coles's tone was light, but his upper lip betrayed him by trembling.

"You don't know her at all." John released Coles's arm and watched him move away. Coles's practiced saunter had a hitch in it.

Lord help me, but I could do violence to the blackguard.

Praying, John breathed deeply. Calm slowly lapped over his heated skin, even if his fury over Coles didn't entirely fade. Perhaps it never would.

At least Coles seemed to be giving Helena a wide berth. And Helena—and the rest of the party—seemed oblivious to John's taking hold of Coles.

"Have you no sense of pretense, man?"

Well, almost everyone had been oblivious. His father-in-law, the Duke of Kelworth, appeared at John's elbow, glowering at him before shooting an equally unhappy glare in Coles's direction.

Since Kelworth had dispensed with pleasantries, so would John. "It was a quiet conversation, Your Grace."

Kelworth harrumphed. "Your hands are still clenched."

So they were. "I suggested we leave the moment Coles arrived, but your daughter refused."

"She was right." With an artificial smile, Kelworth nodded at an acquaintance before turning back to John. "Overt rudeness will cause speculation. So would our abrupt departures from this insipid rout—I didn't even wish to come, but my wife was most insistent. So now, to spare us all from speculation, we must act as if Coles is beneath our concern, as opposed to giving the appearance you might challenge him to a duel."

John glanced at his father-in-law. "Helena told you?"

Kelworth sputtered. "I was tossing ideas to the wind. Truly, Ardoch? A duel?"

"It was a moment of madness." No wonder Helena hadn't taken him the least bit seriously. Now, she looked almost happy, her arm linked with her friend Frances Fennelwick's as they drifted along the wall of French doors to the terrace, which were closed against the cold winter evening.

"Remember the goal, Ardoch. Protecting our honor."

"'Tis more important I protect Helena."

"Aren't they one and the same?"

Not in the slightest, but it wouldn't do to argue with Kelworth here, not about Coles, or about the duke's handling of what happened to Helena.

Kelworth turned away to cough, and something shifted in John's chest. Perhaps it was the lighting, but the duke's skin seemed sallow, his eyes weary and shadowed. Helena was right: her father was not well. And John pitied him.

For his ill health. For having been gifted with three daughters—including Helena—and not truly knowing them at all. For placing his perception of honor above Helena's well-being. Most of all, for not knowing God.

Thank you for sending Helena to me, Lord, to show me how important my children are and saving me from this poor man's lot.

His coughing fit passed, Kelworth occupied himself with brushing a speck of lint from his sleeve. "If you do not want

Helena or any of us to be the subject of gossip, it would be wise to model her actions. And my wife's. See how they circulate the room, as is appropriate, while I do the same."

Indeed, the Duchess of Kelworth spoke in hushed tones to their gray-haired host, Lord Holliver, breaking off to greet the duke's brother, Lord Cecil Stanhope, and his wife, Lady Davinia, but they did not return her falsely bright smile.

There was not much affection between them, to be sure, for whatever reason. John didn't much care why at the moment. The whole idea of more artificial smiles and pretending was beyond wearisome. It was ridiculous.

He preferred a quiet night at home with Helena and the children.

But he was here for his wife, and he knew as well as Kelworth how society worked. "I shall endeavor to behave, Your Grace."

Did the man almost smile? "Then I'll take my leave of you. But oh—have you heard the grim news of the king? It is said he can no longer walk."

Carvey had told him. "Our prayers are with the royal family."

Kelworth nodded, leaving John alone to watch Helena and Coles in turn while making overtures at being sociable. He'd chatted with a handful of fellows when his host, Lord Holliver, joined him with a bow. "Congratulations on your nuptials. Your wife is the loveliest lady here."

For some reason, the compliment sounded both genuine and barbed. Like Helena's family, Holliver probably thought John beneath her in station.

"Thank you. I certainly think so."

"I was curious about her marrying you. None of us knew you'd met, but I understand her cousin is your neighbor." It wasn't a question inviting conversation. More like an observation to himself. Then he glanced at John. "Pardon me. I should see to other guests."

John nodded his farewell, thoughtful. Hadn't Helena mentioned a viscount had offered to marry her and been refused by her father? Was it Holliver?

Quite possibly. John may not be the most intuitive fellow, but Lord Holliver's gaze followed Helena with open admiration. He'd probably fancied Helena once upon a time. John couldn't blame him.

He continued to watch after his wife, seeing her in a way he never had before. This was her life before she married him—parties among the highest born of society, elegance and splendor. Aside from Coles being in the room, Helena was probably enjoying herself more than she had in months.

This was her realm, not Scotland. Drawing rooms, not nurseries. The *haut ton*, not Highlanders. She'd chosen to be here among them tonight, rather than stay at home with him and the children. Even though Coles was here.

He and Helena might be married, might be friends, even, but they were of different worlds. How quickly he'd forgotten.

Helena shivered, but not from the cold in this overwarm room. She was made of ice, stiff and brittle and ready to break. Her face would crack from these smiles, this pretending she didn't want to retch each time Frederick Coles strode past.

Her cheeks pained from holding her smile in place. "If it weren't for you, Frances, I should be in pieces."

"Nonsense." Frances jiggled their interlocked arms. "I shall not let you go, and it shouldn't be too long now." Her steps faltered. "Look."

Frederick slipped to the salon door, glancing behind him. He could be going any number of places in the house, but

Helena doubted he had innocent intent. "Do you think the Thief of Mayfair is about to strike again?"

"And Frederick 'The Finder' Coles will play hero?" Frances's grip tightened. "We will prove to all they are one and the same when we catch Frederick alone, pilfering Lord Holliver's wares."

Helena pulled Frances toward the door. "And he'll be punished, for this crime, at least, if not his others." And he wouldn't hurt anyone else again.

The ladies hurried after Frederick, but the reception hall off the salon was empty, devoid even of servants. "He's upstairs already." Frances extricated her arm from Helena's. "Let's go."

They were five steps up when a short, snub-nosed man dressed in dingy brown ran down the stairs and bolted past them. Frederick followed, a gold chain dangling from his fingers.

"Thief! The Thief of Mayfair!" His brows were pulled low in indignation.

That meant—Frederick was *not* the Thief of Mayfair? It was another man after all?

John rushed from the salon. Lord Holliver was close behind, followed by numerous guests. John reached Helena's side before she could exhale.

He pulled her away from Frances. "Did he touch you?"

"The thief?" Her head shook. Then she realized he meant Frederick, who'd rushed downstairs and was loudly telling everyone he'd interrupted the Thief of Mayfair. Lord Holliver issued instructions for the burglar to be pursued, and servants rushed to and fro while guests thickened the hall. But John still waited, his green-eyed stare intent on hers.

She shook her head again. "*No one* touched me."

His nostrils flared, the only evidence of his emotion. But was it anger, or fear? "You left the salon. And *he'd* left."

Both anger and fear, perhaps. "I'd scarce been gone thirty seconds. And I was with Frances."

"Nevertheless I feared he might taunt you or otherwise cause you distress." Lines of anguish marred his cheeks and encircled his eyes. "Helena—"

"Lady Ardoch." Frederick dared speak her name—not to her, but in conversation with an enraptured crowd. "She saw the thief's face. Miss Fennelwick did, too, and I am grateful such reputable ladies can attest to tonight's events."

The way he looked at her when he called her reputable, as if he was so earnest it could only be a mockery, made her fingers itch to slap him. Her hand lifted an inch.

But every eye seemed fixed on her.

"Is it true, Lady Ardoch?" Lord Holliver's voice was gentle. "You saw the Thief of Mayfair?"

She nodded. "Briefly, but I can describe him to the authorities."

Mama took Lord Holliver's arm. "Her memory is excellent. So is her sister Maria's. Such an observant young lady—"

"How did you manage to come upon the thief yet again, Mr. Coles?" John's even tone didn't fool Helena for a moment. There was a sharp edge to it, like a sword still sheathed, but ready for battle in an instant.

Frederick shrugged, a practiced gesture she'd once found appealing in its apparent humility. "Same as your lady, I expect. I needed air. Oh, Lord Holliver, I was able to pull something from his hand." He held out the chain in his fingers.

When he reached, his coat opened, revealing a warp in the gold-weave pattern of his waistcoat pocket from something tucked inside. And then Helena knew.

The Thief of Mayfair was not one man, but two.

All of this was a performance, intended to place Frederick above suspicion. He'd probably waited for her and Frances—anyone—to leave the salon so they could bear witness to Frederick chasing the thief.

She'd underestimated him. But he'd underestimated her, too.

"Do not forget the item in your pocket." Helena pointed her fan at his patterned waistcoat.

Frederick's laugh was brittle. "I do not—that is—oh, yes. I could not hold everything in my hands. Here." He pulled a gold brooch from the pocket of his waistcoat.

Someone mentioned summoning the magistrate. Papa tipped his head at Mama in the way Helena recognized as *let's take our leave*. Frances had found her father, and they seemed to have the same idea, for they wandered toward the vestibule.

John brushed her fingers with his, a discreet touch that lasted a mere moment but jolted up her arm. "I will call for the carriage."

"Wait." She clutched her arm, as if it would dispel the effect of his touch. "If the magistrate is coming, shouldn't I offer testimony? I saw them."

Them, not just the brown-coated thief. She must be more careful if she didn't wish to give away her suspicions. "I mean the thief."

John shook his head. "If the magistrate needs to speak to you or Miss Fennelwick, he will call on our homes. But I doubt he will do so. Frederick Coles will probably suffice as witness enough."

"Because he's a man?" Such was her lot as a lady, considered too delicate to bear witness to something unpleasant unless she was close to a fainting couch. She scowled.

His countenance softened. "It will be well, Helena. He'll be stopped one way or another. You are safe."

And by *he*, John didn't mean the Thief of Mayfair. He

meant Frederick. But no one was safe, not until Frederick was stopped—*one way or another.* The blackguard was free to harm women and steal. Free to taunt Helena.

Until he was caught in the act of stealing, or with the stolen goods...

John peered down at her, as if her expression was curious to him. "I'll call for the carriage. You'll be home shortly."

Home at the town house on Saint James's Square, but also home at Comraich. The date of her and the children's departure was in but a few weeks, and oh, how she desperately wanted to stop Frederick Coles before she left London.

When John left her side, she watched after him. *One way or another.* He'd said it before about Frederick receiving the justice due him. It seemed he might share her suspicion Frederick was in league with the Thief of Mayfair, and he hoped Frederick would be caught.

But Helena had to do more than hope.

She hurried over to Frances. "May I call upon you tomorrow?"

"For certain." Frances pulled her pale blue shawl tighter about her shoulders. "We have much to discuss, do we not?"

"That we do." Helena lifted her chin. "I might have another plan."

Chapter Twenty-One

"**P**attens are for outside, Louisa, not inside," Helena said for the second time as they stood in the town house vestibule, with the butler Kerr and a footman waiting to receive their outer garments. It was three days after Lord Holliver's musicale. Three days after Frederick "The Finder" Coles gave chase to the Thief of Mayfair, proving they were not one and the same person as she had hoped. Three days since Helena had truly slept well, waking frequently to mull over her plan to stop him.

Perhaps fatigue was why her patience was worn to a wet string today. Still, she strove to keep her voice calm and even as she pulled off her gloves and watched Louisa do nothing about removing her pattens, as requested. "Come, Louisa. Sledding is over, so we must remove our overshoes."

Ignoring her, Louisa marched in place so the metal rings on the pattens' bottoms clanked against the slate floor like broken bells.

"Louisa." John grimaced at the discordant sound. "Enough. Remove your pattens yourself or we shall do it for you."

She marched away from his voice, swinging Tabitha and accidentally hitting Alex in the nose.

"Argh!" He covered his nose with his hands. "Her head's wood, you know!"

Helena gathered Alex close and pulled his hands away from his face. No blood, but the shock must be frightening. "The pain will recede—"

"Bad show, Louisa." Alex reached around Helena and batted Tabitha from Louisa's hand.

Louisa's next stomp landed on something soft.

"Now you've done it." Margaret rolled her eyes. "You stepped on your baby."

"Tabitha!" Louisa's screech could have peeled the blue wallpaper from the vestibule walls.

Iona chose that moment to shake herself, scattering melting snow from her coat all over the vestibule—the floor, walls, lacquered table holding a vase of hothouse flowers and the post, and Helena's face.

Deep breath. Helena flicked the doggy-scented water from her cheek.

Without a word, John plucked the wailing Louisa into his arms and tugged off her pattens.

Margaret gathered up Tabitha, shoved the doll into Louisa's arms and sighed far more loudly than necessary. "I'm going upstairs without you, Louisa."

"Me, too." Alex pulled away from Helena, his nose apparently feeling better. "You hit me in the face."

Callum said nothing, but the moment Alex was up three stairs Callum scooped something white from his pocket and—

A snowball exploded on Alex's backside and ricocheted off Margaret's hip.

Not even a second passed before the entire lot of them began howling. Iona barked, Louisa cried, Margaret screeched and Callum cackled. Alex glared down at him, red-faced again. "I hate you!"

And Miss Munro on her half day off, and Agnes down with the ague. Kerr and the footman's eyes were wide.

Helena met John's gaze. He set Louisa down and—

His lips twitched. "You know what's more pleasant than this? Trying to convince your father and his cronies to listen to my ideas on education reform. And that says something."

A laugh bubbled out. "At least you didn't receive the brunt of the dog's shaking."

"Louisa screamed into my ear, so perhaps we are even." He withdrew a handkerchief from his coat pocket and dabbed her damp cheek with businesslike efficiency. "All right, then. Let's settle this, shall we?"

Helena nodded. "Children?"

Margaret tossed her head. "I'm going upstairs."

"No you're not," Helena called after her.

"Margie, listen to your aunt." At John's loud voice, they hushed—the older three entirely, and Louisa lowered her volume to a whine.

John fisted his hands on his hips. "I've seen better behavior from monkeys. Callum, clean up the snow."

"It's only water."

"And someone could slip on it. Clean it and apologize to Alex and Margaret. In fact, you all owe apologies. Louisa, I know it was an accident, but you must be careful. And when you're told to remove your pattens, do it. Margaret, your attitude is unacceptable. And Alex, you do not hate your brother. Apologize and then the lot of you march up to the nursery to think on your behavior. Later this evening when we've all calmed down, we'll have a further discussion."

They gaped. Was this the first time John had ever disciplined the children like this?

Probably, so they'd better respond appropriately.

"Obey your father." Helena's spine straightened. "Now."

Mumbled apologies followed as each child went about

his or her own business and lumbered upstairs, heads hanging low.

"Oh, my." Helena bit her lip.

"Sorry to leave you with this." John strode to view the damp post. "Carvey and I have an errand."

"Once Miss Munro returns, I have plans with Frances."

He tapped a vellum rectangle sealed with a red blob of wax, pressed with a bird of some sort. "You've spent each day this week with her."

"Yes." Did he suspect they weren't simply chatting about household matters and drinking tea?

"I'm glad you have a friend." He shoved the letter into his pocket.

Should she tell him what they planned to do today? That they sought evidence to prove Frederick was in league with the Thief of Mayfair?

Protective man John was, he'd stop her. He wouldn't understand she didn't do this just for herself, or for Frances and every other woman Frederick might have hurt or might hurt in the future, but for John, too.

He'd promised to protect her. But one of these days, John might not be able to control his anger. No, she'd protect him this way. Today, she'd put an end to their agonizing over the injustice of Frederick wandering free, taunting them, seemingly untouchable.

God, forgive me for keeping this secret from John. But it's better this way, isn't it? John's brow furrowed, as if he debated saying something. Then he shook his head. "Have an enjoyable outing with Frances. I'll change my clothes and meet Carvey, then, and you and I will spend some time with the children tonight to show a united front."

"I look forward to it."

And she did, her nerves calming at the thought of being

together with the children, a team of sorts with John. And hopefully, with evidence to prove Frederick Coles guilty of thievery.

God, let this be the end of it.

Once John left for his errand with Carvey, she didn't have much time. She summoned her maid, Barnes, requesting a particular heavy cloak and bonnet.

"The white ones?" Barnes's brows raised a fraction.

Little wonder. Helena had never worn these items from her trousseau because they were white, a color she'd shunned since Papa's scold on her wedding day that white was for purity.

But the cloak was long and full, concealing her clothing, and the bonnet's wide brim would hide her face. "Yes, please. I'm going out with Miss Fennelwick."

"Do you require the carriage?"

"No, but a footman would be welcome." There was no escaping the need to bring a servant with her, for propriety's sake.

Adam awaited her in the vestibule when she descended the stairs. She forced a smile. "Miss Fennelwick and I will meet to pay a call."

"Very good, milady."

He followed her out through the square and onto the busy streets of Mayfair. Weak winter sun streamed through a dull sky, adding a pale gold glow to the afternoon but little in the way of warmth. Helena hurried along until they reached the corner of Jermyn Street and The Duke of York Street, where she'd planned to meet Frances.

The spot was ideal, since it afforded her an excellent vantage of Coles's front door. His yellow brick house was three stories tall and two windows wide, small but well made, and the rent was no doubt dear in this neighborhood.

But Frederick had a tendency to purchase more than his purse could fund.

Where was Frances? Helena craned to look for her friend's familiar blue cloak.

Meanwhile, Adam loomed behind her. He was the greatest flaw in the plan today—he and whichever manservant accompanied Frances. Ladies did not call on gentlemen unless it pertained to a business matter, as even their footmen knew.

Well, they indeed had business to discuss. The business of Frederick being a criminal.

She and Frances would confront Frederick about his treatment of them. Then Frances, on cue, would require a moment and slip upstairs to search for proof Frederick was in league with the Thief of Mayfair. With such evidence, surely someone would mount a more legal, thorough search, and find enough to convict him of this crime, at least.

"Where are you, Frances?" Her whisper curled like steam in the cold air, but Frances did not materialize, only a short, snub-nosed fellow in dark livery coming from the back of Frederick's house.

Helena gasped. It was him, the Thief of Mayfair who'd run past her on the stairs at Lord Holliver's party. And he was Frederick's manservant. Frederick's only servant, if he'd spoken true when he told her about his financial difficulties.

He glanced up. Grateful for her bonnet's wide brim, Helena lowered her head, waiting a few moments before turning back to gaze at the yellow brick house.

The front door opened. Frederick quit the house.

With panic swirling in her stomach, Helena considered her options. She couldn't confront him now. Even if Frances arrived this moment, Frederick was gone—

* * *

She glanced up at Adam. "We shall continue without Miss Fennelwick. The matter is of the utmost urgency."

"Milady." He hid his hesitation well, but his voice held an uncertain edge.

She strode across Jermyn Street, as stately and dignified as the duke's daughter she was. Then she kept walking, past the yellow brick house and around the corner to the lean passage at the building's rear. Four houses' kitchens and gardens could be reached from this spot, which was why she turned back to Adam. If he lingered here, no one would know which house his master or mistress visited.

She willed her voice not to shake. "Please wait here."

"Milady?" He didn't disguise his hesitation any longer.

"This will take but a moment." She dashed around the corner to Frederick's house. Four more steps and she was at the servant's entrance. Her hand shaking, she grasped the knob.

The door swung inward with a soft moan.

Was this criminal of her, entering like this? Probably, but she went inside anyway. "Hello?"

No answer replied. Frederick hadn't lied. He had only the one servant, and apparently he hadn't laid a fire in the house today, perhaps all week. The air was as cold inside as it was outside.

Her breath created little clouds as she slipped up the back stairs. Her pattens clanked against the floor—oh, how Louisa would remind her pattens were for outdoors! But Helena hadn't time to think of the children now. At the landing, she didn't pause to look about, but it was impossible not to notice the dearth of furniture, the darker patches of floor where rugs had once been and the scent of tallow rather than beeswax candles. The place had an abandoned, greasy atmosphere.

"Frederick, you have indeed fallen on hard times."

Only one room boasted a bed and the remnants of a fire in the grate. So this was where Frederick lived, this single chamber in an empty house. Regal red draperies on the windows and bed gave the room an elegant appearance. The odor of his bergamot scent clung to the air, a reminder Frederick spent what coin he possessed on what others might judge—a dandified appearance and the pretense of having funds.

The taste of salt filled her mouth. She must have chomped her cheek. Swallowing blood, Helena swept into Frederick's dressing room. How much time had she left to search through it for stolen jewelry? Ten minutes? She'd best hurry.

Helena hadn't touched a man's clothes like this before. Not Papa's, certainly not John's. Oh, John. The thought of him pained worse than her bitten cheek. He wouldn't like her doing this. But she did this for him, too. Would he understand that?

She rummaged through the cupboard. There was nothing tucked into his coat pockets, however. Nor in his glove drawer or the pitifully unlocked box that housed a silver stickpin, a quizzing glass and two rings. Amazing. Such things should be in a heavy, locked safe.

Did he have one? She stomped her foot at her foolishness. Everywhere she'd looked was the manservant's domain. After giving the manservant his share of the stolen goods, Frederick would hide his portion. Where would he tuck the jewels away from his servant?

Across the hall sat a pathetic library—perhaps there? Servants did naught but dust the books, since they were forbidden to read them. But Frederick was either a poor reader or had sold off what he'd possessed, for the lone shelf in the house held but five volumes. Helena investigated each, fluttering through the pages in case there was a hiding space cut out of one, something she'd read of in a novel.

A creak sounded, like the house settling in the cold. Or a foot on the stair. Paralysis gripped her. Was someone in the house? She hadn't heard either door open or shut, but she'd been focused on the task at hand.

What if they're back? Helena could hide, a task that would be easier if Frederick owned more furniture to shield her, true. If anyone was in the house, though, it was probably the snub-nosed manservant. He'd left first. She'd conceal herself behind the bookshelf until he busied himself with whatever a servant did in an empty house, and then she'd dash downstairs and out the door and he would never be the wiser. Frederick would never know, either.

She wouldn't have the evidence she wished, but she would escape with her reputation intact.

Still gripping a leather-bound volume to her chest, Helena leaned behind the bookshelf, her wild pulse resounding in her ears. Waited. No creaks. No footsteps. Perhaps no one was in the house after all, and what she'd heard was the house settling. Poor house. So cold, and sheltering such a cruel master. It deserved better, like everyone and everything else that came close to Frederick.

She peeked out from the bookcase. Nothing but cold, empty air.

She must leave. Without evidence, alas, but it had been a wild hope to find the proof identifying him as a thief, declaring to the world he was not The Finder but a liar and a crook.

Her arms shook as she lifted the book to replace it. Before it rose higher than her chin, however, she froze.

She was not alone, after all. And it would have been far, far better to be caught by the manservant.

"Good afternoon, darling." Frederick grinned from the

threshold, his cheeks ruddy from the cold, his greatcoat still on, his walking stick in hand. "What a delightful surprise."

"I can't say I'm surprised." John blew hot breath into his gloved fists to warm his fingers, an act Carvey copied. The cold seeped up John's cuffs and down his collar, despite his scarf and heavy greatcoat. "Since the massacre at Peterloo, parliamentary representation has been a more critical issue than education reform. I understand our friends' priorities, but I wish we could address both."

The meeting with their cronies had been frustrating, to say the least. Almost as frustrating as the idea of Frederick Coles walking free about London.

Carvey tipped his head back toward the house they'd just exited, where several of their friends complained over coffee in a room thick with tobacco smoke and angst. "At least Earl Grey is supportive of your ideas, but he is over-worked."

Weren't they all. "In God's time, Carvey. I must let Him work out the matter."

"And all matters." Carvey shoved his hands in his pockets. "Like this matter with Coles. Have you told your wife yet about this scheme of yours to prove him guilty of black-mailing you?"

John scowled.

"You haven't, have you? You're my closest friend, but you're a fool."

"I'm trying to protect her." John had made that clear, hadn't he?

"I doubt she'd see it that way. You've got to tell her. Today. She's your wife."

It was far more complicated than that. Still, there was no use arguing with a man who'd do anything to see his true love once again, a man who couldn't possibly understand John betrayed his first wife by having dangerous feelings for Helena.

A change of subject was in order. "Let's meet the Bow Street Runner, shall we? Perhaps he has new information for us."

"I'll speak to him." Carvey said with a grin as he turned and walked backward away from John. "You go home and talk to your wife."

John was not certain whether to smile or sigh as Carvey turned about and hurried toward Bow Street and the appointment with the investigator John had hired.

Very well. He'd go home. The prospect of seeing Helena and having a proper talk was both appealing and frightening. Could he tell her about the blackmail, or his certainty Coles was partnered with the Thief of Mayfair, and his plan to prove Coles guilty of one of those crimes so he could be judged and sentenced for something, if not the crime he committed against her?

Was Carvey right, that she might be furious with him for withholding his suspicions from her, even if he'd done it to protect her?

Indubitably. But at least then, there would be nothing between them.

He'd use the time at home wisely, then. He'd tell her his plan to get Coles arrested. Then he'd show her support and solidify their determination to parent together. Their friendship, their partnership, could grow stronger from this.

Perhaps Helena would stay longer in London than they'd planned. She was comfortable here; he'd seen it at Lord Holliver's. This was the life she'd known, among glittering society.

And days like today, when the children misbehaved and she was surrounded by reminders of the life she could have had if she'd married someone like Lord Holliver—a fellow who'd clearly harbored tender feelings for Helena, John was sure of it—she surely wondered why she'd agreed to take on John and his *bairns*.

His shudder was not entirely from the cold. Still, it was a blessed relief to enter the warm house. Kerr took his coat and hat.

"It's quiet." John didn't hear a thing, upstairs or down.

"The children are at their studies with Miss Munro, milord. Her ladyship has not returned yet, but someone in Fennelwick livery delivered a letter, not five minutes ago. He said it was urgent for her ladyship, but if she was not here, you were to read it, milord."

His stomach sank to his boots. Why would the Fennelwick household send an urgent message to Helena, here, if she was with Frances?

He took the letter. Tore it open right there in the vestibule and read, his mouth going dry.

God, let me not be too late.

Chapter Twenty-Two

Helena gripped the book to her chest. Frederick didn't move closer, but smiled at her, gesturing at her ensemble. "You're in white, as you were the last time we were alone. Behind the dovecote, remember?"

Before she could answer, he pretended to smack his head. "Silly me. I forgot you napped."

Like a sharp-edged pick, his laugh shattered the ice that had frozen her into immobility. Heat coursed through her bones. "You gave me laudanum, you rogue."

"And you are here, breaking into my house. You're as much a criminal as you claim I am."

"There was no need to break into anything. The door was open."

He propped his ebony walking stick against the wall. "White is becoming on you. Of course, your penchant for the color contributed to your reputation as an ice maiden. Except with me."

She gripped the book to her like a shield. "You're disgusting."

He divested his greatcoat. "Why are you here, darling? Are you searching my house for something to attest to what happened behind the dovecote? A vial of laudanum won't prove anything. Or are you here because you love me still? Oh, Helena." The words were smooth and sweet as honey as he leaned in, near enough to touch her.

She swung the book at his head.

A tiny trickle of ruby-red blood dribbled out his nose. He swiped it with the back of his hand. "Proud of yourself, darling?"

"Not particularly." She'd hoped to hit him so hard she could dash past him out of the house. She couldn't do anything right.

"Females and books aren't a good combination." He struck the book from her hands, sending it to the floor with a thud. Then he gripped her wrists, securing them in one of his hands while the other hand cuffed her neck. Not so hard she could not breathe. More like a warning that he could crush her throat if he wished. And it certainly kept her from screaming for Adam.

Frederick was so close, his scent filled her senses. The tang of his bergamot cologne, the sweet of his hair pomade, the cinnamon-clove spice of his breath. All pleasant, masking such ugliness.

She kicked. Hit something with her patten-shod foot, because Frederick growled. She yanked and her hand was free, caught again when his hand left her throat, but she didn't stop struggling. Her bonnet knocked sideways and oh, there was his hand on her neck again. Squeezing.

She was so tired. She might die here, foolish and stupid. At least, when she was found, John would know from her bruised hands she fought. With the last of her strength, she kicked again. Her patten flew from her foot and hit the floor with a clatter.

Howling with pain, he released her, but scrambled to block the door. He had her trapped like an animal, but at least she had a moment to breathe. To look for another weapon.

"Such spirit." Frederick bent at the waist and rested his hands on his knees. "If I had known you planned to visit, I would have sent my manservant on a longer errand. But he's discreet. And quite helpful."

"Oh, yes, Mr. Finder." Disdain poured out her mouth. "He did a fine job playing the part of the Thief of Mayfair for you to stumble upon."

"So that's why you're here? To find trinkets to prove I'm behind the robberies? Discover anything, then?" He rose to his full height. "I didn't think so. Now, what shall we do, you and I?"

If only Frederick had not lost all his possessions, there might be something to throw at him. "You stand aside and I leave, that's what we shall do."

"I'm not quite ready." He stepped forward.

She screamed Adam's name.

Frederick laughed. "You brought a servant? Is he outside? The street's too noisy for him to hear you."

He meant to frighten her—and he did. But at once, a feeling fell over her, something like the sensation she'd encountered when she entered the kirk on her wedding day. Something like love, but different. Peace, perhaps.

Adam might not be able to hear her, but she was not alone. She was never alone.

"I can't fight you forever, Frederick, but no matter how you humiliate me, God won't abandon me here."

Frederick's laugh rumbled from deep in his gut. "I heard talk of you becoming pious. I never believed 'twas true."

"God helped me change, and He can help you, too, Frederick."

"Enough." With an angry jerk, he gripped her arm.

Her chances of escape dwindled with every heartbeat.

Yet still the odd feeling of peace thrummed through her veins.

"Why are you smiling?" Frederick's voice was different.

Was she? "After what you did, how you left me, I feared that was all there would ever be of me. A broken, dirty shell, with no emotion but grief and self-loathing and hatred of you. But I do not think I hate you anymore. Instead, I'm sorry for you."

A loud, persistent knock sounded on the street door below stairs. In an instant, Frederick's hand clamped over her still-open mouth. His fingers pressed into her lips and against her teeth. "If you scream again, you will bring ruin upon your household. You know that, don't you?"

Of course she did. Screaming could save her life, but her visit here would be exposed. She would embarrass John, his children, her family and herself. She nodded. Of course she could not scream.

But she could bite. And there was already a finger at her teeth.

John's fist was an inch from the door, preparing to pound again, when the scream reached his ears. Faint among the noise of the street behind him, but definite. Someone in the house cried out.

Helena.

John tried the latch. Locked.

"Ardoch!"

Carvey and the broad-shouldered Bow Street Runner John had hired crossed Jermyn Street, their brows knit in twin expressions of concern.

If they were here, they must have found something, but there was no time to discuss it now. He jerked his head, indicating they should follow him. "I'm going 'round back."

They caught up. "Calm, man." Carvey tried to be soothing.

"Helena's in there." John might have said more had he not run into someone in familiar livery. "Adam?"

"Milord." Adam startled. "Her ladyship said—"

"Never mind what she said. I'm going in." John hurried to the kitchen door, his body tensed in preparation to break down the door.

"Allow me, milord." The ox-shaped Runner set his shoulder to the door and his hand on the latch. He almost fell inside when the door gave way under his hand.

John bolted past him, following the sounds of scuffle upstairs. It wasn't hard to find them. Coles gripped a struggling Helena, one hand clamping her arms, the other covering her mouth. Her bonnet was off, her hair a wild mess.

John saw nothing but Helena's face. That, and the ebony walking stick propped against the wall. It was in his hand in an instant.

One hard swing to the back of Coles's knees. With a cry, Coles dropped to the floor. Blood dripped down Coles's hand.

Helena said something. Everyone said something. But Helena's blood on Coles's hand spoke louder than their words. He shoved Coles to the ground with more vigor than necessary, twisting his arms behind his back.

He glanced up. "Restrain him, Carvey, before I do something I will later regret."

"You trespass in my house," Coles cried from the floor while Carvey and Adam held him down and the Runner pulled a length of twine from his pocket. "How dare you bind me?"

John was already at Helena, cradling her cheeks, smoothing her hair, lowering the collar of her cloak to examine the angry pink marks blooming there. His hands could not be still while he took her in and pushed down the near-overwhelming desire to punch Coles in the kidneys. "Where are you bleeding, sweetheart?"

"I am not."

She had to be. His fingers ran the length of her arms, the back of her head, her lips. "There's blood all down his hand."

"Because I bit him." She swiped her mouth.

The Runner laughed.

"That was you screeching, Coles? You scream like a suckling pig." Carvey climbed off of Coles's back.

"I'll have you before the court for this, Ardoch." Coles staggered when the Runner hauled him upright.

"I cannot wait for the day, Coles." John sheltered Helena under his arm, close against his side. "Already the magistrate comes to arrest you."

A flash of fear dimmed his eyes, but it was quickly masked by a too-wide smile. "For this? I'll tell the magistrate Helena came of her own accord and you beat me in a jealous rage."

"Carvey and the Runner know it's untrue."

"They also know she came alone, and when word spreads, you'll be the laughingstock of London."

A knock sounded below.

"The magistrate."

"I shall let him in." Adam first bent to retrieve Helena's bonnet, which she shoved atop her head. Then she reached for something off the floor—a patten?

Perhaps John should feel more satisfaction, but all he wanted was to take Helena home. "I doubt you'll speak of my wife at all to the magistrate, Coles. You're about to be arrested as a thief. Frederick 'The Finder' Coles is, in fact, the Thief of Mayfair."

Coles's grin was the most annoying thing John had ever laid eyes on. "Tear the house apart. You'll find nothing."

Helena gripped John's fingers. "That's why I'm here, John. My search was fruitless. Without evidence, how will he be convicted?"

"Because his manservant, who played the part of the Thief of Mayfair, fenced off the items." John turned his back on Coles and faced Helena again, touching her face and neck again to make sure she was hale. Then he tied the white bow of her bonnet under her chin. "I've had the chap followed for some time now, since before Holliver's rout."

Carvey cleared his throat. "The servant just now attempted to sell a ruby exactly like Lord Bridgewell's. Two Bow Street Runners and I watched the whole thing. One of them took the servant into custody, and we are here for Coles."

"Preposterous. It was my ruby." Coles wrestled against the binding at his wrists. "I may sell what I wish."

Helena snorted. "If you'd had a ruby, you'd have sold it instead of your furnishings."

John caressed her shoulder, but his gaze fixed on Coles. "Once Lord Bridgewell identifies the ruby, you'll be done for."

"My manservant stole it, then. I always knew he was a sneaky fellow."

The Bow Street Runner yanked Coles to his feet. "Enough of this hum. We know the funds for the stolen goods went to an account at Travers & Sons metalsmiths in your name, not his. And Travers himself has stated you've collected. You're as guilty as he is."

Coles's smile died at last.

John held his hand up to forestall the Runner, who jostled out the door. "One last thing. You used Travers & Sons for your ill-gotten funds, so it's only a matter of time before I prove you used them for the money you received through blackmail. Admit to it now, Coles, and I'll see to it you aren't transported to a penal colony."

Coles's jaw gaped. "I don't know what you're blathering about."

"You know." But at Coles's befuddled expression, John's stomach sank.

A call from below, and the Runner lifted his brow at John. "Need more time, milord?"

John shook his head. He'd wanted the blackmailer to be Coles. Hoped it was him. He squeezed Helena tighter to him.

The Runner's gruff voice faded as he urged Coles downstairs. Carvey followed, leaving John and Helena alone.

John took a long, deep breath, recognizing for the first time the cold of the threadbare room and the tallow smell of the place. Coles's debts must be significant, indeed. "If he'd been the blackmailer, he would have taken the money."

"What blackmailer?"

He still had the letter in his inner coat pocket. "Allow me to tell you at home. I don't wish to stay in this place a moment longer than necessary."

She sighed, but nodded. "Is it safe to go down? I'd not wish to cause talk if the magistrate sees me."

He straightened the mess he'd made of her bonnet bow. "It's safe. You are with me."

"How did you find me? Oh, you didn't. It sounds as if you've been following Frederick and his servant."

"Carvey and the Runners came for Frederick after apprehending his servant. I came for you," he clarified, tucking her hand into his arm. "Miss Fennelwick sent a hasty note. She received a call from your grandmother, of all people, and could not break away from the dowager duchess's inquisition despite her best attempts. She hoped her message might reach you in time, but if you were out, she instructed the letter to come to me, and the postscript was most illuminating."

"Was it?"

"Espionage on the highest level. I admit I'm impressed."

"Not angry?" They started down the staircase.

"A little, I suppose, to cover the fear. Things could have gone much differently here today. It was God's grace that I received Miss Fennelwick's message in time, instead of staying out with Carvey as I'd planned. That Carvey and the Runner were here for Coles and I intercepted them outside the door." He slowed their steps on the stairs. "If I'd known what you were about—"

"My decision to come here alone was rash, but yes, Frances and I did have a plan that was perhaps not the wisest course. I wish you and I had told one another what we were about."

Although she was tucked against his side, he could feel her heart tugging away from him. "I trust you, Helena, but I wanted to protect you."

"And I wished to protect you." She chewed her lip. "You've saved me too many times."

"We both wished to see him brought to justice. And now he is."

She smiled, but said no more as they exited the house. They kept to their own thoughts until, trailed by Adam, they arrived home, which had never seemed so warm or sweet smelling. They divested their damp coats and hats. He reached for her hand. "May we speak in the library, please?"

"We have a conversation to finish."

"Two items of post arrived, milord. One was said to be urgent." Kerr's voice held them back. "They await your lordship on the salver in the library."

"Thank you." John led Helena to the library, shut the

door and pulled her close. Her hair reeked of Coles's bergamot cologne. "Shall we call the physician to look at your neck? 'Tis bruised. Does it ache inside?"

Her head shook. "I wouldn't wish to explain the bruises. They'll fade."

"I pray the memories of his hands on you fade as fast."

"Oh, John." She buried her head against his waistcoat. Could she hear his heart pummeling his chest? His arms tightened. Surely she was not unaffected, not repulsed by him to curl into his chest like this.

His lips were against her hair. He could easily kiss her again, starting at the top of her head. Then he'd lift her face and follow the trail of her cheek to her lips.

"The post." Her voice was muffled against his chest.

"Leave it," he said into her hair.

"Kerr said 'twas urgent."

So he had, and John had no business entertaining the notion of kissing her again. His hands fell. "Do not leave. Please." He wasn't ready to part from her just yet.

The top letter was sealed with red wax and stamped with a falcon. He offered it to Helena. "I'm being blackmailed."

She didn't take the letter, but stared at it. "Someone knows what Frederick did to me. You are paying to prevent a scandal."

"I don't care about a scandal. I've been paying to protect you." He stared into her eyes, hoping she could see how much he hated hurting her. "Read it."

At last she took it. She touched the falcon-crested seal, ran her finger under the flap and opened the missive. And squawked like a macaw.

"Fifty pounds and your vote in Parliament, else all London will know of my disgrace?"

"A trifling sum and a pointless request. There was no need to make me vote for the acts when they would carry with or without my vote." John's head shook. "What is more interesting is the blackmailer has yet to collect any of my payments. They sit, as instructed, at a metalsmith near a bazaar on the edge of Mayfair. I can only conclude the blackmailer is less interested in my money and votes than with toying with me."

"So it was you I saw!"

"When?"

"At the bazaar we visited with Frances. We were eating cakes and I thought I saw you. And Carvey."

"I was there to investigate the metalsmith. I'd sent Carvey to follow Coles."

Helena's eyes brightened with moisture. "You told Lord Carvey what Frederick did to me?"

"No—not that. I told him I suspected Coles of being the Thief of Mayfair, and he guessed I suspected Coles of blackmailing me, but he didn't ask why, and I didn't tell him."

Helena chewed her lip. "Can you not find your blackmailer's identity from the metalsmith?"

"I hoped so, which is why I went to Travers & Sons that day, but as I said, the funds have yet to be recovered. The proprietor has no idea what to do with them, nor does he admit to ever agreeing to be a go-between."

Helena laid the note on the rosewood secretary. "The blackmailer asks for payment he never collects and votes he knows will not count. I agree, he is set about wickedness and torment, rather than gain."

"Which, I confess, made me think of Frederick Coles. He's proven a master of manipulation and degradation." A vast understatement. "But now we know it is not he."

"Then who?"

"I won't stop investigating until I find out. In the

meantime, I will keep paying. I'm so sorry to hurt you this way—"

"You, hurting me?" Her brows pulled into a V. "I'm the one who's sorry."

"You've nothing to be sorry for."

"This is because of me. I'm costing you money and agony."

His head shook. "You are far more valuable than whatever the author of these letters wants. That's why I hid it from you in the first place. I did not wish to embarrass you or hurt you. Please say you can forgive me for not telling you."

Her brow relaxed. "It seems we are still always apologizing, are we not?"

"I say let's stop here and now. We are a team, remember? Partners?"

"Oh yes, and as partners, we have children upstairs to speak to about their behavior."

That wasn't quite what he meant, but she reached and picked up the remaining post. "See to this urgent message, too, so we might talk."

Or he could wrap her in his arms again, before they spoke to the children. He broke the seal with too much vigor. Then his desire extinguished, like a pail of sand dousing a flame.

"The Duke of Kent is dead." His Majesty the King's son. The Prince Regent's younger brother. The father of a baby princess, Alexandrina Victoria, who might well be queen someday.

The Duke of Kent and John had been mere acquaintances, but the shock of his loss was nevertheless strong. A man he knew was gone.

Her hand went to her mouth. "How sad."

"It happened Sunday. I'm afraid we are now a house in mourning."

"Of course." She was all efficiency as she nodded. "The children and I have garments at the ready." Every noble household did.

"I must discern how I am to pay my respects, if I can. The prince is ill and His Majesty is confined to his bed." His hand twitched to take hers, to offer and receive comfort.

She'd already stepped away. Out of reach of his embrace, almost out of the room. "If you must dine with your peers, I understand. Your duty to the Crown is keen at a time such as this."

If his cronies gathered to honor the duke, his absence would be noted. Nevertheless, his wife had been attacked today. "I will not leave you, after what Coles did."

"I'm fine, although I should like to clean my teeth. His skin might be stuck there." She grimaced.

"You are becoming in white. Your cloak and bonnet." Why he tried to hold her with compliments, he didn't know. She'd see through them. "I'm glad to see you wear the color again."

She nodded her head in a gesture of thanks, but she could not meet his gaze. "I won't be wearing these again, though. Barnes shall have them."

"Of course. Forgive me. They are ruined by his association. I only meant—"

"I know." Her hand went to the door latch. "If I do not see you until tomorrow, I understand. You have your duty."

"I'm sorry I cannot be here with you and the children tonight." For so many reasons.

"I know that, too. Thank you for coming for me today."

"I'll always come for you."

Did she understand what he was saying? Could she see his heart pounding through his chest?

"You are too kind to me," she said, clearly not understanding what he meant. And then she was gone, leaving him with nothing to do but curse his stupidity and go upstairs to change into something black.

Chapter Twenty-Three

"A dinner party, at such a time as this?" Mama's delicate brow quirked. Perched in the settee of her pale green sitting room, she looked the picture of a fine lady in mourning, her pale, flawless skin a contrast to the dull black crepe of her gown. "The Duke of Kent has not been dead a week, and you suggest a party. We would be judged as the worst of His Majesty's subjects."

"Not a party. A family dinner with you and Papa and the girls." Helena's hands fidgeted on her lap, rustling the black bombazine of her gown. "The children and I are returning to Scotland shortly, but you haven't yet been to our home."

"Really, Helena." Mama crinkled her dainty nose as if something smelled off. "That spencer is out of touch, and tight. How old is it?"

"Two years." Since the last time she'd needed mourning clothes. And yes, the velvet jacket was close-fitting. She'd gained a few pounds since her marriage. But her short, shallow breaths could also be attributed to Mama's critical eye. Back to the dinner—

"You must have the *modiste* make up new mourning attire for you. Ardoch can afford it. At least your bonnet is acceptable."

"What vast relief." She shouldn't have spoken with sarcasm, but she couldn't stop herself. Her black chamois gloves and slippers, fortunately, escaped Mama's notice. "What of dinner, Mama?"

She had to try, one last time, to smooth things with her family, to show them she loved them. If they ever wondered about her, she wanted them to know she was happy. With the children, and with John, too.

At the thought of John, her cheeks heated. Mama's eyes narrowed. "You're flushed. Are you sickening?"

"Just overwarm, Mama." She forced a smile. "So will you come?"

"Perhaps. I'll ask your father."

Helena recognized the dismissal in Mama's tone, but Helena couldn't leave yet. "I had one other reason for calling. The girls are out, you said?"

"We are alone." For the first time, Mama's eyes met hers fully. "What is it?"

"Frederick Coles."

Mama groaned.

"John wrote to Papa of his arrest. Is it not good he is in prison, and on a charge unrelated to what he did to me?"

Mama rubbed her temples. "It is well and good, but you must cease bringing him up in conversation. It seems you relish the attention of it all. Your papa told me you had a hand in the arrest. I'm mortified."

Helena's stomach recoiled, as if she'd eaten something old. It was no use, trying to meet Mama in the middle of anything.

She sat a moment, collecting her thoughts, before she forced another smile. "I must not overstay. Evening is almost at hand. May I leave a note for the girls before I leave? I'd like to wish them well."

Mama nodded, but there was a decent chance she'd

throw Helena's note in the fire once she wrote it. Helena moved to the escritoire anyway. Mama reached in front of her to open the drawer where the foolscap paper and other accoutrements were kept, as if Helena did not know this for herself. No matter. She took a pen from the ink-and-pen stand and got to work while Mama returned to the settee across the room.

There was not much to say. She wished them well, and at the end, she noted her sisters would remain in her prayers. While she hesitated over the wording, a drop of ink fell on the page, smudging that most important sentence. Sighing, she opened the drawer for a new sheet of foolscap. Her hand was on the stack when she saw it.

A desk seal set with a faceted bloodstone handle. The image on the seal looked to have a wing, which was not Mama and Papa's usual seal. She tapped it, adjusting the angle.

Not just a wing. An entire bird. Like the one on the blackmailer's letters to John.

Her heart pounded against her rib cage, painful and fast, while she stood there, staring at the seal. She could pretend she never saw it. Or steal it as proof. No, she couldn't steal it. The options whirled through her head as her legs began to shake.

"Almost finished?" Mama stood.

At that moment, Mama looked so beautiful and familiar, the woman who gave Helena life and taught her to be a lady. Helena loved her, even if Mama was ashamed of her now.

In the end, all Helena could do was grip the desk seal and hold it out. "Mama?"

Mama's mouth set into the practiced smile she'd taught Helena so well. "It was my father's. Do you remember your grandfather?"

The Earl of Terrence, Mama's father, died when Helena was seven. "Not well."

"When he was young, his family called him Terce, shortened from Terrence. Tercel is a word for a male falcon, and he adopted it as a nickname of sorts. He thought this seal so amusing with its falcon on it, but I never liked it. I should throw it out. Here, I shall do so now." Her voice was false and bright as she extended her hand for it.

Helena swallowed. Considered her words with care. "I cannot."

Mama's demeanor changed in an instant. Her jaw clenched and her eyes narrowed. "Don't be ridiculous, Helena. Give it to me."

Instead Helena gripped the bloodstone seal as if it held an antidote to the sick feeling coursing through her. "Why would you blackmail my husband?"

"Blackmail?" Her look of shock came a second too late. "That's quite an accusation—"

"I have seen it with my own eyes, Mama. You disguised your penmanship, but I imagine if I look at the letters again I will see your hand there. This is the seal. It's you. Why would you betray me, your own daughter? Why do this to us?"

Mama's facade fell. Her shoulders squared and the look she cast on Helena was pitying. "You wouldn't understand."

"I insist you give me the opportunity." Her hand clutched the seal.

Mama threw her hands in the air. "Very well, then. It is probably best you hear this. Learn what you've done to us."

"What do you mean?"

"My father forced my marriage, you know. It was my duty to ally our family with Kelworth, no matter how much I dreaded marrying him."

Him—Papa? A fresh wave of pain threatened to sweep

her legs out from under her. "Was there another man, Mama?"

"Oh, yes."

"But you grew to love Papa."

"I married him out of duty," she said, avoiding Helena's question. "That is what we females from the best families do: we marry whom our fathers determine to be best in terms of strategic alliance. You were born for far better than Ardoch. I invested in you. Trained you. Cultivated you, but you wasted all my efforts, all those years of grooming to marry someone important. No, you had to go and ruin yourself with Frederick Coles, leaving you no recourse but to marry Ardoch. We've been mocked by our dearest friends." Mama was no longer beautiful, with anger contorting her features.

"So what is this, then?" Helena held up the bloodstone seal. "Punishment? Frederick's act of violence was not enough to put me in my proper place for not wanting to marry Bowden? You want to humiliate my husband, too? Was it the sport? Did you laugh at us? It wasn't for the money." A new thought occurred to Helena, one that made her toes curl in her slippers. "How would you know how John voted? Someone has helped you. Someone in the House of Lords." Not Papa, surely?

Mama rolled her eyes. "No one helped me. But I did hope to embarrass that husband of yours. It would make Lord Holliver feel better about himself."

"What has Lord Holliver to do with this?" He'd been here, calling on Mama, though, hadn't he? Whatever this was about, Helena's insides churned and her mouth went dry.

"Perhaps if your father hadn't been so set on Bowden, he'd have accepted Holliver's suit." Mama didn't answer the question, and the way she spoke was almost wistful.

"He's of lower rank, true, but he's young, despite that gray hair of his, and he's certainly wealthy enough. Then we'd be fine now."

"We are fine." This made no sense.

"I am not. Your father is dying."

Hot tears stung Helena's eyes. "I feared as much, but—"

"I didn't give your father an heir, did I? You have no brother, so Cecil is heir presumptive. He and his horrid wife will get everything. This house, like every house I've lived in since my marriage, is entailed property and will go to him. I will be at the mercy of your dreadful Uncle Cecil and Aunt Davinia when Papa dies, with naught but a stipend. I need more, so I've striven to get into their good graces so they won't cut me out without a farthing when Papa dies, but it isn't working."

So that explained Mama's attempts at friendliness with them at Christmas and Lord Holliver's party. "You blackmailed John for the money, then. You never intended to reveal my disgrace, when, by extension, the name of Kelworth could be affected by it."

Mama examined her buff nails. "Oh, I need money, true, but that wasn't why I did it. I wanted you and your husband to go away, to frighten you all the way to Perthshire. You see, if I cannot be supported by Cecil, I must marry my remaining daughters well with the expectation that I will live with one of them, in the manner to which I'm accustomed. I've convinced Lord Holliver that since he could not have you, he can have Maria. He likes her well enough, but your being here has reminded him how much he still cares for you. And he's not happy you rejected him."

"I didn't do that, Papa did."

"He doesn't see it that way. He confided his frustration to his friend Frederick Coles, certain that you could never be wooed, and next thing he knew, you were fawning over Coles."

Helena's hand pressed into her roiling stomach. Holliver was Frederick's friend, the one who'd said she was too good for anyone. An icicle, Frederick had said. It was his words Frederick took as a challenge, to prove she would fall prey to his charms. Helena stood still, but inside, her organs writhed.

She would not cry, not here, not in front of Mama. She strode to the door.

"Leave the seal." Mama's final words to her, spoken with stern authority.

Helena placed the falcon seal on the little table by the door and walked out.

Directly into Papa.

Chapter Twenty-Four

John glanced out the nursery window at the dark street below, searching for their carriage. Where was Helena? She'd been gone a long time—

"Oomph." A body plowed into his legs from behind.

"It was Callum," Alex cried.

"'Twas the dog," Callum countered.

Iona panted, the picture of innocence. John grinned. "'Twas all of you, I suspect."

"Not us." Dressed in her tiny nightgown and nightcap, Louisa toddled toward him, one hand clutching Tabitha, the other held in front of her to feel for obstacles. "Margaret and I were perfect ladies."

"That's right." Margaret folded her arms. "We don't wrestle with the dog before bed."

This seemed to renew the boys' attempts to climb John like a tree.

"You are the wildest lot in the square, and it's nearly bedtime."

As the boys moaned, Louisa reached for him. "Are you going to bed, too, Papa?"

"Not yet. I await Helena's return from her mother's so we can dine together." Normally they dined before the children went to bed, but when in London, Helena had reverted to keeping London hours. Still, she should have been back an hour or more ago.

Louisa's hands roamed his sleeves. "You forgot your buttons."

"How observant you are, little one. Mourning coats have no buttons on the cuffs. 'Tis a way of showing respect to the deceased."

"We've not worn blacks since Queen Charlotte. Louisa just doesn't remember." Margaret's tone held an air of authority, but it was not as superior as it had been a few months ago, to John's relief.

Callum rolled to his back on the floor, wrinkling his nightshirt into a twist. "When we are back at Comraich, I wish to play with the paper theater."

"Cinderella." Louisa lifted a wet finger into the air.

"Yes, yes," Margaret agreed. "But *Hamlet* next. We've had our fill of *Cinderella.*"

"When we get home I will check the cows for you, Papa." Alex nodded. "Just as you taught me and Callum. And tell you about the bad bull. We will write of how things progress."

How grown up they were. The knowledge was bittersweet. "You are all ready to go home, then."

"London smells bad." Louisa scrunched her little nose.

Just then, Agnes entered the nursery with a stack of linens—an excuse, perhaps, to remind him the children should be abed.

"London will be more fun when I'm old enough to attend the parties." Margaret returned his embrace.

"Give me a horsey ride before bed, Papa." Louisa patted his thigh.

"Very well." He took a chair and pulled her onto his lap. "This is the way the ladies ride, primmy, primmy." He wiggled his legs, then knocked them about with more vigor. "This is the way the gentlemen ride, jimmy, jimmy. And this is the way the butcher boy rides, obbly-oi, obbly-oi!" He bounced Louisa about, setting her shrieking.

She'd never go to sleep now.

A flash of black at the door drew John's gaze. Adam stood in the threshold with an odd look, as if seeing his master giving horsey rides was difficult to reckon. He recovered at once. "Milord, Lady Ardoch is arrived, accompanied by His Grace the Duke of Kelworth. They await your lordship in the drawing room."

The boys crawled upright. Louisa slipped off his lap. "Mama!"

Mama.

John's heart swelled and then, when it felt it couldn't get any fuller, cracked in two. Joy for Helena. Grief for Catriona, who would wail to hear her daughter call another woman by that name. An odd mixture of both emotions for Louisa, who had come to love his wife.

The other children were silent. Neither of the lads protested, as they had at the wedding. Margaret's mouth was shut, but she didn't grimace. The older children might not be able to call Helena *Mama* or *Aunt*, but they did not hate the notion anymore, either.

"Will she kiss our cheeks tonight?" Louisa puffed hers out.

"Of course, although if His Grace is here, it must be important and we should attend to him first."

"We will behave whilst he is here," Margaret assured him, eyeing her cousins. "His Grace has not called upon Helena yet, so she must be pleased. We should not ruin it for her by causing a ruckus."

"The duke doesn't like noise." Louisa's voice followed John out of the room.

Indeed, Kelworth did not. He didn't seem to like a lot of things. Then why had he come?

John hastened downstairs. Helena sat on the settee, dabbing her eyes with a large, black-trimmed handkerchief. Kelworth perched in a stiff pose beside her, but he held her hand.

John's lips popped apart. A thousand questions rose to his lips. Kelworth's attendance, his hand on Helena's, the stricken look in his eyes. What cause? He settled on the most important. "Helena, what has happened?"

She waved the handkerchief. "I'm so happy."

He exchanged a look of disbelief with Kelworth. Then he bowed. "Your Grace. I've forgotten my manners."

Kelworth stood, disentangling himself from Helena. "Lord Ardoch." Then he peered down at Helena. "You are not happy, daughter."

"I am." She sniffed. "You are with me, Papa, and your defense of my character gladdens my heart in a way I cannot express in words."

John knelt at her side, offering a dry handkerchief from his pocket to supplement the damp one, which, presumably, belonged to Kelworth. "I, too, am grateful, although I'm befuddled."

"She's overwrought." Kelworth took a seat in a wing chair, leaving the spot beside Helena for John. "It had been a most eventful afternoon."

"Coles was released?" John popped to stand again.

Helena took his hand and with a gentle tug, pulled him to sit. "No. It is Mama." With a guilty look at her father, she recounted the day's events. The falcon seal. Mama's blackmail, because she wanted Helena to go away. Kelworth stood silent, but there was betrayal behind his too-blank expression. He had heard it with his own ears, having returned home earlier than expected and catching the end of his wife and daughter's conversation.

Then, spoken with the high-pitch harbinger of more tears, Helena spoke of the duchess's resentment toward Helena. "She begrudged me not making a dynastic marriage. But there were joys in her life, John. Papa is a good man. And me and my sisters—why could she not have been happy with us?"

"I pity her." John squeezed Helena's hand.

"I'm sorry, Papa." A few tears clung like jewels to Helena's lashes, but she had stopped crying.

"I am the remorseful one." He stood and paced. "I didn't realize how harmful our actions were. I thought if you married Bowden, you'd have been well-provided for. And close by." His voice cracked.

And not married to a Scot. John dared not smile.

"When you told us what Coles did to you, I wanted to take a whip to his hide, but we could not expose you to the scandal of seeing him brought to justice. I suppose my exasperation was revealed in other ways." Kelworth brushed a shock of blond hair from his brow. "Such as how I treated you. I didn't know how to, well, go about things, and I'd wanted the best for you."

Releasing John's hand, Helena rose, stepping forward with her arms extended. "Papa."

Their embrace was awkward. Kelworth hugged like a marionette, his arms not quite going around his daughter, his joints stiff. But it was probably the first embrace Helena had received from her father in a long time, if ever. John blinked something from his eye that was absolutely not a tear.

Helena blinked a few times, too. "I love you, Papa."

"Yes, well." He pulled away, unable to say the words back. "I should return home to see to your m—Her Grace.

And I apologize, Ardoch. For the blackmail. Not for disagreeing with you at Westminster."

He couldn't hold back a chuckle. "Indeed not."

Helena sniffled. John dug his handkerchief from his coat pocket and dabbed the last of her tears. "With Coles caught, will you stay in London longer?"

Blinking, her brow puckered. "He was never the reason we decided the children and I would return to Scotland without you. You have work to do, and we—well, I think the children are ready to go home."

He stepped back, shoving his handkerchief in his pocket. "The *bairns* are anxious to be reunited with their paper theater, aren't they?"

Helena met his gaze. "I think I need to go home, too."

Comraich. She'd called it her home. The sound of it warmed him, and it wasn't any use thinking it was because he was glad she'd settled into their new life together. It was something far more dangerous than that.

These feelings he'd developed for Helena—well, he'd never felt such emotion for Catriona. Never hated the prospect of telling her goodbye like this.

"I should probably bid the children good-night, if they are still awake." Helena was still speaking when a knock sounded on the door.

John stepped away from her. "Come in."

Adam approached with the salver, which bore a single familiar card. "His Grace, the Duke of Kelworth."

"Again?" He exchanged glances with his wife. "Show him in at once, Adam."

Kelworth lacked breath, coughing. John ushered him to be seated, but Kelworth waved his hand, recovering quickly. "I just heard in the square—His Majesty King George is dead. The regent is now king."

No one moved. John didn't think he even breathed. "Lord, have mercy."

Helena's hand was at her throat. "I shall write condolences at once."

Kelworth nodded his approval, and then looked to John. "I'm out to learn more information, if I can. Would you care to accompany me?"

Helena waved him away as Catriona had once done to him. "Go. I will see you tonight. Or tomorrow. You must not neglect your duty."

The gesture took him back to a time when everything he did was for duty, not his heart. He married Catriona out of duty, served out of duty. Perhaps he needed the reminder that he still had a duty, and part of it was upholding his word to Catriona.

Which was probably why it was best Helena returned to Scotland as planned. So he could be apart from her for a while, and rein in his emotions before he fell all the way in love with his wife.

Helena kissed the children good-night, ate a light meal and began writing out letters of condolence to the royal family. The night grew late, but John didn't return home, so she went to bed.

The next morning, she was up early, but John had already risen and left, so she began preparations for her return to Scotland.

Over the next few days, John wasn't home much, but Helena understood the gravity of the situation. In between matters of state, he'd ensured the Crown's case against Frederick Coles went as it should, and now Frederick was imprisoned in Newgate.

John's absence made it far easier for Helena to stay busy and keep her mind off John. She bid farewell to Frances and took the children on last-minute errands. Soon enough, the day for their departure arrived, crisp and clear, perfect for travel. Voices clamored through the brisk February air on Saint James's Square as the servants secured their baggage and Alex and Callum tossed snow at the girls.

The tidy town house would be quiet once she and the children ascended the coaches and found the North Road. John would be alone except for Iona—the children insisted he keep the dog as company—but he would undoubtedly be lonely. She could prevent it by staying.

But he needed to work. That was their original agreement, wasn't it? That he would reside in London and she would care for the children at Comraich.

Now, they stood outside the house and he embraced the children and Tabitha three times each, kissing their brows and bidding them farewell.

When the children settled into two carriages—the boys with Miss Munro and the girls in the carriage they'd share with Helena, John gazed down at her, his expression businesslike. "If the weather continues to hold, you will be home shortly."

"I shall write when we arrive."

"Please." John glanced back at the house. "Things will be quiet here now. Too quiet."

"You won't even notice we're gone. You'll be quite busy." There would be the king's funeral and matters of state to deal with.

But there was also new work. With the death of the king, the session of Parliament would die, too. John, as a Scot, would not be allowed to keep his seat, as Papa would. John must soon vote for another Scottish lord to take his place in the House of Lords, a bitter decision.

He wouldn't be able to introduce his petition on education reform. He'd have to leave it for others to do. He'd scarcely had any time to do the work he'd long prepared to do. Poor John.

He looked down at the snow for a moment before meeting her gaze, but his look was no longer businesslike. It was intense, shooting fire through her core. "Be assured, I'll notice you're gone, Helena. All of you."

She licked her dry lips. "We shall miss you. I shall miss you."

Perhaps she shouldn't have said it, but it was true.

He looked about to say something, but shouts escaped the boys' carriage. They turned, and Callum shooed the dog out the open door. "You can't come, Iona! You stay with Papa!"

Iona stared at the carriage, her head tilted.

It was best Helena go before the dog tried again, or someone cried over parting from her. "I should go."

"God be with you." John handed her up the first carriage step, then stopped. Pulled her back down.

"John." At her gasp, the servants peeked at her, then looked away.

He embraced her, hard, lowering his head so his lips brushed her ear, just under the brim of her bonnet. "So much has happened these past few weeks, with Coles and your mother and your father, but I hope when you are alone at Comraich and you think of them, you remember to see yourself as God sees you. As I see you. A new creature, worthy of love and hope. Wear white again, Helena."

Then he let her go.

"Mama," Louisa's high voice shouted out the coach. "I cannot find Tabitha's fancy gown."

The one with the ruffles.

The coach rocked. "It is here," Margaret shouted. "Louisa brought too many toys. I have no room for my legs."

Perhaps it was a good thing the boys rode with Miss Munro on this leg of the journey.

John smiled down at her. "I can only prolong this good-bye for so long. Just remember, Helena, you are—"

Her breath caught. What would he say? That she was in his prayers?

"A gift." He kissed her hand. "Godspeed."

Chapter Twenty-Five

Helena was outside London before the girls settled down and she was able to think about what John said right before sending her on her way. *You are a gift.*

To him? Because her care for the children freed him to do his government work, as they planned back in July, when the weather had been warm and the heather grew thick among the green around Comraich, and her greatest hope was to love the children and be left alone by John?

So much had changed since then.

She was afraid of him—of all men, after Frederick. She felt broken, iced, unloved and unwanted by her family. She was relieved John would be gone so much of the year.

She didn't feel any of those things anymore, not with God's healing in her life, and the way He'd filled her heart with love for her new family.

Including John.

Heat suffused her chest, spreading down her limbs. She loved John. Really loved him. Not as her friend. Not as her partner in raising the young ones.

As her husband.

She'd known she was in danger of falling in love with him, but she'd been foolish to think she could prevent it.

This wasn't mere attraction, or even gratitude for all he'd done for her. She loved his gentleness, his strength, his humor, his smile. She loved him from the very marrow in her bones.

Her posture straightened with resolve. Her love would change nothing. She wouldn't let it. John had promised Catriona to never replace her in his heart. He was a man of his word, so even if he came to care for Helena, he'd never act on it.

Much as she never wanted to be apart from him, this separation might be the best thing possible. God might use the time to heal her of her impossible love for John, so she wouldn't yearn for him and something she would never have.

Louisa patted Helena's cheek, demanding her attention. She dipped her head. "What, sweetheart?"

"Tabitha needs a proper coat, too. Like ours."

Helena fingered the tiny flannel coat. "What is wrong with it?"

"It has a button on each sleeve. Papa says buttons aren't worn on cuffs in mourning."

Margaret shoved Louisa's felt toys off her side of the seat. "Rip it off and then sew it back on once mourning is over."

Louisa harrumphed, sounding so much like the Margaret of old it took considerable effort not to laugh.

Thank you for these children, Lord. For my new life.

She was grateful the entire trip home. The Lord provided clear weather and a smooth journey, and the children didn't bicker much despite being confined to the carriages for several days. Soon, they were back at Comraich, requesting the paper theater be brought down from the attic.

Helena wrote to John first thing, a longer letter than necessary, perhaps, but he'd want to know about the children.

She also wrote of her plans to visit the tenants, many of whom were ill, according to the housekeeper.

She would keep as busy as she could to distract herself from thoughts of John.

Perhaps she overexerted those first few weeks, because one afternoon during a paper theater performance of *Cinderella*, her skin began to ache. So did her head, right over her eyes and at the base of her skull.

When the performance ended, her applause sounded weak, even to her.

"You didn't like it?" Alex, clutching the paper board character of the prince, gaped at her.

She forced a smile. "Forgive me, of course I loved it. Marvelous, everyone."

"What's wrong?" Callum squinted. "You're yellowish."

"I'm fine." But when she stood, dizziness overtook her, and she plopped back into the chair.

She was not fine. Not at all.

After a few days with only Iona to keep him company, John felt the quiet in the house on Saint James's Square would drive John mad. By the week's end, he'd taken to eating at the Clarendon Hotel with Carvey. Tonight, however, several days after Helena and the children returned to Scotland, he had a houseguest, and a most welcome one at that.

John offered his Perthshire neighbor Tavin Knox his usual wing chair by the fire, sitting his bones down in Helena's chair. "You are good to stay with me."

"On the contrary, you're good to offer, since I do not keep rooms in London anymore." In his black mourning garb, Knox looked different from how he did in his usual vibrant colors. Less sociable. Perhaps even dangerous.

"You're here for the king's funeral, I take it?"

"And a matter for the Home Office. I cannot explain further, however. Forgive me."

John learned of his neighbor's occupation as something of a spy when he and Mrs. Knox purchased the adjacent property in Perthshire and set about restoring the old castle ruins. "I would not dare pry, except to ask of things at home. How is your family?"

"The nephews are taller, the baby grows plumper and Gemma thrives." His small smile conveyed deep emotions. "Only the Crown's call could tear me from them."

"And Helena? Did you see her before you left?"

He'd received her letter informing him of her safe arrival a few days ago. He'd worn the foolscap soft from so many readings. Had they received any of his letters yet? He'd started writing the day after they left, filling the missives with tales of Iona's antics rather than the details of his political discussions and lonely meals.

Knox's smile widened. "Briefly, before I left. They seem well. Helena is changed since your marriage. I confess I hoped you would make a match of it. I wasn't certain at first, when you mentioned looking for a convenient wife. But when I came to London and Helena was in need, as it were, I knew she should wed you."

"Thank you for trusting me."

"'Twas more than that. I thought you might be good for one another. And I see from your faces I was right. She is as miserable apart from you as you are from her."

John's gulp of coffee burned down his gullet.

Knox studied his boots. "I know it can't have been easy for you, having been wed before."

"I beg your pardon?" John had never spoken to anyone but Helena of his promise to Catriona. Had she told her cousin?

"Vows are made to be kept, and I'm certain you will

never forget your first Lady Ardoch. You vowed to honor her until you were parted by death, and you did. I'm certain she would wish you happy."

Would she?

Catriona's face flashed before him then. Not in her haggard delirium at the end, but in their early days, before the troubles that came after Louisa's birth. She'd been pleasant, if not a friend. No confidante, Catriona, but she cared for him as he cared for her. That Catriona smiled at him in his thoughts.

Then a rush of memories filled him, one after another. Walks in the garden. Dancing a reel at the neighbors' summer ball. Their wedding day, when he promised to care for her. Recalling her now, and his parents and their expectations, too, there was far less pain than usual. Did that mean he was free to love Helena?

John shifted his legs, unsure. But it was healing. What a surprise, considering he mourned so much right now, including his short career in the House of Lords. All he'd wished to accomplish, and now his chance was dead with the king.

But God would give him something to do, and for the first time in his life, he didn't mind not knowing what the future held. Carvey was right: John was a changed man.

"I say," Knox intruded upon his thoughts. "What time do you leave for Windsor on the morrow?"

"Eight." John smiled as they spoke of safer things. The king's lying-in tomorrow at the Royal Apartments in Windsor, where he had died. The funeral and internment at Saint George's Chapel the following day. The news that the king's heir, Prince George, was gravely ill. There was talk of burying two kings within days.

But despite the grief and uncertainty in the country and in his heart, something shifted in John. He felt hopeful.

God would make clear His purposes for John—and his relationship with Helena—when He saw fit. In the meantime, John had work to do.

Through the busy following days, John prayed about his feelings, Catriona, Helena, work, all of it, his emotions unchanged, but still feeling hopeful.

His hope deflated when he arrived back to the town house several days after the king's funeral to a letter from Comraich.

Helena was abed with fever and delirium.

The letter crumpled in his fist.

Chapter Twenty-Six

Helena's hand pressed flat against her bodice, as if by constraining her rib cage the ache would lessen. A feeble act, as every breath was agony.

She swayed into Margaret as she succumbed to a fit of coughing, then righted herself at once. Margaret wouldn't like the touch. But Margaret took her arm and held her upright until the coughing passed.

Each cough reminded her of Papa. Her illness wasn't like his, though, and she was blessed to be improving. Unlike him. Had he grown sicker since she'd left? *God, help him to know you.*

"Better?" Margaret asked once Helena caught her breath.

"Much." The damp, cool March air soothed her raw throat like balm.

"You shouldn't have left the house yet." Margaret was bossy as ever, although concern furrowed her brow. "It's starting to rain, and you're still weak."

"This seemed a good idea an hour ago." Helena tipped her head, indicating they should continue up the road back to the house. The gatekeeper's cottage was off a dirt track past the end of the drive. Not so far she should feel this tired.

Then again, she'd been quite ill.

She could have sent a servant with the soup for poor Mrs. McGregor, the gatekeeper's wife who burned her arm and juggled half-dozen children under the age of twelve. But she'd grown weary of her bedchamber walls, and calling on tenants was a privilege and a duty for the lady of the house. It was also far more enjoyable than she'd anticipated it would be. She'd never expected to feel such pleasure at becoming part of the village community.

Margaret peered under Helena's bonnet brim. "The doctor wouldn't like you being out yet. Neither would Uncle John."

"What's a little rain?" Nevertheless, the sound of her boots on the drive's gravel was a welcome sound. Almost home.

The rain fell harder. It was much like the day she first met John. Not as warm, of course, since it was spring now, but as wet, and the lower third of her white cloak was flecked with mud.

Back when she met John, she wouldn't have imagined she'd someday stride arm in arm with Margaret. An everyday thing, but so precious. This was all she'd hoped for: a home, children to love and who, miraculously, loved her in return. God had given her far more than she deserved.

They rounded the copse of trees, and Comraich's blue freestone walls came into view. They'd not taken more than a few strides when the front door opened and a furry wheat-hued creature bounded over the gravel toward them.

Margaret hopped up and down, but Helena froze. The dog. Iona. That meant—

John strode out the door, Louisa in his arms, the boys at his flanks. And—Papa, too? What were they doing here?

Callum cupped his mouth with his hands to yell at her. "Papa is home!"

Indeed he was, tall and hale and stomping toward them, passing Louisa off to Margaret with a kiss for each. Mercy, he looked wonderful. Except for his glower.

"What are you about, woman?" His rough words were not the reunion she expected.

"I—"

In an instant, she was lifted off the ground and hoisted in his arms, basket and all. She'd dreamed of curling against his chest when they reunited, but never in her imagination had it been like this, with servants and Papa watching and the children clamoring around them and the dog weaving between everyone's legs.

"John." She pushed at his chest. "Set me down."

"I will, where you belong." He carried her into the house. "What's in the basket?"

"Nothing now." Margaret must be behind them, so close was her voice. "We took soup and a salve to Mrs. McGregor. She burned her arm."

"Foolish female." His voice rumbled under Helena's cheek as he mounted the stairs. "You, not Mrs. McGregor. You're the one needing soup."

Servants stood out of the way in the hall, their gazes downcast. Heat crept up Helena's cheeks. "John, really."

He pushed open the door to their sitting room. Barnes poked out of Helena's dressing room, and then, wide-eyed, stood back.

"I shall summon you if her ladyship requires you, Barnes."

"Yes, milord." She dashed out. John had Helena through the dressing room in three strides and crossed into her bedchamber. None too gently, he dropped her onto the pale blue coverlet and took the basket from her arm.

"John." She scuttled onto her elbows. "How rude. You're never so gruff."

"Sorry. I'm not usually so terrified." He was already at her feet, tugging the laces of her boots.

"You are not terrified."

"Every day, since I married you." His warm hands rubbing her stocking feet felt better than a coal brazier. Then they were gone, and he leaned over her, loosening the ribbons of her bonnet. His gentle fingers left trails of fire on her neck, but it was nothing compared with the blaze in her core when he drew close, his gaze on her lips—

He kissed her brow, nothing the least romantic about it.

"Are you checking me for fever?"

"Yes. You're fine." He shifted back.

"I thought that was established already."

"Not to my satisfaction. You are cold and wet." His words were brusque but his touch was tender as he unfastened her cloak and tossed it onto a chair beside her bonnet. He was so close, she could see every plane of his angry face. The blond stubble shadowing his clenched jaw, the soft hair curling about his ears. And then she couldn't see anything because a fit of coughing overtook her and her eyes began to stream.

John dabbed her cheeks with his handkerchief. "I'm calling for the physician."

Helena rose from the bed and flapped her hand. "He was here this morning. He said I'm recovering well."

"You should change into dry clothes."

"I do not need to. My cloak took the worst of it."

He glanced at it. "You wore that cloak the day we met, when you fell down into the ditch."

Doon, doon, doon. She'd missed his voice. "It's a fine cloak."

"I'm glad you wear white again."

"If the color is a symbol, it is not of purity or my lack of it. It is a sign of God's grace. I am new." She grinned, reaching to don her house slippers. "I may wear whatever color I wish. Tomorrow it may well be green."

"Indeed, and now that the matter of your wardrobe is established, we can move onto other matters." He reached for her hands and led her to the settee near the hearth, where he pulled her down beside him. He smelled of horse and dust and the spice that clung to his clothes. "Can you guess, lady wife, how I felt receiving a letter from Kerr? The butler had to write because my wife was too ill to lift pen to paper."

"I sent you a letter. Four days ago." When she could sit up without feeling dizzy.

"It crossed me on the road, then." He settled closer to her. "I was worried."

"I'm sorry, John, but I'm fine now."

"I'm glad you are, but I'm not sure I am." But he smiled, belying his words. "Marrying you, I expected life not to change much. I'd stay in London and the children would be safe at Comraich. But we hadn't been married a full day when you challenged Catriona's rules. Remember?"

How could she forget? "You didn't want us playing nine pins on the lawn."

"Because I knew bad things would happen if I raised the children in a way she didn't wish, and lo and behold, when I relented a few weeks later, Louisa encountered the bull. 'twas awful."

This wasn't making her feel any better. "But good things happened, too. Look at Louisa."

"You're right. The children are healthier, happier and more independent. I'm a better father, I think, because we've adapted some of those rules. I've learned circumstances change, necessitating an alteration of how I view my promises to Catriona." His gaze met hers. "But my promise never to replace her in my heart isn't one I can break."

She knew this going into their marriage, but hearing

him restate his intention to keep their marriage convenient stung. The old feelings of inadequacy and rejection made her skin hot and itchy. "I understand."

"I'm not sure you do." His warm fingers intertwined with hers. "Despite our promise to keep things, well, as they are, I've fallen in love with you."

He what? Her lips popped apart.

"I'm sorry if this distresses you, Helena, but you must know my feelings so there are no secrets between us. I've struggled against my feelings because of my promise to Catriona as well as my promise to you, for a friendly marriage, no more. I convinced myself I didn't love you, which would be easier for both of us, wouldn't it? Then that letter from Kerr arrived, and at once I understood. Catriona will always be in my heart. She's the *bairns' mither*, but my love for you is something altogether different. Something I've never felt before."

Oh. Oh!

"I love you. More than I've ever loved anyone." John's gaze seemed to burrow into her being, leaving her breathless. "I want a real marriage, and yellow-haired children, if God wills, who take after their brave, beautiful mother. But I will never speak of this again if you wish to keep things as they are. Nothing needs to change—"

"I want it to change." She blurted it so fast it was almost funny, but he looked as serious as when he'd confronted Frederick Coles.

"You do?"

"I love you, John."

Words she feared never speaking to him. Words she never expected would make a man look as happy as John did right now.

Then she wasn't looking at him at all, because his lips met hers in a kiss that was nothing like the first kiss he gave her in the alcove on Christmas. This one left her breathless, and not because of her recent illness. At length his lips left hers to roam her jaw, her chin, the hollow of her throat, before finding her lips again. And again.

"I need you, Helena." His words were intoxicating and warm against her cheek. "I needed you to love. To love me. To make me a better man. And I think you needed me, too."

"Not just for your roof and name and protection. I needed you so much, John."

John's head tipped back and he looked deep into her eyes. "I want to be your husband, Helena. If you'll have me." He spoke it like his wedding vow, his voice clear.

"I will." Her vow matched his.

For better, for worse. For richer, for poorer. In sickness and in health, which she must recover at once so she might start her marriage aright.

They stood together. Arm in arm, they went out to find the children and her father. Helena felt like a bride at last.

Epilogue

August 1820

John took Helena's face in his hands and grinned down at her. "Are you certain?"

"I am." A thrill of joy shot to her toes. "A school on Ardoch land for poor boys and girls is a wonderful idea. You know Frances and I have been corresponding with ideas for ways to improve girls' education."

"And Carvey wishes to help, too. It sounds as if we have the leadership and funds to create a fine institution. Thank you for your support, darling."

"No thanks necessary, but you may repay me in kisses later."

"Your wish is my command." He settled for kissing her hand now, as they were out on the green behind Comraich, the children busy at nine pins with Papa while Iona snuffled through the grass. Papa smiled at the children. Alex issued instructions to Callum for a change. Margaret looked up to wave at them. Louisa dropped Tabitha to the grass, took the ball and tossed it at the pins.

Helena's heart swelled within her ribcage. "You thought you could not serve unless you stood in Parliament. Yet look at you, starting a school, helping fund the blind school in Edinburgh, continuing to petition your peers to work for educational reform. You've influenced Papa, you know. This morning he said he'd make a large donation to the blind school in Liverpool."

"God's grace indeed."

And God's healing. Papa's visit in March when Helena was ill seemed to have had a positive effect on his health, and his cough almost vanished. His energy had improved, too, but both worsened again when he returned to London. He'd determined the foul city air to be responsible for his malady, so he'd returned quickly to Comraich. He hadn't coughed much since, and he and Helena had continued to repair their relationship.

Perhaps in time, God might work out healing between Helena's parents. For now, however, Papa was growing in knowledge about God, and he'd begun praying for his wife. Mama was not yet ready to reconcile with him or Helena, though, and remained in London with the girls.

Helena would keep praying.

Her gaze returned to her husband. "The school will be wonderful, I'm sure of it. I'm sure of two other things, too."

"And those are?"

"I'm happy. You took a broken, spattered girl who fell in a ha-ha and helped her become someone new."

"I hauled you out of the ha-ha, true. But you and God did the rest. You helped me, too, you know." His eyes warmed, deep in hue as the green coat he wore. "And the other?"

"You were right. I think today is the day to tell the children our big news."

His exuberant grin made him look so much like Alex and Callum that Helena laughed.

"Everyone," he called. "Hurry here."

Papa's brows knit. "What's the matter?"

Margaret held Louisa's hand while they jogged toward them. "You're red, Uncle John. Is it the heat?"

Louisa tugged free and cuddled Helena, patting Helena's midsection. "It's a brother."

They were all quiet for an instant. Then the noise began again.

"Or a sister," Helena clarified. "In February."

"How could you know such a thing?" John scooped up Louisa. "How do you know where babies live before they are born? Never mind."

"A baby?" Callum's mouth twisted like he'd eaten an unripe berry.

"A baby," Alex marveled.

Papa nodded, a pleased turn to his lips. Iona barked.

Margaret—the poor orphan relation who'd viewed Helena with scorn for so long—held back. "Do I get to hold him?"

"Of course. He is your brother. Or sister. He or she will look up to you and love you." Helena wrapped her arms about Margaret, who returned her embrace and started to cry. Helena patted Margaret's back. "The baby is ours. All of ours." She could tell Margaret understood. They did not require blood to be a true family.

Then the boys were in her arms, and everyone touched everyone else. After a minute, Callum waved his arms. "Nine pins. Are we playing or not?"

"Playing," Helena answered. "Me, too."

"I suppose I shall have a hand in it, as well," Papa said. "I have not played since I was Louisa's age."

Alex whooped. Louisa followed his example, and Iona started barking in earnest.

"We will be the loudest family in Perthshire." John sighed. "Our neighbors will complain of the noise."

"Can you hear us, Perthshire?" Callum shouted. Their laughter echoed off the stones of the house.

After her turn, John touched Helena's arm. Just a discreet touch, with the promise of more to come. "A year ago, you needed a home. I needed a mother for my family. God gave us so much more."

"A family. A husband and a baby. My father again. And more love than I know what to do with."

Which is why, she supposed, they had a lifetime to share it.

* * * * *

Dear Reader,

Thank you for choosing *A Mother for His Family*! When I decided to write about a woman who'd survived a terrible ordeal, I knew I wanted her to experience Jesus and His healing, and to see herself in His eyes for the first time. I also wanted her to find a life of joy and fulfilment with a man of faith who found himself challenged to grow in the Lord and as a family man as a result of their relationship. I've been eager to write a marriage of convenience story with a nursery full of children, and some of my favorite scenes to write included Margaret, Alex, Callum and Louisa. I hope you enjoyed reading about Helena, John and the children as they forged a family and found a happily-ever-after.

If Gemma and Tavin seem familiar, you may have met them in *The Reluctant Guardian* when they had their own adventures! Like Helena and John, they learned that while we humans often make plans, God's plans are often better than we can hope for or imagine, and He has great things in store for all of us when we follow Him.

One last thing: in 1793, the Edinburgh Asylum for the Relief of the Indigent and Industrious Blind became the world's third establishment dedicated to the welfare of the blind. I fictionalized it for my story, but I truly appreciated learning about the efforts of its founders. I'm also grateful to the folks who helped me with the character of Louisa, especially Laurie Alice Eakes and Kathleen Fuller. However, any errors in the book, in this or any area, are mine alone.

I love hearing from readers, and if you'd like to say hello, please drop by my website, www.susannedietze.com, or my Facebook page, SusanneDietzeBooks.

May the Lord bless you and keep you!
Susanne

Get 2 Free Books,
Plus 2 Free Gifts—
just for trying the
Reader Service!

Love Inspired HISTORICAL

If you loved this story from
Love Inspired® Historical
be sure to discover more inspirational
stories to warm your heart from
Love Inspired® and
Love Inspired® Suspense!

Love Inspired stories show that
faith, forgiveness and hope have the power
to lift spirits and change lives—always.

 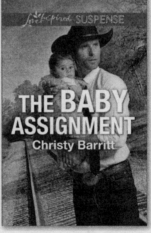

Look for six new romances every month
from **Love Inspired®** and
Love Inspired® Suspense!

Looking for inspiration in tales
of hope, faith and heartfelt romance?

Check out **Love Inspired**® and
Love Inspired® **Suspense** books!

New books available every month!

_____

CONNECT WITH US AT:

Harlequin.com/Community

Facebook.com/HarlequinBooks

Twitter.com/HarlequinBooks

Instagram.com/HarlequinBooks

Pinterest.com/HarlequinBooks

ReaderService.com

LIGENRE2018